Spartes Connection

by

Keith Hoare

Spartes Connection

By

Keith Hoare

***

Published by: Ragged Cover Publishing
ISBN - 978-1908090-676

Chapter 1

Liberty Parsons lay on her bed, listening to the shouts and screams of children playing. How she longed to join them, but locked up inside a house, that was never going to happen.

For Liberty, it had been this way since her current owner purchased her nearly six months ago. Aged fifteen and taken from her family at eleven, she had been with a number of owners, each change she prayed that this man would treat her better. It never happened; these men were demanding, enjoying punishing a girl, for what was often a minor misdemeanour, while begging his forgiveness.

Since the age of eleven, Liberty had only known a life of being locked up, beaten, and raped, yet still a child, she longed to play on the beach, paddle in the water, before she died. Liberty knew it might never happen; in the eyes of the world, children like her did not exist.

Soon she would be sixteen and after talking to other girls at the communal orgies, they would all participate in, it was well known that once a girl became sixteen, she would disappear, never to be seen again. Many had ideas of what happened to the girl, from allowed to return home to being killed, which Liberty thought to be more likely. Every child used by these perverts, would know at least by sight, their abusers, if not their names. To be allowed to walk away would leave every abuser vulnerable, if the child talked to the authorities. Because of this, Liberty was already counting the days to her birthday and death. She may never have joined children playing on the beach or swimming in the warm water, but she would be free from a living nightmare.

Sitting at the window of her bedroom, reading a book, Liberty was alone in the house. Her owner had gone out, locking the bedroom door as usual. She was not bothered. In fact, she was used to it. Over the years, to pass the hours of boredom, Liberty had read a great deal. She had thoughts of escaping, but every house they had taken her, she always ended up discounting such thoughts. This house, like others, the windows had several vertical bars attached to the wall on the outside. Her bedroom window would only open a few inches, to let fresh air in during the heat of the day, but that was all. Her bedroom looked out on the back garden, if you could call it that, being more a dumping ground, overgrown and surrounded by a high wall. Beyond the wall, she knew there was a busy road, and what she believed was the beach when at night, lying on her bed, she would hear the sound of crashing waves. Where she was in the world, she had no idea, but suspected as the sun shone virtually every day and going dark early, this had to be a country around the Mediterranean.

At that moment, a football came over the wall, hitting the side of her open window. This surprised Liberty. Nothing had ever happened like this before. She could hear people arguing from beyond the wall, then a lad's head appeared, followed by a scrambling and cursing as the lad attempted to climb over the wall, assisted, she assumed, by others.

"Give me a bloody chance to get a grip," the lad shouted back in English. Then he had hold of the top and dragged himself up and over, dropping into the garden.

He looked around for the ball.

"It's under my window," Liberty called.

The lad looked across to where a girl's voice came from and began to make his way over.

"Thanks, it's shitty around here. Doesn't anyone do the garden?" he asked, at the same time picking his way between the rubbish towards her.

She watched as he came closer. He was a good-looking lad, around five feet ten, thin, with curly blond hair, aged around sixteen. "Shouldn't think so, well I've seen anyone. Tell me; with you talking English, what country is this?"

He frowned. "Excuse me, are you putting me on?"

"No, I only wondered, but if you're not going to tell me, it doesn't matter."

"You're in Portugal on the Algarve, just outside Albufeira. Dad has a villa here, well not a villa as villas go, more like a concrete bunker with a flat roof, but it's cool and we have a swimming pool. What's your name?"

"Liberty. What is yours?"

"Russ, I live in Norfolk."

"Is that in England?"

He looked at her. "Like, yeah. I thought you were English, you speak it well."

"I was born there, but I moved to Italy when I was a baby. I can speak Italian, French, Spanish, German, and English, but prefer English."

"Bit of a bummer, being able to speak all those languages, now you live in Portugal."

"I suppose. Then I was in Seville early this year, before my current owner brought me here."

Russ seemed confused. "Why do you call your parents 'owners'? That's a strange description."

She looked down. "I've not seen my parents since I was eleven. Since then, I've been passed around."

"Oddball life, but if you're cool with it, I suppose it's okay. Why not come and join us? It's crap sitting inside on a day like this. We've got a football game going, before going back into town to pick up burgers then down to the beach?"

She looked at him with obvious sadness in her eyes. "I'd like that, but I'm not allowed out. Anyway the doors locked. Maybe I'll join you some other time?"

"Yeah, okay," he said, while parting overgrown

3

shrubs looking for the ball.

"Bloody hell, that hurt," he cursed, pulling out a six-inch nail. "You should be careful, leaving things like that hanging around."

"Sorry, if you give it me, I'll put it in the bin, so no one else gets stabbed."

Russ passed it through, found the ball, and turned to leave. "I'll see you around."

"You never know, thank you for talking to me."

Russ threw the ball over the wall before looking for a way back over. Finally, he moved a tipped over oil drum closer to the wall, turning it upright before climbing on and pulling himself up on the wall. Seconds later, he was gone.

Liberty sat staring at the wall, in a way hoping the ball would come back over, but it never did. Tears were trickling down her cheeks. How she would love to go with them to the beach. She looked at the six-inch nail. He was right; it could cause injury with its sharp point. Liberty was about to throw it in the bin, when she hesitated. This could become a weapon, maybe not a very good one, but there may be a situation when such an item was needed, not that she could see what. Deciding to hide the nail, while considering her next move.

***

Russ, along with Adan, Henry, and Cassondra, were sitting on the sea wall munching burgers. The others from the football game had already headed off home.

"Forgot to tell you, I met a girl in the house where I got the ball. The stupid girl didn't even know what country she was in, going on about how she didn't live with her parents but with her owner. I asked her to join us. After all, it's crap sitting inside all day, but she said the door was locked."

"That's a strange conversation. Was she putting you

on, just to get a conversation going?" Henry asked.

"No idea, but she looked weird, you know, pale, like, not all there."

"Are you sure you're not winding us up, Russ? That's Blake Fellers house, and he doesn't have a daughter," Cassondra commented.

"How do you know?"

"You forget, Russ, I live here. That man taught us for three years before they kicked him out, accused of spying on the girls in the changing rooms."

Russ shrugged. "Kicked out or not, he's got a young girl in the house our age. Anyway, she seems okay with it, not blubbering or asking me to get her out. She's probably a relative of some sort."

Adan finished eating and stood. "Come on, this talks too heavy for me. Race you to the edge of the water.

They were all up and running, Liberty forgotten.

Chapter 2

Blake Fellers, the man Cassondra said lived at the house where Russ met Liberty, arrived back home. Dumping a bag containing food on the kitchen table, he went through to bring Liberty out of her room, in order to make dinner.

She began the preparation while he sat reading. Placing the paper down, he gazed across at the screen of his security system. While it required a password to open up, a small icon in the screen's corner showed something had triggered his camera surveillance system. This happened at times and would always be worth investigating. He made a mental note to do that after dinner. In the meantime, he decided to quiz her.

"Has anyone rung the doorbell today?" he asked.

"No, were you expecting someone?"

"That's none of your business, just answer the question, nothing more," he came back at her curtly.

She never replied. He would turn anything she said into an argument, giving him an excuse to beat her.

Blake was confused, why had a camera triggered if no one had come to the door. He went over to the unit, keying in the password and opening it up. This was confusing. The camera that triggered the alarm was in the yard. He began playing the recording and soon came to where Russ appeared on top of the wall before jumping down. However, what he was doing and why he was there was not immediately apparent, mainly because he had gone out of sight of the camera. As Blake ran the recording on, he saw the boy drag the oil drum over to the wall before climbing back over. What he did not see was Russ, while out of sight of the camera, throwing the ball over before moving the drum to climb out.

"I asked if anyone had come today. Why did you lie?"

"You didn't. You asked about the doorbell. Why, has someone come to the door without ringing the bell?"

"Don't be fucking clever with me. You know a kid came over the back wall into the garden, so why didn't you mention it?"

"How would I know? I have been asleep all afternoon. I got little sleep last night with your friends passing me around until the early hours. Then why would someone want to climb over the wall, short of attempting to break in? Unless you're suggesting an intruder has, and I should have seen them?"

While her explanation sounded logical, if there was a possibility of this lad coming back, he could not afford for him to see Liberty. She only had to blab and the police would be knocking on his door.

"After dinner, collect everything from your room. You're moving into the cellar."

She turned and stared at him. "But it's damp and dirty. I have done nothing wrong. Can't I just go there when you're out?"

"No, I don't want any sign that you're living in the house. Do as you are told, and get your clothes together. Unless you want me to drag you down and throw your clothes after you?"

"No, I'll do as you ask and take everything I have downstairs," she answered, resigned to going into the cellar, no matter what. Although in reality, beyond the shorts and T-shirt she had on, all she had was a sexy set of underclothes, two short dresses, fancy high-heeled shoes, a few well-read books, and a tiny stuffed toy.

***

Following dinner, Liberty was in her room pushing everything into a polythene shopping bag. She was close to tears, desperately wanting her sixteenth birthday to come, but that was still at least two months away. Until then, the nightmare of what was happening to her would go on.

Blake came through. "Come on, move your arse. You have company later and I want you under a shower."

"I've got everything. I just need my bedding."

"Give me your bag."

She handed it to him and he tipped the contents out onto the bed.

"What's this, a bloody stuffed toy at your age?" he commented, picking it up and throwing it towards the rubbish bin.

Liberty stared at her small stuffed teddy bear face down at the side of the bin. "I want Teddy. You've taken everything else from me," she said, her voice faltering.

He grabbed her long hair, yanking her head back, with his face inches from hers. "I've taken everything? You had nothing to take. I have fed and dressed you, given you a roof over your head. So grow up and accept you are no longer a child but a whore, to do my bidding. That's the cost of living under my roof."

Even though she was terrified of this man, Liberty stood her ground. "I pay with my body for what you claim you give me, but Teddy is mine, not yours, so I want him."

He pushed her away. "Get your fucking stuffed toy then. As for talking back to me, get rid of the pants and bend over the side of the bed. You know the rules and you've broken them."

Liberty went over to the bin, bending down to pick up Teddy. Then she saw the six-inch nail glinting slightly behind the bin. Instinctively, she picked that up as well; hiding it in the same hand, she was holding Teddy.

"I don't deserve punishment just for asking for my own property. I'll not remove my knickers," she said bravely.

"You won't, won't you? That is yet another misdemeanor, which attracts harsher punishment. So expect my trainer across your bottom. Have you learned nothing over the time you have been here? I tell you, you never tell me. Do I make myself clear?"

"Very clear, except why should I be punished for wanting Teddy with me?"

As far as Blake was concerned, he had heard enough, the girl needed to learn respect. To do that, he had to teach her a lesson she would not forget. He came up to her, grabbing her hair and pushing her shorts and knickers clear of her bottom. Liberty was in a panic, still struggling, even with his firm grip of her hair. Somehow, she twisted around to face him, lashing out to free herself, dropping the stuffed toy as she raised a hand to push him away. However, this was the same hand gripping the nail, and its sharp point caught him under the chin, sinking deep into the soft tissue. Liberty suddenly felt damp around her hand. Letting go of the nail, she pulled her hand away in panic.

Blake screamed in agony, releasing her, trying to push her away and find what she had used to attack him. But the nail, while at first only painful with no actual risk beyond intense pain and minor bleeding, caught an artery as he pulled at it, followed by blood spurting out of the wound. Almost immediately, Blake felt faint from the loss of blood, slowing his aggressive and defensive actions down, before crumpling to the floor.

He lay there, staring up at her. "Help me, I beg you," he gasped.

She looked down at him, wiping his blood from her face with her arm. "So you can beat me? Help yourself; I'll not lift a finger."

"If I die, the police will hunt you down. You will go to prison for the rest of your life. Give me assistance and I'll claim it was an accident."

"Why should I worry? If you'd not forgotten, I will

be sixteen in two months. No girl lives beyond sixteen, they are killed."

"That's not true. You go to a brothel to live a better life."

To be told that she would not die, but destined to work in a brothel made her feel sick to the stomach. She had been counting the days to her death and release from the nightmare she had lived for over four years. Now, with what he said, it would never end.

"You don't have to go. I could keep you here, tell them you'd taken your own life," he persisted.

"Where's the better life? Beaten and demeaned, or shagged seven days a week in a brothel? You are stupid if you think I would accept either. I would rather go to prison; at least I'd be safe, or a bloody sight safer than in a brothel. Die like a man, Blake Fellers, knowing I was the last girl you will ever abuse." Then she bent down, picking up the stuffed toy before sitting on the edge of the bed watching, as he attempted to crawl along the floor towards the hallway and through into the lounge for his mobile telephone.

With the loss of blood, Blake never got to the lounge, before passing out. Liberty had not moved, gripping the toy and staring vacantly ahead. How long she sat there, she had no idea, brought out of her trance when the doorbell rang. She knew the person at the door would be the man Blake had told her she was to entertain later. She ignored the bell, even when he began calling Blake's name through the closed door. Eventually, it fell silent. He had finally given up and left, maybe believing no one was in.

Removing her clothes spattered with Blake's blood, she walked through to the bathroom, washed the clothes in the sink hanging them over the side of the bath, before stepping into the shower. Coming out of the bathroom, with a towel wrapped around her, she looked down at

Blake. He had not moved, then with never seeing someone dead before, Liberty was not completely certain if he was. Opening the cellar door, she dragged him through and down the steps, leaving him at the bottom, before coming back out and bolting the cellar door. At least, safely locked up, if he was not dead, he couldn't escape.

Laid on the bed, Liberty felt scared. Had she actually killed Blake? If that were the case, would anyone believe it was not intentional, after dragging him into the cellar? In her mind, doing that, a claim of self-defence would sound hollow. Liberty had no idea in what she should do, eventually falling into a troubled sleep.

***

The following morning Liberty had come to a decision. She looked around the rooms, going through drawers finding a few euro. Then, wearing a skirt and T-shirt, which was not much better than the shorts, along with underclothes she placed inside a plastic carrier bag with Teddy, Liberty left the house, heading towards the beach. No matter what happened to her, she wanted to experience the sand running between her toes, the water swishing around her legs. Beyond that, she had no plan, no idea where to go, or how to survive. She was free, with little or no remorse about what had happened to Blake. The man had treated her like a piece of dirt under his foot. He deserved all he got. Not that she accepted it was her that caused the fatal injury, but more his ripping at the nail that had done the real damage.

Chapter 3

The day after Liberty left Blake's house, and with not getting an answer from Blake's mobile telephone his friend, Alex Candor, returned the following morning. He was just about to knock on the front door, when to his surprise he found the front door partially open. Pushing it wider, he called Blake's name several times before venturing inside.

He first saw the dried blood all over the hallway, with scrape marks of dried blood leading to the door of the cellar. Immediately he assumed the girl may have been injured, or even killed, but why leave the place in such a state? He called Blake's name, again no response.

With trepidation, Alex grasped hold of the basement door, slid the bolt free, and pulled it open. Switching the light on, he looked down the stairs, stepping back in horror and surprise. Blake was at the bottom of the steps. Alex could see he was dead, without going closer.

Alex closed the door and began looking around the house. Where was the girl? Had she escaped, had she been snatched, or was she down in the cellar with Blake? He had no idea, but either way he called the police, told them what he had found and left the house, sitting on the outside wall to wait for them. He decided against mentioning anything about a girl living at the house. If they found her in the cellar, as far as he was concerned, he knew nothing about her.

Blake's death was fast becoming a murder case and it got around the locals in Albufeira like wildfire. He was well known, with teaching so many children before being forced to resign.

***

In Russ's house, the family sat down for dinner, his father entering the room last. "The police cars further down the road, according to Duarte next door, is because they've found a man dead. He says he's been murdered," he commented, at the same time sitting down.

"Murdered? That is not good for a tourist area that prides itself on low crime rates. Was he local, or a visitor?" his wife asked.

"A local so Duarte said. Taught at the school for some years, a man called Blake Fellers."

Russ's ears pricked up at the name. "What about the girl in the house? Was she killed as well?"

"Why do you ask? Did you know the family?" his father wanted to know.

"No, our football went over the wall and I went to fetch it. She was in the house and we spoke for a minute. I asked if she'd like to join us, but she said she couldn't leave the house."

"That must have been awful. When you talk to Duarte again, Daniel, ask him if she's alright," Russ's mother commented.

"I will, not that he mentioned anyone else was in the house. I hope she's not dead and the police are saying nothing."

***

The following day, Russ's family were out in the back garden. Both Russ and his brother were playing in the pool, while their parents sat on loungers reading, when the front doorbell rang.

Daniel walked through to open the door. Outside, two uniformed police officers and a man in a lounge suit stood there, he was the one who spoke.

"Good afternoon. Mr Bewley, I am an investigator from the Polícia de Segurança Pública looking into the death of a certain Mr Fellers. I believe you, or your son, may have vital information that can assist us in finding his killer?"

"Then you've been talking to Duarte next door, when

I asked if he knew anything about the girl in the house?"

"We have. May we come in?"

"Of course, come through. We're all in the garden."

"Perhaps we should remain in your lounge and you bring your son inside?"

"I'll fetch him. Is it alright I remain, he is a minor?"

"That is in order. At this stage, we are only here for information."

For the next twenty minutes, they quizzed Russ. The man in the suit making notes.

"Thank you, Russ, for an explicit statement. Are you certain this girl never mentioned her surname, and she was around sixteen?"

"I am, although thinking about it, she seemed a very young sixteen, so she may have been younger."

"When she said 'her owner', did you not think it a strange word to use? Why not an uncle, a brother, maybe father?"

"I did, but she told me she spoke several languages and I suppose in a way I thought she'd got the wrong word, or interpreted her answer in a mix of languages. Then I was in a rush to get back to the game, so it wasn't a long conversation."

"And none of your friends saw the girl?"

"No. We talked about her, that's why I recognised the name, when dad mentioned the murder."

"Very well, we will leave it there. Thank you for your help. Please mention nothing about the girl to anyone, particularly the press. She maybe in great danger, if it became known we were looking for her."

"We understand. In fact, we will be leaving for the UK on Saturday. Do you require our address, in case you need Russ again?" Daniel asked.

"Yes, we'll take your UK address. If she is picked up, there may be a possibility you are asked to identify the girl calling herself Liberty. Although we may do this primarily by photo, but if it becomes a court action, you will need to return, Russ."

"That's fine. Whatever I can do to help, I will. She seemed a nice girl, but never smiled. I hope she's alright."

The police left the house; the investigator stood for a short time with the uniformed men. "We must find this girl. She is the key to what happened in that house."

"I agree. At least now, we know she exists. Forensics will go through that house with a fine-tooth comb. If she lived there her prints and DNA will be everywhere. So when we pick her up, there will be no doubt as to her involvement," one of the other men agreed.

Chapter 4

While Liberty fulfilled her dream of walking on the beach and paddling, she had become more and more convinced that Blake was dead, not that she'd shed a tear over his death after the way he'd treated her, but it was essential to leave not only the area, maybe even the country with no delay. With that in mind, she carried on along the beach towards the town centre of Albufeira, asking a local street vendor where the railway station was. The woman directed her to a bus stop where the bus passed the railway station in Ferreiras. At the station, Liberty carefully checked a map on the station wall as to where to head, before deciding it would be best to go to the main railway station in Faro, where there should be a better choice of destinations.

In Faro, after looking at the destinations of trains leaving the station, Spain seemed the obvious choice. At least she could speak Spanish and blend in; Liberty used the last of her money, after buying a pair of cheap jeans and trainers, for a train ticket to Seville. However, with the train not departing until late afternoon, a journey of four hours would bring her into Seville just after nine at night, giving her little chance of finding somewhere to sleep. Liberty was not concerned in spending the rest of the night on the streets, at least she would be out of Portugal.

***

Leaving the railway station in Seville, it was already going dark. Liberty walked a short distance, finding a van selling coffee and snacks, on the point of closing.

"How much is your cheapest hot drink?" she asked in English.

The owner looked at the young girl, who was obviously tired, and very short of money to be asking the price.

"I'm packing up, but I can do a coffee for a euro," he

16

replied. This was a third of the normal cost, but he would only pour it away later.

Liberty pulled out a few coins and offered them to him. "It's not quite a euro, but it's all I have. What will it buy?"

He filled a paper cup, adding sugar and milk, passing it to her. "Put your money away. I will not see a child unable to buy a drink. I've also a sandwich left. So rather than throw it away, if you like salami, you're welcome to it."

"Yes please," she answered, taking the cup, sipping the hot coffee.

"Where do you intend to sleep tonight?"

"I'm not sure, but I'll find somewhere."

"It's far too dangerous to be out on the street all night for a young girl. There is a shelter in Perafán de Rivera. I could call them and see if I can get you a bed. Do you want me to do that?"

In the past, he had seen many runaways wondering around the station area, often directing them to a shelter. But at this time of night, most shelters would be full. Although the one he intended to call had an emergency bed available, providing it had not already been taken.

She nodded her agreement.

Taking out his mobile phone, and quickly finding the shelter, he dialled the number, speaking to them in Spanish.

Liberty, not admitting she spoke and understood Spanish, listened carefully. She had no trust in anyone offering help. However, everything she heard seemed to confirm he was talking to a shelter. He stopped talking for a moment and looked at her.

"They will keep their emergency bed for the next hour. I will give you the directions. What is your name and age, so they know who to expect?"

Liberty stood for a moment, her mind racing. Should

she give him the name used by the trafficker who took her, or her real name? Blake was dead, and then she had given the lad Russ her name. He could tell the police, where no one knew the name she had been born with. "Zoey, I'm fifteen?"

He passed on the details and cut the call. Drawing a simple map on the back of a flyer, he handed it to her. "It is around three and a half kilometres away, taking about three quarters of an hour walking if you keep to these directions."

"Thank you for your help. I really appreciate it, as well as the coffee and sandwich."

"You're very welcome. Now get off and take care, Zoey. Do not let anyone distract you. Go directly to the shelter. You can't afford to dawdle."

"I will, but tell me, why are you giving me help?"

"A fifteen-year-old girl, alone in Seville, broke with her only option being to sleep on the street. Do I need to answer that question, Zoey?" he answered with a smile. "Now get yourself off."

***

After a few errors in following the map, Zoey knocked on the door of the shelter with only minutes to spare. A man came to the door, followed by an elderly woman.

"Can we help you?" the man asked.

"I'm Zoey. I believe you have a bed available for the night?"

"We do, Zoey, come in. You are cutting it fine. Any later, we would have had to release it as available."

"Sorry. I got lost twice. I've walked from the station."

"At least you're here now," he answered.

She followed both of them into a small office.

"My name is Rodrigo, this is Mariana. We do not question why anyone needs a bed, Zoey, but you should understand we are making available our emergency bed.

It is in a single room at the top of the building. It cannot be used by the same person for more than one night. That person has to take a chance, like others wanting a bed for the night, when we open at six tomorrow evening. There is a problem in your case. In view of your age, we're not allowed by the authorities to place you in a mixed bed dormitory, so after tonight you cannot return to the shelter."

"I understand. I'll be moving on anyway."

"Can you tell us where you're heading?"

"I don't know. I'll just have to ask around to find somewhere to sleep."

"Do you have any money?"

She shook her head.

"We'd like to help, Zoey, if you'll allow us. We are in contact with several charities and groups who help minors. Would you like us to contact one for you?" he asked.

"Who are these people?"

"That depends on why you are homeless. As a minor, if you have run away from home, then we have contacts with church groups who will look after you. They would find you accommodation, even talk to your family and attempt to heal any rift. If you have no family, again there are housing groups who have shared houses. The last option, which is very rare for a girl coming to our shelter, is if you have been the subject of abduction, then the charity 'Lost But Never Forgotten' becomes involved. That is one of the largest charities in Europe, with three enormous complexes in Spain, on the coast between Marbella and Malaga. It is a private charity, and they only take persons who have been subject to abuse at the hands of human traffickers. They wouldn't take you otherwise."

She shuffled uncomfortably, not really wanting to tell them where she'd come from.

Mariana could see her hesitance. "Zoey, in this shelter we meet hundreds of people, each with their own, often harrowing, story of hardship. We do not judge, no matter what has happened in a person's life. You can tell us to mind our own business, use the bed and leave unhindered tomorrow. But for a child, beyond shelters, as Rodrigo has told you, there is help to keep you off the street while you sort your life out. Again, they do not judge and only want to help. If you would like us to call one, we need only a hint of your personal circumstance, then we can contact the ones who deal with that issue," Mariana told her.

Zoey knew she needed help; she could not even feed herself. "I've been with a paedophile ring since the age of eleven. Would any charity take me in?"

Both looked at her in astonishment. Never had they faced a girl in that situation.

"My god, Zoey, this is serious. Do you believe you are in danger of being snatched back?" Mariana asked, obviously anxious.

Zoey gave an indifferent shrug. "If they can find me, I suppose it is possible."

"LBNF has to be contacted immediately, Rodrigo. I do not believe it is safe for Zoey to be here. Do we have their call centre number handy?"

"We do. I'll call them."

"While Rodrigo contacts LBNF, Zoey, how about you and I go through to the kitchen and open a tin of soup with a slab of bread? You must be hungry," Mariana suggested.

"That sounds great. I've only had a small sandwich all day."

After they left, Rodrigo dialled LBNF's help line.

"Lost but Never Forgotten. How can we help you?" a friendly female voice answered.

"This is Rodrigo, the manager of the homeless shelter in Perafán de Rivera, Seville. We've had a code red come in."

A code red to the LBNF help line, known by most shelters and groups dealing with the homeless, meant they had someone in imminent danger and in need of Unit T's help. Unit T was a European based part military unit formed to combat human trafficking in the EU. Working closely with LBNF, they maintained a small Dark Angel unit in Malaga's Torre del Mar complex. Partly to look after high-risk victims of trafficking in a secure area of the complex, but also geared as a first response unit ahead of help coming from Unit T's base in the South of France, if a situation required it.

"I understand, Rodrigo. Can you give me more information about that person?"

"Her name is Zoey, aged fifteen, and she has been in the hands of a paedophile ring since the age of eleven. Somehow, she escaped and a street vendor outside the railway station called and asked if we could provide a bed for a young girl for the night. We would never leave a child on the street and released our emergency bed. When she arrived and told us where she'd come from, I knew she could still be in danger if they were looking for her. Shelters are normally the first places traffickers search. We could not protect her. That's why I've requested a code red."

The girl was typing as he spoke. "Please hold, I'm putting you through to Unit T control."

There was a brief delay before a man came on the phone. "This is Unit T. A Dark Angel unit is on its way from LBNF's Torre del Mar complex in Spain. They will be with you in around two and a half hours. Can you lockdown until Unit T arrives?"

"At this time of night, we're full and the shelter is now secure for the night."

"Very well, although we may request a police car outside until we arrive. I will inform them not to enter the building. I'll text you a unique password which our Unit T unit will give you to allow entry."

***

After coming off the phone with Rodrigo, Unit T's duty officer called the intelligence unit. If Rodrigo was correct that Zoey had been in a paedophile ring for such a long time, Colonel Harris needed to know urgently. Zoey would be extremely valuable and this was a chance in a million. Information from the girl could break the ring.

Karen Harris joined Unit T at eighteen, rising quickly in the ranks to take command. A year before she had stood down as commander, but circumstance forced her to return as an advisor. Karen had turned the unit around and she worked well with the current commander.

"Sorry to call, Colonel Harris. We have a code red from a shelter in Seville. Would you believe a fifteen-year-old, who has been with a paedophile ring since eleven, walked into a homeless shelter? They realised she could be at very high-risk and called LBNF for help," the intelligence officer told her.

"For a girl to be in a ring for such a long time is absolute gold. We can smash it. What's our unit's ETA [*expected time of arrival*]?"

"Around two and a half hours, from Torre del Mar. The shelter's locked the building down."

"Call the local police and have them secure it outside. Nothing and no one goes in or out of the shelter until Unit T arrives."

"I've already called them, Colonel."

"Good, keep me informed. I want to know immediately when she's under our protection."

***

Rodrigo came into the kitchen. "I've called in a code red, Mariana."

"How far are they away?"

"Torre del Mar, so it's about two and a half hours."

"Who is coming?" Zoey asked. "Not the police, I hope?"

Mariana smiled. "No, Zoey, it will be a Dark Angel unit from Unit T. Unit T is an EU military unit, far more powerful than the police. You will be very safe and well looked after, believe me. Once you told us where you came from, all shelters have a number to call to instigate a code red for any person caught up in human trafficking. The people you have been with will almost certainly be looking for you, and they can be extremely dangerous. Anyway, now you've eaten, I think it's time you got your head down for a couple of hours."

"Thank you for everything you're doing for me. I really am exhausted. It's been a very stressful day."

"I can imagine. Do you have any valuables, such as a mobile or similar? We always put them in a sealed envelope in the safe, ready to collect when you leave. It is safer that way in any shelter. You never know who is sleeping next to you. We get many on drugs and they will take anything sellable for their next fix. Not that you will be in a dormitory, but we still ask for valuables."

Zoey looked down with sadness in her eyes. "I have nothing, only Teddy and a few coins."

"And Teddy is?" Mariana asked.

Zoey took the stuffed toy from her plastic bag. "This is Teddy, he's been with me since I was a baby."

"That's fine, Zoey. If you come with me, I will find you a towel and toothbrush, and show you where to sleep.

Ten minutes later Mariana joined Rodrigo. "The girl's completely shattered. She could hardly keep her eyes open."

"You should get your head down for a few hours, Mariana. I will wait for Unit T. We also have not one, but three police cars parked outside. Unit T's taken Zoey's safety seriously."

"After what she's been through, they should. Four years being passed between paedophiles does not bear thinking about. She must be a very strong-willed girl to be in a state of mind to make an escape. I wonder where she originally came from and where her parents are."

He sighed. "Once Unit T takes her, we'll never hear about her again. She'll get a new name, and a new life."

"She'll need it. Zoey will never be safe."

Chapter 5

Rodrigo saw two Range Rovers draw up outside the shelter, via the outside cameras. A female soldier climbed out along with two male soldiers from one vehicle. She went across to the police car showing them her ID. Four more soldiers came from the vehicle behind and spread out across the street. The police left and the woman came to the door, ringing the bell.

"Yes?" Rodrigo answered over the intercom.

"Unit T, Lieutenant Campagna."

"Can I have the password?"

She gave it, and soon he was down to open the door. The three soldiers came inside.

"Where is Zoey?"

"She's asleep. How about a coffee, while I call her? She has agreed somewhat tentatively to leave tonight, but she may need convincing you are, shall we say, the goodies?"

"Let's see how she reacts shall we, most girls in that position will know about Unit T and LBNF, but can still be very untrusting of any help offered. Many have heard it all before and been let down. But for us, coffee would be most welcome as well as the lads outside if possible?"

"No problem," Rodrigo answered, taking mugs from the cupboard.

"Do you know anything about Zoey?" the lieutenant asked, as Rodrigo poured them coffee.

"Nothing, beyond the fact she claims to have been in a paedophile ring for four years. We don't ask questions of people coming to the shelter. It makes them nervous and defensive, particularly if to feed an addiction they have committed criminal acts. Then we have a few who would prefer to leave rather than answer any questions. Although there are exceptions, particularly with children, we try to help them. In fact, most are desperate for help but won't admit it, so it's often a softly, softly approach."

"Understandable."

"Will she be going to, Torre del Mar?"

"I don't have that information. I've been ordered to collect the girl, confirm we have her, and wait for further orders."

"That's fine. I'll call her."

Zoey came into the kitchen carrying her plastic bag.

Lieutenant Campagna came up to her, pulling her ID from her breast pocket handing it to Zoey.

"I'm Lieutenant Kum Campagna from Unit T, Zoey. I understand you have been a victim of human trafficking. I am here to take you to a place of safety. Unit T holds an EU mandate to control the rise of human trafficking in the EU. Do you have any questions?"

Zoey looked at the soldiers and Rodrigo, before passing the ID back to Kum. "I've never heard of Unit T, so how do I know you are who you say you are, beyond an ID that could be easily forged?"

"That's a good point, and by what I've heard has happened to you, trust in anyone offering help is bound to be looked upon with caution. We are here at the request of the shelter who, concerned for your welfare, believes you are in a great deal of danger. We are not forcing you to come with us, Zoey. It is entirely your decision. If you refuse our help we will walk away, the same as the shelter will not prevent you from leaving in the morning."

Zoey said nothing.

Kum could sense the girl wavering. It was time for a different approach. Unit T needed this girl badly, but they could not drag her out of the shelter against her will. If they did, it would be unlikely she would impart the information they know she will have about the paedophile ring.

"If you've never heard of Unit T, let me tell you

a little about us. Just before you were born, a girl was abducted and taken to the Lebanon to be sold. The girl's name - Karen Marshall - except today she is called Harris. Her family believed she was dead, so Karen knew no one would be coming for her. However, she escaped and sold her story to the papers. Not to make money for herself, but to help others who had been mixed up with human traffickers. In fact, she made so much noise over the issue that these girls were not being helped, and were effectively forgotten; the EU formed a special unit named Unit T to sort out the worsening trafficking situation. Karen joined that unit and eventually became our commander. Karen went one-step further. She created the charity Lost But Never Forgotten to help the girls Unit T pulled out, by giving them a home and a future. LBNF does not judge, does not look at victims of trafficking as second class citizens. The charity rebuilds lives, makes a girl proud of herself, helping with their aspirations, be it education or just to become a mother and have a family. Over the past sixteen years, LBNF under Karen's direction has become one of the largest charities in Europe. In the complex, at Torre del Mar, where I am based, every girl lives with two others in an apartment where each has their own bedroom. Most work locally, the complex has a hairdresser, a shop, a restaurant, a swimming pool and even a private beach. Karen also owns a private hospital next door, which the charity uses. That complex, Zoey, is one of three Karen owns, as well as hundreds of apartments and villas across Europe. We know what we are doing, as well as the type of people who have imprisoned you. They will be concerned you have escaped. Have no doubts, they will send people to find you. These people know all the areas you would attempt to hide. Most of the places they search are areas the homeless and users of drugs congregate. There will be ones, to get their next fix, who will be prepared to sell information about your whereabouts. Believe me, there is no place to hide. They will find you. Only under our protection, or in a LBNF complex, will you be safe while we round up your abusers? I can assure you no trafficker group would dare to go up against Karen and attempt to take you. If they tried, she has the power and the facilities to crush them."

"What you are telling me is frightening. Never being allowed to watch television, or read a newspaper, all I got were books. I suppose if I had, I'd have known about Karen Harris and Unit T."

"You would have, believe me, she is never out of the papers, and you can be sure your abductors know about her. So, are you going to take your chance on the street, or come with us?"

Zoey stood for a short time, wanting to believe her and the offer of help, but frightened what would happen if they found out about Blake. "May I speak to your alone, please?" she asked Kum.

"Of course, can we use your office, Rodrigo?"

"No problem. You know where it is, Zoey."

Once in the office, Kum closed the door. "Why don't we sit down?"

Once sitting down, Kum waited for Zoey to speak.

"If I tell you something, you'll not hand me over to the police, will you?"

"That is not part of my orders, Zoey. It is for officers beyond my rank to make such a decision. But I will tell you this, during my time at Unit T, I know of no person caught up in human trafficking being turned over to local police, just because they have committed a criminal offence in their attempt to escape. Karen would make such a decision and she is the sort who would consider the circumstances leading up to any criminal act, before involving the police. Then, if she did, Unit T would provide legal support. They would not leave you alone. So are you going to tell me what has happened, or would you prefer to wait until you are back at Unit T?"

Tears trickled down her face. "What if someone may have been injured and I mean really injured when I tried to escape? Would Unit T support me then?"

"I'd not worry too much about that. Most girls in my experience, who get out by their own volition often end up in a scuffle, a few have actually hit their captor over the head with whatever was at hand, some even end up in hospital. But the law is clear on that, you can take actions to defend yourself. In your case, I'm assuming you were attempting to escape, or protecting yourself from a beating, struggling with the person?"

The room fell silent. Kum would not push Zoey either way, knowing the girl's escape, might have resulted in a serious confrontation.

Zoey looked down at the floor, tears running freely down her face, her voice a whisper. "I'm so frightened about what will happen to me. I don't know what to do for the best."

Kum stood and came to her side, placing her arm around her. She could feel the girl shaking. Such was the reality of what she had done, which was now coming to the fore. "Place your trust in Karen, Zoey. In all my time with Unit T, I've never known Karen let a girl down, no matter what she had done."

"I need to tell someone. I only wanted to keep Teddy. Blake had taken everything else. Teddy's been with me forever; it wasn't a lot to ask, wanting to keep it, was it?"

Now Kum realised why the girl was in the shelter. She was still a child holding onto her past with a stuffed toy. For someone to take it from her would have been the height of stupidity. She could also see how such a confrontation could have quickly turned violent, leaving the man badly injured, allowing Zoey to walk out of the door unhindered. It was time to take charge of the situation and bring her in. The girl could not cope alone.

"Come on, Zoey, we should leave. Karen will understand and be on your side, that I'm certain."

"You really think so?"

"I do. In Karen's sixteen years fighting these people, do not believe for one second she has not had girls in similar situations. She will have, and know what to do."

"I'll come. I have nowhere else."

Kum took her back into the kitchen. "Zoey is coming with us, Rodrigo."

"It's the right decision, Zoey, believe me."

Zoey said nothing. She knew there was no option.

One soldier offered Zoey a black short-sleeved jacket and helmet.

"Can you put on this bulletproof jacket and a helmet?" Kum asked Zoey. "These are just precautions. We are not expecting opposition with more of our troops outside securing the area, but we take no chances. My orders are to collect and keep you safe until you are inside the Torre del Mar complex, or at another location."

After Zoey thanked Rodrigo, she left with Unit T.

Once in the vehicle, she was able to remove the helmet and jacket.

Lieutenant Campagna called ahead to Unit T control, confirming they had Zoey.

"I have an update for you, Lieutenant, from Colonel Harris." The controller began. "You are to take Zoey direct to San Pablo airport. A Unit T aircraft is on the tarmac and ready to depart."

"Copy that."

Sitting by the side of the driver, she turned to Zoey. "Looks like you've got your very own aircraft, Zoey. You are to meet Karen at the Unit T camp."

"I've never been on an aircraft."

"Then you are in for a treat. It is not a commercial flight. You will be travelling in the executive jet that belongs to Karen."

"She must be very rich?"

Kum smiled to herself. That was an underestimation. "Something like that, Zoey."

The journey to the airport was relatively short and soon the two vehicles passed through the security gate, going directly to a private jet waiting on the tarmac. Zoey thanked them and went aboard. Minutes later, the aircraft was on the move, heading back to Unit T.

The Dark Angel unit was ready to return to Torre del Mar and breakfast, except Kum had one last thing she needed to do before they left the airport. Having the driver leave the vehicle, Kum made a call to Unit T, asking to be put through to Karen.

"In view of the time, I need to check if Colonel Harris is available to talk to you, Lieutenant. Is this the number she can call you on?"

"Yes, but I really need to speak to Colonel Harris urgently."

"Very well, I'll be back to you. Otherwise Colonel Harris will call you direct."

Kum waited. She knew Karen would still be up, but she hoped the call back would not be too long.

Suddenly, the phone rang. Kum picked it up. "Lieutenant Campagna."

"Colonel Harris, Lieutenant. You wanted to talk to me?" Karen asked.

"Thank you for calling me back so quickly, Colonel. I'm sorry about the time, but I thought it important you should know of a conversation I had with Zoey."

"The time is of no consequence, Lieutenant. I can be contacted at any time. Do we need to go to a secure line?"

"I'd prefer it, Colonel. Then you can decide if what I'm about to tell you remains classified."

"Very well, I'm switching us to a secure line."

Kum waited and listened as the telephone pipped several times, then Karen was back.

"We're secure, Lieutenant. What is it you consider important about Zoey?"

Kum told her exactly what Zoey had said, adding an observation. "I really believe the toy she calls Teddy was the catalyst in her leaving, Colonel, and suspect the man's badly injured. You should know the police may have a warrant out on her."

"Thank you for the information, Lieutenant. I will take it from here. You have done an excellent job of bringing her in. Your conversation with Zoey must not be part of your official report. It never took place. Do you understand, Lieutenant?"

"I understand. Colonel, she seems a nice girl and to have been with such people for so long, it must have been a living hell."

"Believe me that would be an understatement of what she would have gone through. Most girls brought out at that age, even after only a year, often revert to drug addiction to block out the past, but by the sound of it, Zoey is clean. That is some tough girl. You should now call it a day, Lieutenant, and thank you once again for making me aware."

***

The aircraft was the height of luxury, the seat Zoey sat in, padded soft leather that wrapped itself around her. Once the fasten seat belt light went off, the only other passenger on the aircraft, a girl who had shown her to a seat and now sitting on the other side of the aisle, turned to her.

"I'm Jasmin Dlamini, Zoey. Karen has sent me to meet you in Seville and see you safely back to Unit T. We have a flight time of around two hours. Would you like a drink or would you rather get your head down and try to sleep?"

"I've never got much sleep in the night, so I'm used to staying awake, but a drink would be nice. I will have anything that is going. There is no preference for me."

"That's fine, I'm having a cappuccino. I will make you the same. Do you take sugar?"

Zoey nodded her acceptance.

Jasmin, a white South African and an attractive girl in her late twenties, worked alongside Karen. Her background was that of a contract killer, first being very successful with her partner Nick, then later after Nick's death, alone, with many cartels using her services. However, on a contract to kill Karen in the past, circumstances changed and both she and Karen had to work together to get out of a dangerous situation. Since then, Jasmin joined Unit T and became a Dark Angel soldier. She often worked alone out in the field, or alongside Karen.

"Tell me, Jasmin, you all seem to have taken a great deal of trouble for me. Does this always happen?" Zoey asked, when Jasmin returned with the drinks.

"We look at a victim of trafficking, unlike most in the world, as first and foremost a human being, and someone's daughter, who through no fault of their own, desperately needs help. So answering your question, yes, Karen will go to any length to bring a victim of trafficking out. In your case, you are different. To be with a paedophile group as long as you have and get out is extremely rare. You will also have a great deal of information that may allow Unit T to bring the ring down and pull out more victims. So you can understand why you're not going directly to a complex, but Unit T itself."

"I suppose you're correct. Spend years among them, they become complacent, talk too much so I know many names, besides, show me their photos I could identify them. But what happens to me after you have all this information? Am I on my own?"

"Before I answer, Zoey, do you have a family? If so, how is it you ended up with paedophiles?"

Zoey sat silent for a moment. "It seems so long ago, Jasmin. On my eleventh birthday, I remember going to bed. Thinking back, I was more tired than usual and over the following months concluded they had drugged me. Anyway, when I awoke, I was in the back of a van with another girl who I knew from school. That journey seemed to go on for an age. It was hot, we had no water and both of us were still wearing what we had gone to bed in. They took us to a house. Both of us were told by a man who called himself Beacher, our parents had been in debt to him and we were their payment to get out of it. From now on, he owned us. I could not believe my parents would have sold me, but with no other explanation, it seemed they had. This was brought home to me when I was given a plastic bag with a few of my clothes inside, to find at the bottom of the bag Teddy, he had been with me since I was able to walk. It is an odd name for a teddy bear, I know, but I never thought of calling him anything else, he was always Teddy to me. I think mum must have put it there knowing it meant a great deal to me."

Zoey took her teddy bear from the bag she had brought on the aircraft to show it Jasmin. The stuffed toy was only around five inches high, but Jasmin could see how much it meant to her, in the way she held it. This little toy was her life, her connection to her childhood. Little did Jasmin realise the significance of such a bond, leading Zoey to a violent confrontation, rather than lose it.

"They put us to work," Zoey continued, still holding Teddy. "At first serving drinks to clients in a large room, waiting for their turn to go in a room with the older girls.

That was our first so-called indoctrination, walking around a room, wearing a crop top, knickers and very short skirt, with high-heeled shoes. Refuse to go in and they had a stick that if it touched you, an electric shock went through your body. Believe me; you did not want many of those before you would do anything they asked of you. Walking round, men would put their hand up your skirt, squeezing your buttocks; some would even pull your knickers down, before grabbing you and forcing you to bend over their knees, for what they called a gentle spanking. Gentle was laughable. It bloody hurt. It was not long before we were being taught how to keep a man happy. After the so-called training, at the end of the night, they paraded us around the room naked for a man to bid for you, the winner taking you to his bed. By then we were all sleeping with different men every night, cleaning the house in the day. After a few months, they sold me to my first permanent owner and I never saw my friend again. They probably sold her like me. Then when my owner tired of me, which was usually around six months, I would be taken to meet other men in the group. There would be around ten or fifteen men, all there to exchange the girl they had. That was my life, and I eventually accepted it. What else could I do? There was no escape."

"Can you answer me a question? This man you knew as Beacher, was he of Mexican descent with a surname of Marinez?"

Zoey thought for a moment. "Funny you say that. My friend thought him Mexican. I was not sure, not having met any Mexicans. I never knew his surname, but it has been many years since I saw him. All I remember is his beatings and spending a week in his bed while he claimed I was being broken in for use by the clients. That was just an excuse. All he wanted to do was shag me as often as he could before he tired of me and took another girl."

"We hear that a lot, Zoey. Do you reckon you could identify Beacher if you saw him again?"

"I think so. His voice, his mannerisms, would give him away." Then she hesitated and smiled. "Besides, when he drops his pants, you'll find he has a penis that's got a bend on it. The girls in the room, we all used in the day, would make fun of it. I know it was stupid, but with no telly or even something to play music, we found other ways to entertain ourselves, often telling the other girls the night's experience with certain clients, their habits and parts of their anatomy we could make fun of. Then, knowing their habits, such as the likes and dislikes of the men, by playing on their preferences it would save punishment if we knew what he liked to do. Believe me; such information was important, most men would complain about anything. They got to watch the girl being punished, enjoying hearing her screaming."

"An interesting way of checking we have the right man, I think. I must tell Karen that. You seem well educated. Have the men you've been with arranged that?"

She sniggered. "You are joking. Clean, cook, shag, is all I ever got from them. But I enjoy reading; have done since I could virtually walk. Most houses they took me to had books, and my owners would let me take one or two at a time to my room. I also leant to speak languages, more by necessity when my owner did not speak English. Many of the books were in different languages, but I muddled through them until I could actually read the language. I'm self-taught and speak many languages." She gave an indifferent shrug. "Goes to show, with no distractions and years of boredom, you can learn anything. It also became a sort of fad of mine to see if I could follow the stories when I had no pictures, particularly if I found a dictionary on the bookshelf."

"With mentioning various languages, it seems you

36

were living with men from different countries, did you travel abroad, or remain in one country?"

"Different countries, I think. No one ever told you where you were going, or even what country you were in, but you could often tell by the weather you'd probably crossed a border."

Jasmin was surprised just how calm and articulate Zoey was, as if she had accepted that was her life. However, while she was recording the conversation for Karen, she did not think it was worth delving deeper. Karen had her own ways and often preferred to do that herself.

"You asked earlier what would happen to you. Now I know there could be problems in you being returned home, Zoey. You will come under the care of LBNF, not abandoned. There you will complete your education, as well as being given the choice of what you would like to be. LBNF will send you to the best universities in the world to achieve your dream. No pressure, if you would rather be looking to get married, we are okay with that. The thing is, Zoey, you will never be alone again and believe me; someone close to a billionaire in Karen Harris, supports LBNF, so cost is never an issue."

"Why does she do it, with that sort of money, Karen must have the world at her feet?"

"She does, but she has never forgotten what it was like for a girl on her own, her life controlled by people who only want to make money from her. She wanted every girl finding herself in that position to keep believing we will come to take her home."

"Are you the same as Karen?"

"No, I'm here for a completely different reason, but I'm the odd one out. My job these days is to protect Karen. That can be a daunting task, believe me. She leads the pack, not runs behind. Most of the girls who work with Karen have been victims of human traffickers."

"Could I join her?"

"Why not, prove you are up to it and Karen would never say no, but one step at a time, you're not sixteen, as well as been shut away from the real world. Once you understand, maybe your priorities will change to becoming a lawyer, or social worker, fighting for victims of trafficking in other ways."

Jasmin passed Zoey a magazine. "You may be interested in reading a little about LBNF. The magazine is printed each year explaining LBNF's goals, as well as what they have achieved over the past year. I think it will surprise you, what you are becoming part of. The girls themselves put together this magazine and very professional it is, as well as having a worldwide circulation. Such is the demand from people interested in what Karen is doing. This one has an in-depth interview with Karen, that, believe me, is very rare and a journalist would kill for such an interview."

She took the magazine and looked at the picture on the front of Karen with two other girls. "She's very attractive. I can understand why they wanted her. The long-legged attractive girls were always in demand at the parties."

"With your help, such cowards, who can have a sexual relationship with a girl when she's under duress, their days are ending, Zoey. Karen may be an attractive woman, and more suited to be sunbathing on the deck of a multi-million pound yacht, but that is not the real Karen. The real one is extremely dangerous and many in the past have found she's not one to be crossed."

Chapter 6

Beacher Marinez, a Mexican who broke from a South American cartel to come to Europe and make money in fields he knew best, such as the supply of drug and young girls to paedophile groups, was watching the television reporting Blake Fellers murder. In the same room was another man called Javier Schneider, from Germany.

"Wasn't Blake part of the Spartes paedophile group?" Beacher commented, after the report finished and he turned off the television.

"He was, in fact, the group leader Virgilio was in touch a few days back, saying they are losing five girls, coming up to sixteen and asking for replacements," Javier answered.

"We should do nothing until we know just what has happened and they're no girls involved."

"I'll give Virgilio a call," he answered, pulling out his mobile.

There was a delay before Virgilio answered. "You need me, Javier?" he asked.

"Yes, Beacher and I have just watched the news talking about a the murder of Blake Fellows. Did Blake have one of our girls?"

"He did, and she's missing. We are certain the police don't have her. There's been no announcement."

"What is her name?"

"Liberty Parson's, she's aged fifteen and due back to you in two months."

"Just hold for a moment, while I tell Beacher."

Javier muted the phone. "They've lost Liberty. She could be on the run."

"Shit, that's all we need. We want the eleven girls they still have back immediately. They should go to ground until we can find Liberty. We also need to have our people out looking for her. She will not get far, that is certain. A girl of fifteen will know a great deal about the Spartes, not that she's likely to remember her time with us."

"I don't know about that. If I remember correctly, Liberty was one of the brighter girls."

"Then it's imperative we find her."

Javier went back to Virgilio. I have spoken to Beacher. As a matter of security, we will collect the rest of the girls so we can keep them secure. I suggest all the group goes to ground for a short time until the police find Blake's killer. We will put our people on the job to find Liberty. I think we'll all sleep better once she's back with us."

"That's fine. I will talk to the group. If Liberty has anything to do with Blake's death, she must be punished."

"More than that, Virgilio, we have a client who would delight in giving her a send off in style, so to speak. He also does it with invited guests, if your people would like to join him?"

"Book us in. Blake was a good friend of us all. He didn't deserve to die."

"I'll do that. Keep in touch if you hear anything. We'll collect all the girls tomorrow, so let your members know."

After he went off the phone, Javier looked at Beacher. "I assume you got the gist of the conversation? We must protect ourselves, Beacher, in case Unit T gets hold of Liberty. These days they have, or rather Harris has, a considerable informer network. She could pick up a fifteen-year-old sleeping rough by chance. It'd be like her birthday to have Liberty."

"You're right; Harris wouldn't be able to contain herself, although Liberty is more likely to point the finger at the Spartes first. Have some of our people monitor Spartes members. If Unit T makes a move to pull any of them in, Virgilio is the only person within Spartes who can direct Harris to us. He'll have to meet with an accident."

"What of the girls, do we ship them all into the US, rather than just the ones of sixteen? They would be too risky to offer around in Europe?"

"We may as well. Five were already due to be sent, so what's a few more?"

"Okay and a contract killer for Virgilio, so we stand away?"

"Yes, who do we know?"

"Most I knew are dead, or languishing in prison. I have a contact in the Bear Cartel. He should know who is available as well as reliable. I'll call him."

Chapter 7

Major Uwe Lang, commander of Unit T, walked through to Karen's office.

"Good morning, Colonel, I understand our Spanish team collected a girl on a code red last night? What do we know?"

"Good morning, Major. Yes, LBNF instigated the collection and called me. Apparently, we have a fifteen-year-old girl called Zoey on the run from a paedophile group. I understand she had been with them for four years. I listened to the recording this morning between Zoey and Jasmin Dlamini during the flight from Spain. This girl knows names, can identify individuals and with her being with them for so long, we'll get firsthand knowledge of how they operate."

"It sounds too good to be true. It is also your field of expertise, Colonel. I'd like to stand back and control only raids, if that will be acceptable?"

"Of course, Major Lang, in fact, I am hoping your teams will be busy as we pull members of the paedophile ring in. Any distraction taking me away from digging deeper into the operation that brought her into the ring to start with is not good. My immediate concern is the safety of girls still with them. Zoey will not be alone. The paedophiles will go to ground, panicking because of Zoey's escape and knowing if they can't find Zoey, the police or we will."

He looked concerned. "When you say, go to ground, is there a possibility girls still in the ring may be killed?"

"It has happened. During my time in Unit T, while we lose victims for various reasons, twice I have had multiple losses in an operation. You never forget the time standing there looking at the victims, some as young as ten. Both times, the traffickers killed the girls so they would not be captured with them. There was not much justice as far as I was concerned, even though the perpetrators were killed, those children did not deserve to die."

Lang shook his head slowly. "Sometimes I despair of humanity in what they are capable of. Since you returned, the more I see and hear, the more I realise what you have had to contend with, when here was me, happy a girl had escaped and we've brought her in, only to be told it may write the death sentence for many more."

Karen shrugged with indifference. "If she'd escaped and not come to us, the other girls would have still been at risk, Major. You can never save them all. Often, the losses can be greater than the number we pull out. The sad part in this case, the girls left behind are not even sixteen, some possibly a great deal younger, but at this stage, all is not lost. Even though they are at risk, we are dealing with traffickers supplying the child rings, and they will see value in them. With such a possibility, the trafficker who sold them to the ring, may want the girls passed back to be sold on, while he considers the implications of losing Zoey."

Lang smiled inwardly; again, he believed Karen knew more than she was admitting. "By what you are suggesting, I suspect you already have a good idea who supplied the girls to the paedophile ring?"

"Possibly, the name Beacher came up in the initial conversation between Zoey and Jasmin. When Jasmin asked if he was Mexican, Zoey told Jasmin she was with him only for a short time four years back, but a girl she was with at the time said Beacher was definitely a Mexican. Zoey also came up with an identification mark that only a girl raped by him would know. Such knowledge would be useful to bring him in for an interview. While Beacher is a general name in South America, I believe he is in fact a Beacher Marinez. Unit T has known about him for some years, but never been able to pin anything on him. Marinez is a nasty piece of work who brought to Europe a level of violence gained from working as an enforcer and punisher in a South American cartel. We also believe he still works with them, supplying drugs into Europe. That would not involve Unit T, but if Zoey can identify him as the one who took her, even raped her, before passing her on to a paedophile ring, then we will have enough to charge him in connection with the human trafficking of minors. That is one man I'd dearly love to take off the street, but we have no idea where he lives and only old photos of him from the USA, yet his name keeps coming up."

"Would one girl's word hold up in a court case?"

"Unlikely, although in the past we have secured a conviction on one girl's word, but there were special circumstances in that case. In Zoey's case, she was with him nearly four years back, a good defence lawyer could rip her testament to pieces. The point is, Major, before we make a move, Zoey's experience with him, according to Jasmin, sounds like she was only one of many girls at the time she was there, which points to quite an operation going on. If we can find more of them, our case will become that much stronger."

Lang shook his head slowly. "That is an area where you excel, Colonel. I would not know how to begin such an investigation. All I could do was go in and drag the man out to place before the courts. You can build a solid case and really nail the bastard."

"Perhaps, but let's not get ahead of ourselves. To take him down, Jasmin and I will covertly enter the seedy world of the criminal cartels and snoop around. What we find will determine how to go forward."

"Like I said, that is your expertise. When you begin your debrief of Zoey? I'd be interested in listening in, to understand the criminal world more."

"Following lunch with her in the restaurant, I will use the interview office in the suite set aside for girls we bring in, where there is a full camera and recording system. I'll have extra seating placed in the monitoring room so you can watch the interview."

"So the time in the restaurant is to relax the girl?"

"Not so much relax more to get an understanding of her level of intelligence in a general environment. With most young girls, the experience can be traumatic, take them to the edge of sanity, even questioning their own inadequacies, as to how and why they fell into the trap. One moment they can be very lucid, the next they break down completely, often needing a sedative to calm them. Zoey, according to Jasmin, had come to the same opinion as me, after I had listened to the recording of their initial conversation. Both of us believe she is stable because of how long they had Zoey, and her acceptance of that life, clutching to the past with the only item she had to remind her; a teddy bear. The significance of that stuffed toy is paramount in getting her to open up."

"Well, if anyone can get her to open up, you can. I'll leave you to it and perhaps we'll meet later and decide where to go from there."

"Before you go, we have a more immediate problem, which for the time being cannot appear on our official interview report."

"Should I know this?"

"You are Unit T's commander. Of course, you should. I am not here to keep things from you. We have to work together, so I want you to understand the thinking of a girl on the run."

"I appreciate that, Colonel. What is it I should know?"

"Early yesterday we received information about a Blake Fellows from the Portuguese police."

"I saw that memo, and thought it strange they had sent us notification that they were conducting a murder investigation. Was his death important to us?"

"It would not have been, apart from closing any further investigation concerning him. In fact, Fellows was among a few people Unit T was investigating, suspected in being part of a paedophile ring. It was early days, but we had sent out the usual request for any information about him from Interpol and the Portuguese authorities. I had kept him on the list as being a person of interest to us, so the Portuguese informed us of his death."

"And you believe Zoey could be involved, or am I getting ahead of myself?"

"Maybe; we know Zoey came from the railway station in Seville. We also know a train arrived minutes before from Faro station in Portugal. This maybe coincidence, but a suspected paedophile is dead, a girl arriving claiming she had been in a child ring since the age of eleven does not happen every day. I called the Portuguese police for further information; ostensibly, my inquiry was to close our file on the man. The information they gave me is that they were looking for a young girl, who they believed was in the house where Fellers died. A witness said she had told them her name was Liberty. This pointed to a girl being held by Fellers. How he allowed the girl to talk to a stranger is not clear. Then Zoey, knowing what had happened, may have changed her name. She has not given us the name of the person she was being held by, or where she had actually come from. Until I understand Zoey, and her thinking, I intend to delay requesting further information from the Portuguese. I've told them at this stage, we only required confirmation that they have identified the body in the house as Fellows, and we'd be in touch if we needed more."

"Does this pose difficulties for us?"

"If Zoey admits she was in the house and had a part

in Fellers death, possibly. Until then, we treat her as a victim of trafficking. The information she has, outweighs the demise of a paedophile who could have been raping the girl day after day, week after week. However, if after a discussion we consider her explanation to have been self-defence; either Unit T will step in and sort the situation out, or LBNF."

"And if you think she killed him and it wasn't self-defence?"

"Let's not go down that path. While children can kill, I cannot see it being premeditated. There had to be a reason she turned on him. After all, she had been in the ring for four years, not knowing any other life. For her it would a have been a day-to-day existence. In my mind, it is perfectly possible that Fellers was fatally injured in a scuffle between them, but first, we must be certain this is the girl they are looking for."

Chapter 8

Arriving at the camp, Zoey had been taken to the purpose-built victims' unit. This unit comprised of a large lounge, single bedrooms, games room and its own dining room, served from the main camp restaurant. It would be rare that a victim of trafficking would remain here much longer than a week before being moved to LBNF, where obtaining documents for the victim to return to their own country, would begin. LBNF was all right with this arrangement because Karen, some years back, had negotiated with countries whose nationals, snatched within the EU, will fund their stay with LBNF while waiting for repatriation. If victims could not return home for various reasons, they would be looked after by LBNF.

Zoey slept until eleven. She had taken a shower in the en suite bathroom, where she found a packaged toothbrush. Wearing the same clothes she arrived in, Zoey wondered into the main lounge. The woman, who ran the unit, met her in the lounge taking Zoey to the camp shop. There she was able to select a new wardrobe along with other personal items, even makeup if she wanted. Apart from the usual shorts, jeans and trainers, she also chose two dresses with shoes to match, along with undergarments and night clothing. With not getting up until late and being told she was to join Karen for lunch, Zoey decided against breakfast, apart from a can of pop. Now she was back in the victims' suite dressed in one of her new dresses, waiting for Karen to collect her. Zoey had become more and more in awe of Karen, after reading yet another earlier LBNF magazine she had found in the magazine rack inside the suite, as well as a Unit T magazine printed for staff and residents in the camp. Only now was she realising just how high the rank of colonel was in the army, as well as how important Karen was to the camp.

Karen, in her military uniform, entered the suite, walking over to Zoey. "Hi, you must be Zoey? I am Colonel Karen Harris, but you can call me Karen. Everyone else does, providing they are not in the military," she said with a smile.

Zoey stood. Taken aback at how friendly Karen seemed. She had expected someone more reserved and staid in her approach. "Thank you for my clothes. I really appreciate being allowed to actually choose what I'd like to wear."

"You're very welcome. We can't have you wondering about in second-hand clothing."

"I've been told we are having lunch together? Is it in here, or somewhere else? With not knowing, I've tried to dress appropriately."

"The dress suits you. You have good taste. I was thinking of the camp's restaurant. They can normally find me a table. Shall we go? I'm starving, being up since six this morning."

Zoey did not believe for one moment a person of Karen's rank, would not to have a table laid out for her, but she never commented and left the building with Karen.

"What is going to happen today?" Zoey asked, as they walked towards the restaurant.

"After lunch, we'll go through everything that has happened to you since they snatched you from home. Most girls find it a little daunting, forced to relive episodes of their life they would prefer to forget. Unfortunately, that must happen. There are other girls out there, still held by the paedophile criminal group, waiting for our help. You may add to our own intelligence and end their nightmares. If you want a break, just tell us, there's no pressure."

Before going into the restaurant, Karen diverted through the regimental gardens, sitting down on a bench, urging Zoey to do the same.

"I've brought you to the gardens, out of earshot of others, for a good reason, Zoey. We are not the police; neither do we have allegiance to any EU security services. I tell you this because no matter what you tell us, we never pass it on. It is up to EU countries to pursue their own criminal investigations. We won't help them out."

"Can you do that?"

Karen smiled. "I can do what I want. We are a military operation, so all our work in human trafficking violations across EU countries is classified. You need to understand, users of girls at your age and younger, come from all lifestyles. I have prosecuted lords, captains of industry, doctors, politicians and everyone in between, down to the person in the street. To share what we know with outside security services is to forewarn sometimes very influential people who can disrupt investigations. That will not happen on my watch. So they all sit there, complaining we tell them nothing, with often the ones who complain loudest being the ones engaged in illegal activities with children, or older girls snatched from their homes."

"I didn't realise it was so widespread, mind you, I know lots of names, most boasting just how much money they have, or claiming they are in government and trying to get us out, but wanting to be told what other men do to us. It was all shit. It would turn them on when we told them. Sometimes they would want us to re-enact the action so they could understand. Just dirty old men, really."

"Then you can understand why we are secretive and tell people nothing? Which brings me to your situation? I want no lies, Zoey. Like I said, I could not care less what you have had to do, but time is of the essence. They will know you are gone and the other girl's lives in the paedophile ring are now at risk. Every scrap of information must be the absolute truth, no fantasy, no downgrading, believing we will think badly of you, or your actions. We are not here to judge. All the interviewers are female and, like me, have been in the hands of human traffickers, sometimes more than once. We know how helpless you are and given the opportunity of escape, when a chance to do so arises, or planned, you grasp it with both hands, no matter what."

"I won't lie to you, but what happened in the last days you must realise I had only two months left before my sixteenth birthday and I was counting the days."

"Why is sixteen important?"

"That's when they get rid of you. It was talked about between girls you met at gatherings when you went up for exchange, sixteen is the day you die, you know too much and no matter what they tell you, they would never risk you in a brothel, or use you outside the paedophile ring." She hesitated a moment. "I was looking forward to it. After living the way I had for four years, any dreams of a family, or a life where you are not just a plaything for an old man, is gone. You just want out, even when the only release is death."

Zoey had decided to ignore Fellers claim that she would have gone to a brothel. She never believed it anyway. The man was desperate for help and if it meant telling her lies to help him, what would that matter.

"Well now you have that future, Zoey. I can promise you that. Come on, it's time to eat."

When Karen walked into the restaurant, the room fell silent, with everyone standing. Normally, if she went in, she would not be in uniform. This time she was, and her rank had to be acknowledged.

"At ease," she ordered, and the restaurant reverted to normal.

The restaurant manager came up to her. "Your table is ready, Colonel, if you would follow me?"

Zoey smiled to herself, she knew Karen would have

a table.

They both sat down. "Marvin knows what I have, Zoey, but you're welcome to go to the self-service and find something you'd like, or have the same as me."

"I'd like to look. I have never had a choice before. I've read about self-service, but I don't understand how it works."

"What do you think, Marvin? Would you mind showing our Zoey the ropes?"

"Of course I wouldn't, Colonel. Come on, Zoey; let's find you something you really like, shall we?"

As they walked away, Zoey asked him a question. "Why did everyone stand when Karen came in?"

"The rank of colonel in a military camp commands acknowledgment and respect, Zoey, particularly when in uniform."

"But I was told by the lady who runs the victims unit, that Karen is not the commander anymore. Was she sacked? If so, why is she here?"

"It's complicated Zoey, and not my field. Save to say, Karen stepped down as our commander and moved to the EU main building in Brussels. The rank of colonel is too high to command a unit like Unit T, so we now have a major. Karen is here as an EU advisor, but of course, she still keeps her military rank, making her the senior officer in the camp. While she won't interfere in the day-to-day operation of Unit T, she will have control of operations going on out in the field."

"I wish I'd not asked. It all sounds very complicated."

"Don't worry about it. As far as you are concerned, Karen is in charge of your situation. Now it's time to sort out what you're having for lunch."

Zoey returned carrying a tray, on it a plate piled with chips, beans and a burger, jelly and cream for afters, with a soft drink.

Karen looked at it. "Are you sure that is what you want?"

"Of course, I've read about burgers and how all the kids love them, but never had one, and I love chips. This couldn't be a better dinner for me."

"Yes, I was forgetting you've grown up in an older male dominated world. Burgers wouldn't be on their list of favorites, neither would jelly."

She looked at Karen. "You don't mind, do you? I'll take it back if I've got the wrong food."

Again Karen realised how obedient she was, if the person she was with did not agree with her. The indoctrination seemed to be complete, to have a child so scared of upsetting their owner she would immediately become subservient and apologise. It was becoming understandable how they could keep a child so long without problems.

"God no, often you'd find me and Jasmin sitting on a wall outside a burger bar enjoying just what you've selected. It's just that with such a large choice, I was a little surprised you chose that."

Zoey relaxed and started eating. Shortly, she stopped for a moment. "Do you really sit on walls eating burgers, or are you putting me on? After all, I have read about you in the LBNF magazines. You are mega rich. Why would you be happy with a burger?"

They had given Karen steak and onions with chips. She finished what she was eating and looked at her. "I am, as you say, supposedly mega rich, if the press is to be believed, who incidentally seems to know more about me than I do. I was brought up in a semi-detached house. We had nothing and a chip shop supper was a luxury once or twice a year. It was only when I left home I inherited sufficient money to secure LBNF's future. I spend very little on myself, really, because I am not interested in showing off, by having big parties, super cars on my drive, and extravagant properties all over the world. I have a house here with another in Brussels and London for my work, as well as a holiday home in Corsica. My cars, I have three, all at least ten years old, that still run well. I know many people with far less resources than me, living the high life with all the trappings. It is a state of mind, when you spend lavishly to impress, but the reality is you lose sight of the value of money, believing if you pay more your get better. That is not always true; all you do is walk around with a large 'M' for mug pasted on your forehead. So now, you know all about me. This afternoon will be your turn."

"You'll not like it. My life has been pretty pathetic as well as traumatic."

"No, Zoey, four years of your life have been traumatic. For the rest of your life, you are part of the LBNF family and it's time to live again, but this time free to do as you want."

Chapter 9

Beacher Marinez arrived at a large warehouse outside the docks in Leixões, Portugal. Going through to the back office area, he met Javier.

"How many have arrived?" he asked.

"We have six from local men, two are on their way, and three are still with their owners, who are refusing to hand them over. I've arranged safe houses for the ones who are here and on their way."

"You go with our people to fetch the last of them. Any objections treat the owners as a security risk and put a bullet in their heads. I am not messing around. Our contact in Unit T has confirmed, less than an hour back, they have Liberty. How the fuck Harris could move that fast and pull her out, I do not know, but she has and will soon act on information extracted from Liberty. We will not have much time. First she will be pulling in the paedophile's, giving us a breathing space to get the girls out of the EU, before anyone points a finger at us."

Javier seemed confused. "Liberty couldn't know much about our current operation. It's changed so much since she was with us."

Beacher sighed. "Harris has a massive intelligence operation with covert operators and informers. Liberty may only fill in a few blanks, but that could be all Harris needs to complete the picture. Don't for one moment think she doesn't already know about us, she will."

"Why should she? She's raided none of our locations?"

"She'll know, but that woman will not only be looking into the movement of the girls, Harris will be following the finance, our contacts, so when she strikes, she takes everything. It's how Harris works and how she's been able to amass a personal fortune while doing it."

Javier grinned. "You're suggesting she's not that honest?"

"Suggesting, no, telling you, yes. I have met many who say the same. Harris goes for the money, ploughing it into her charity, as well as pocketing a lump herself. Well, she is not getting any of our money. We have not spent years accruing a fortune just to let her get it. So we move the girls out fast, then sit back and wait. She'll not hang around long before moving on to more lucrative criminal groups."

"Very well, I'll take Jake and Andre. We should be back in three or four days. When are they loading?"

"Seven days' time, so it'll be tight if you face any delay. This is important. If you cannot meet the loading, the girls have no value. We will be stuck with them for a month. That cannot happen if you get my meaning?"

"No problem. I should make it."

After Javier left, Beacher called his contact at Unit T.

"Can you talk?"

"Yes."

"What's the chance of getting someone into the camp?"

"There are ways. The camp is not that secure unless it goes on lockdown. These days, lockdown is rare since the new commander took over. The operations he has instigated since coming amounts to one, even that was a farce, the man is a buffoon. Harris's command was very different. The camp would always be secure when she ran it."

"I'm told Harris is back. Has nothing altered?"

"No, she's only here as advisor, not in command. Why are you asking? Who wants to come in?"

"That is my business. Your job is to get him in, your fee, ten thousand euro in gold sovereigns."

"And I just get him in. I'm not assisting in any way?"

"All he will want is a map showing the layout of the camp, and then you're done."

"I can do that, when?"

"Tonight; where does he meet you?"

"The forest bordering the camp has tracks used as firebreaks going through. It is close to a thousand acres. The forest surrounding Harris's house is completely out of bounds, but I can give him a route that avoids getting close. He must not deviate from the route I give. Dark Angel units patrol the forest area around the house. Stumble on one of them and he may as well go home. It would activate an emergency shutdown of the entire area. Years back, a cartel believed they could take on Unit T in their own backyard, so to speak. Harris was able to field nearly a hundred troops for a running battle going on in the forest. They eliminated the cartel. Although the cartel destroyed her house, she rebuilt it and the area around the house is now very secure, with Harris going on to purchase all the forest. Now it is used by Unit T troops for training. But at the moment there are none out on exercise."

"What doesn't that woman own?"

Rolando laughed. "When you're as wealthy as Harris, you can own what you want. Believe me, a thousand acres; she'd buy out of petty cash."

"Maybe, but back to business, the person you are to meet will come on an electric motorbike following the firebreak tracks. When he arrives and has completed his job, if you decide you want out that is fine. You can leave with him. I have a ship departing shortly. You could be on that with an extra hundred grand in your pocket as a bonus and gone forever."

"I'll think about it. When can your man be here?"

"Three hours."

"Have him set off and text me his number. I will text

him a 'three word' location. If he has the what3words app on his phone, he'll know exactly where I am."

"Never heard of that app, but if you say it works, why not? Just get the job done."

Rolando Christopher, aged twenty-seven and a trained Dark Angel soldier, cut the call to Beacher. Already he was spending the money Beacher had offered. For some time, he had been getting nowhere in the military and once, while on holiday, he had met Beacher. They got on well and as soon as Beacher found out he was in Unit T, he became more than interested. By the time the holiday was over, and with Beacher supplying young girls for the nights, Rolando was hooked, particularly when money was forthcoming for what he saw as minor information passed to Beacher on movements within Unit T.

***

Just after nine thirty in the evening, Rolando began crawling under the camp fence in a far corner of the campground, dragging a backpack after him. This, for soldiers who had been in the camp for a few years, was a known way out when they did not have a pass, avoiding the MPs at the camp entrance. Sprinting a short distance into the forest, Rolando dragged out one of five bicycles hidden in the undergrowth. Soldiers used these bikes to get to the town around ten miles away, frequenting the bars to the early hours, before returning to the camp the same way. Peddling for a good fifteen minutes, he was soon at the location where he was to meet the man sent by Beacher.

He had been there for twenty minutes when two electric motorbikes approached silently, one man on one, two men on the other. The man on one came to a stop and pulled off his helmet.

"The name's Marcel, Beacher sent me. Are you Rolando?"

"Yes, but I thought there was only one coming?"

Marcel shrugged. "What's it matter? One or three, you've still got a seat on the pillion if you are coming with us after our operation."

"I will come with you, except I've only brought one uniform for you to use. So if they saw you on camp, no one would take much notice of a private wondering about."

"Good thinking, I'll use it. The other two lads are my backup. They can stay out of sight. How close can we go by bike?"

"With these types of bikes within a hundred yards from the fence, then the track becomes too narrow."

"That's fine. Climb on behind me," Marcel told him, replacing his helmet.

In minutes they had arrived, hidden their bikes and after Marcel had changed into the uniform, they made their way to a gap under the fence, all crawling through.

"Where is the victim's suite in relation to us?" Marcel demanded.

Rolando stared at him. "You're going after Zoey?" he gasped.

"That's who she calls herself, is it? We know her as Liberty, but yes, who do you think we've come for?"

"You'll never get close. She's guarded."

"That is my problem, not yours. Now point the bloody place out."

Rolando showed him the route to take. "I'm remaining here. I'm not going near the victim's suite."

"We don't want you to, but Franco here will remain with you, in case you change your mind and decide to raise the alarm."

"I'd not do that. I want out, but I don't want to get in a gunfight with my friends."

Marcel shrugged, told one of the men to follow behind him, and they set off. Both pulling handguns out and screwing on silencers.

Soon they were at the side of a building, looking at the entrance to the victim's suite.

"Guarded, that's a laugh, with only one security man sitting at a desk. Watch my back, I'll go inside," Marcel told the man with him.

Walking purposefully up to the door, he stopped to allow the man inside to see him. The guard pressed a button to release the door, allowing Marcel inside.

"What do you want? My shifts got another hour to run."

"Bloody charming, I was told different. Who do we have in the suite?" Marcel asked, carrying on with the deception.

"One girl, but she's out tonight at the club cinema. Due back shortly."

Marcel realised, with the soldier being so open and talkative, he did not consider that the person standing in front of him offered any sort of threat. After all, they were deep inside the camp, so there would be no reason to. This may be why he was not being asked for any ID. Such complacency, for Marcel, was playing into his hands. He glanced towards a door to one side of the desk. "What's in there?"

"It's the storeroom, have you never been in here before?"

"No, have we time for a quick look around?"

"Why not, as I said she won't be back for another half hour."

They both went into the suite. It impressed Marcel how large and well fitted out it was, even commenting to the guard.

"It was all down to our last commander, Colonel Harris. She would often have ten or twelve girls here. She hit so many criminal groups and cartels, her own charity was at capacity, which delayed moving them on. That was until the last complex Torre del Mar came online. That complex is vast, according to some lads coming back after a stint there. More than two or three girls, here at the same time, would be rare. So, where have you been working?"

Marcel took a flyer with his answer. "I normally patrol in the forest area."

"Wow, I always wanted that. I'm told when Karen's away, the lads get to use the outside pool."

"I wish, I was on remote patrol. We'd better return to the reception, if she's due back," Marcel suggested, not wanting any possibility of MPs coming into the suite with Zoey.

As the guard led the way. Close to the door through to the reception, Marcel pulled out a stun gun, pushing it into the man's neck, pulling him back from the door, as he slumped to the floor. Dragging him further into the suite, Marcel secured his hands behind his back with large tie wraps, taken from his pocket, before doing the same to his ankles. Finally, after sticking duct tape over his mouth, he dragged the man into a bedroom, closing the door and jamming a chair to stop the handle being used.

Back at the reception, he sat waiting for Zoey to return, at the same time calling the man with him stood opposite the entrance watching, giving him an update.

Fifteen minutes later, a jeep stopped outside, with an MP driving, Zoey at his side. She climbed out and he remained there until she was in the suite's reception before driving off.

"Was it a good film?" Marcel asked.

"Yes, thank you. Is the door open?"

"No, I'll come and let you in."

As they entered the suite, Marcel slammed the door behind them. Zoey turned to look at him, somewhat surprised he was still in the room.

"What is your name?" he asked.

"Zoey."

He shook his head slowly. "That isn't your name. It may have been when you were very young, but our good friend Beacher changed it, if you remember? So what is it?"

The mention of Beacher made her go cold inside. Who was this man and why was he in the suite? However, Zoey had spent such a long time in the hands of traffickers; she did not have the strength of character to argue a direct question.

"My name is Liberty."

"That is correct, I don't want to hear you calling yourself Zoey, or any other name that comes into your head, understand?"

"Yes."

"Now we understand each other; I've come to take you back to Beacher, who is not too pleased with you killing Blake. After all, he was paying Beacher each month for your company."

Her mouth dropped. The fear of being taken to face Beacher terrified her. "Please don't send me back, I beg you. It was an accident. I never wanted him to die. I was happy there and worked hard to please him. You can punish me. In fact, I will do anything you want of me. I've been told I'm good in the bedroom, so no matter what you want, I'll not disappoint you, but don't take me to Beacher."

"What do you know of pleasing a real man? You've only been with old men, used as a plaything."

She looked down. "I suppose, but that's not my fault, I can only go where I'm told. I was eleven, underdeveloped and a child, when Beacher taught me how to look after my owner. Now I am fifteen, nearly sixteen with an acceptable figure, willing to learn as well as being submissive. What more would a man want?"

He said nothing.

Liberty was desperate for him not to take her to Beacher. She pushed the straps of the dress off her shoulders, allowing it to fall to her feet, before stepping away from her dress, wearing just bra and knickers. "You can see I'm not lying. I have a nice figure for my age. There is a bedroom through that door. Let me show you what I have learnt over the years. I can't offer anything else apart from promising I'll be attentive and submissive for as long as you keep me."

"You're correct, you have a nice body. It is a pity it was being wasted on old men. When we leave here, we will be stopping in a hotel overnight. Prove to me you can shag and I mean really shag, you'll not go to Beacher, I'll keep you."

"Thank you for giving me a chance. I promise I'll not disappoint."

Taking a plastic bag from his pocket, he handed it to her. "It's time we left. I want you in jeans or shorts, what clothes and personal items you have, that will fit in this plastic bag, you can take with you."

Immediately, she picked up her dress running into her bedroom. In minutes, she was out holding the bag, wearing jeans. He took it from her and looked inside before handing it back.

"Are you going to give me any trouble when we leave?"

"No, Sir, I'll give you no trouble. I know my place."

"See you don't. It's time to go."

Leaving the victim's suite, they crossed the road and joined the other man, before retracing their steps back to where Rolando was waiting.

"You've brought Zoey. How are we going to get her away? We have no room?" he gasped.

"That's easy. We leave the least valuable person behind, and unfortunately, dollar for dollar, Liberty is worth a hundred grand, while you are worth minus a hundred. No contest, don't you think?" Marcel came back at him, pulling his still silenced gun from his pocket and shooting him in the chest. As soon as he fell to the ground, this was followed by a shot to the head.

"You can see, Liberty, because of your escape, people die. I hope you feel good about this. Get yourself under the fence."

They travelled on the bikes for over an hour before pulling onto a side road and then down a farm track before stopping in an open area, where a car was already parked.

"Liberty, into the car," Marcel told her. She ran over and climbed in the passenger side.

"Good job, lads," he said, handing each a bundle of euro. There's more money for you both when she's sold."

"We'll be looking forward to it. Call us when you've done a deal," one said, and then they both turned, heading to the two bikes.

Marcel smiled. *"You wouldn't answer if I did,"* he said to himself, raising his gun and shooting both in the back, before walking over and finishing them with a shot to the head. Reaching down, he retrieved the payments he'd just made, and walked back to the car, climbing in the driver's seat."

"See, Liberty, yet more people have died because of you."

"Why?"

He looked at her. "Do you want to go to Beacher?"

She shook her head.

"In that case, everyone who knew I'd got you out can't be allowed to blab to Beacher. All you have to do now is prove to me people were worth dying for you. Can you do that?"

"Yes."

"We'll see." He started the car, and they turned back

to the main road, setting off towards Paris.

Chapter 10

The telephone ringing wakened Karen just after six in the morning. On answering, she was told what had happened at the camp. Now Major Lang was requesting she attend a meeting at nine o'clock. They would send a car for her. Karen sighed inwardly. This cannot be happening.

Karen, in uniform, entered Major Lang's office.

He stood as she entered. "I have fresh coffee, Colonel. May I pour you a cup?" he asked.

"Thank you. Do you have a time line for what transpired?"

He brought her coffee over and they both sat down.

"I have. My initial report is inside a folder on your desk. Summing it up, I found a catalogue of stupid errors. Such as the soldier on the reception of the victim suite not even checking on someone coming to the door, be it by showing an ID, or even contacting security as to why his replacement was there an hour before he went off shift, before letting him in. Soldiers, who have been in the camp for some time, also knew there was a way out under the fence that was used to visit the town, when the soldier did not have a pass to do so. Then the MP, who brought Zoey back to the victim's suite, did not even sign her in, just watched as she went inside before driving off. I take full responsibility for shoddy security, Colonel, which should never have happened. During a perimeter search, which located the breach in the fence, they found a soldier in civilian clothing. Alongside him was a backpack full of his personnel items. It would seem the soldier intended to leave, but that is only a surmise. A soldier has died on my watch; security's breached, as well as losing the girl." He passed across to her a letter. "It's my resignation, effective immediately."

"I agree, by what you have told me, there has been

66

a breakdown in security procedures that allowed Zoey to be snatched, but your resignation is unnecessary, Major. A review of security would be far more preferable than a change of command."

"No, Colonel, the safety of each person in the camp is ultimately my responsibility. I never really believed what you kept telling me of the dangers victims of trafficking faced. In fact, in my mind, you were exaggerating. Because of that attitude, I was becoming, like others, complacent about what should have been a priority in protecting a very high-risk asset, who was also a vulnerable child in our care. How you control the security in the LBNF complexes with so many at risk girls, I cannot imagine. But for me, as a professional soldier all my life, there is no room for a lax operation, resulting in the death of a soldier. I have informed senior officers in my country and been recalled to face a disciplinary hearing, making it impossible for me to remain as Unit T's commander. With an officer on the camp holding a senior rank, you are required under military law to take command of Unit T until a replacement is in post. I'm sorry our association had to end this way, when I finally began to understand what you've had to face over the years, and I respect you for what must have been a tough job, given the opposition from others in the military."

"You are correct; it has always been a problem since I took command. Although I saw in you a very competent commander, who once you understood, could take Unit T forward. I too am sorry it ended this way."

Ignoring Karen's assessment of him, Major Lang continued telling her about the handover arrangements he had already put in place. "I have asked my adjutant to set up a meeting of all military personnel in the sports hall for eleven hundred hours. There I will announce my stepping down as their commander and you taking command. Then

I will leave you to address the unit. I have booked a seat on the service aircraft for Paris later today. My belongings will be sent on to me. I trust that is in order?"

"It is, Major." Karen picked up the cup and sipped her coffee. She considered the man spineless, bailing as fast as he could. She also believed, what transpired here, once he was back in Germany, would be swept under the carpet. His usefulness in remaining here to monitor what was happening had ended and they, or rather someone, wanted him out. Probably to be replaced by a man more pliable than Lang. He was a soldier and followed orders to the letter, making any control of him difficult, if not impossible, without written orders. She replaced her cup on the saucer. "There is one thing I would like to know. Before you leave the camp, who did you talk to in Germany?"

"General Gomeric Busch."

"Was this the same man who wanted you to remain, when I returned as adviser and you had asked for a reassignment?"

Lang knew why she asked. Karen had a particular interest in the man who had convinced him to remain and effectively be an informer of anything she was undertaking, but he had not disclosed to Karen his name.

"You have never pushed me for the name of the man who wanted me to inform on you going forward, and I respect that. You have also shown to me what people were saying about you, particularly that you were as bad as the criminals you had taken down, was not true. In my mind, you are a remarkable woman who does not deserve the accusations men were throwing towards you. I was being told that some very important people are involved in certain ways that the public and media could construe as criminal, yet it was the only way of getting things done. Then to be reminded that I rely on what is happening in these shady deals to keep my job and a good salary. That, for me, was a shock, but to be further told that such dealings was how you had accumulated your wealth and they were doing the same. After all, in their view, no one goes from nothing to be worth close to a billion, particularly with a full-time job in the military."

"I documented my inheritances as required, but criminals will always attempt to distort truths to convince others because they make their money illegally. You mentioned that you spoke to a General Gomeric Busch, is he the officer who also suggested I was a criminal?"

"Correct. Although, I have disclosed nothing to the General, which could be why this security breach is very useful in getting me out, with a replacement that may be more accommodating."

"It wouldn't surprise me, Major. I also appreciate you confirming a name. Everything, however small, adds to the picture we are building. I am also surprised a General is talking to you. After all, in the German army that is a rank six stages higher than you are, so why would he involve himself? The only reason I can see is the people telling him to become involved, are politicians, or very wealthy business people, who have an interest in keeping tabs as to what I am up to."

"May I ask what your approach will be going forward?"

"It's no secret how I operate. I bring a person of interest to book by the use of informers and covert operators who infiltrate. It works. Criminals become complacent, believing they are untouchable. Until we walk in the door and take them away. Even then, most never see the seriousness of their situation, believing they will get an insignificant punishment and walk out. That is until we take their world apart by impounding assets. Believe me, it's then when they squeal, offering information to save their own skins, knowing if they can't come to a deal, when they finish their sentence, everything will be gone."

"It sounds so simple, but I suspect very complex. I hope you find Zoey. That girl has gone through hell. She deserves a new life."

Karen stood. "In my experience, once they get out of her what she's told us, we will be very lucky to find her alive. Zoey is far too dangerous for them, when they risk entering this camp to snatch her. She knows too much, but I will not give up on her, until I know either way. On another point, when you address your command, I will not be there. After you leave, then I will go in. I think it is best that way."

"Very well, Colonel. We may have been together for a brief time, but I'll not forget you."

Karen nodded and left the office.

***

Karen entered the sports hall. Every soldier stood at attention. She walked up to the Regimental Sergeant Major; he saluted.

"Is every soldier here, including ones off duty, but still in the camp?" she asked.

"No, Colonel. Soldiers conducting security jobs around the camp and off duty personnel are not here."

"I understood Major Lang had requested every soldier in the camp attend? Send people to find them. Lock the main gates if necessary and place civilians there. I'll return in fifteen minutes, those not here by then place them on report," then she walked out.

Immediately, he was shouting to officers and MPs to move themselves and bring every soldier into the hall.

Karen was back in exactly fifteen minutes. Stepping up on the stage, she looked around the hall, but she did not have them stand at ease, although the regimental sergeant major was waiting for her nod.

"A soldier died last night, a fifteen-year-old girl,

locked in a life of hell with a paedophile group since the age of eleven snatched. Not at one of LBNF's complex's, or off the street, but from inside this camp. Your commanding officer was required to resign his post and perhaps face a disciplinary board. I hope you all feel proud of yourselves, because believe me, I do not. You make me ashamed of stepping in as commander once more. Such complacency in security means we will be extremely lucky to find the girl alive. It also means, I have to risk the lives of people working out in the field trying to locate her, before I can order a Dark Angel unit in," Karen hesitated. "Those among you, who worked with me when I was last in command, know I treat everyone as equals and a responsible adult. But let none of you believe, because of that approach, I am a soft touch. I am not. I have seen too many excellent soldiers, too many covert operators out in the field, the same as victims of trafficking, die, to be complacent with security, on or off the camp. Until a permanent commander is in post, I am in command, any further lax in security procedures, or soldiers leaving the camp without permission will not be subject to internal discipline, those soldiers, no matter what their rank will stand in front of a military tribunal facing a court martial. We have standing orders for a reason, not to make life difficult, but to keep people, be it civilian or military, safe. Following your dismissal, all officers are to review their own areas and procedures, then report to me in twenty-four hours. Think about what I've said, those who can't follow orders, go home, we don't want you, the army doesn't want you," then she left the stage and walked out of the building.

After being dismissed, most stood around, stunned by her words. Those who had been here when she was last in command had never seen this side of her. She seemed cold, hard and annoyed she had taken back command. None doubted she would not carry out her threats.

Chapter 11

Marcel lay back, watching Liberty walk through to the bathroom. For the last hour, he had been working her hard, and like she claimed, she had grown up during her time with Spartes and really knew how to please a man. While he did not intend to keep her around, he could see real value in her, particularly being at an age buyers of young girls would snatch his hand off when offered for sale. At that moment, the mobile rang. He looked at the caller ID. It was Beacher.

"Marcel here," was all he said.

"Where are you? I cannot even get an answer from Rolando, or the lads. Then you've not been answering your phone," Beacher burst out, obviously annoyed.

"Yes well, if your man in Unit T had been straight and not led us into an ambush, you'd have the girl by now," he came back at him.

"You're telling me, Rolando, set us up?"

"Not telling, he did. Both lads were killed. The last I saw of Rolando was on the ground, in agony, with a bullet in his gut. I cannot see him lasting. I had to shoot my way out, and only just made it to the bikes we had hidden. As for the girl, fuck knows where she is, probably still with Unit T. We never got close enough to snatch her."

"Shit, that's all I need. What are you doing now?"

"I've a job outstanding, so I'm going on that. Why?"

"We have a contract you've not fulfilled."

"Find me a way into the camp and I'll see it through. I told you before you gave me the job, I don't kidnap, I kill people, neither do I trust people I have never met. But with us doing a lot of business in the past, I agreed to help you out of the shit with this girl. It has proved my rule to be correct, never work with, or rely on others. So if you've a single contract, I'll take it, providing it does not include me working with so-called trusted people."

"Where are you?"

"In Paris, why do you want to know?"

"Then I have a job, and one you can work alone. Javier has problems. He is still in Spain collecting one of three girls from an owner who would not let go. He was then to drive back to Chartres for the last, but will not make the boat if he does. Chartres is only an hour from where you are. Fetch her and kill her owner."

"And if the girl is trouble and won't come?"

"Then kill her too. She knows too much anyway."

"Fifty grand and I'll take the contract."

"Okay, but don't hang about. With Harris still having Liberty, time is of the essence in closing all loopholes."

"Send me a text with the address and his name. Make a fifty percent payment into my usual account. I will text you when it is done. A couple of hours and your problem will have gone away."

With a deal agreed Marcel cut the call. He could not believe it, a chance of another girl along with extra cash in the bank. Things were looking up.

Liberty came through from the bathroom after a shower, with a towel wrapped round her. She stood for a moment, looking at him shyly. "Was I what you wanted and you won't send me to Beacher?" she asked quietly.

"You have certainly learned how to please a man, I'll give you that, but will you be loyal, not wanting to run away all the time?"

She gave an indifferent shrug. "I didn't want to leave Blake. Our argument was that he wanted me to live in his cellar. I would have gone, but he was in one of those moods he kept having, not letting me take Teddy. He tried to snatch it off me, and injured himself with a nail I had picked up off the floor to throw away. I could not stay in the house on my own, so I ran. It did me no good, you soon found me. Then I do not want to end up on the street again, with not enough money in my pocket to buy a drink. Even Unit T wanted to lock me up, maybe send me back to Portugal to face the police. I have no idea. So look after me and I will be loyal and keep you happy. I can offer no more." Liberty hoped she had said enough, and he would not take her back to Beacher.

"Very well, I'll give you a month to prove yourself. Get dressed, I've a job and you're coming with me."

As she dressed, the text came through of the address in Chartres. Marcel checked his bank account. The twenty-five thousand was already in. With Liberty ready to leave, they left the motel.

***

Théo Deschamps came through from the lounge to find Avril, a girl supplied to the paedophile ring by Beacher, standing at the sink rinsing the dinner plates. He watched her with a hint of a smile on his face. Aged, fourteen, long blonde hair, tall, slim, Avril, was everything he wanted from a girl. However, a call from Virgilio, the leader of the group, informed him that Beacher wanted Avril back. This annoyed him; he was not ready to let her go. So he had refused, telling Virgilio, he had no intention of losing Avril until her time was up and looking at her now, wearing heeled sandals, a very short skirt, showing off her slim legs, he knew he was right. In his mind, Avril, although needing a great deal of control, was close to perfect. He had at least two months before she would go to another in the group, until then, she would remain here.

Avril heard him come into the kitchen, and turned. "Do you need me, Papa?" she asked. Théo always insisted she call him Papa. Why, she had no idea, in her mind he would never replace her own father.

"We are going away to the cabin for a few days tomorrow. We will be leaving early, so when you have finished, it is an early night for us both."

She smiled sweetly. "If that's what you want, I'll not be much longer. Do you want me to wear my new nighty with the matching panties?"

"Yes, but don't waste time, already you're turning me on with just the thought," then he left the kitchen.

Avril sighed. Since she had turned eleven, this was her seventh man from the paedophile ring, and the only real life she could remember. Her childhood before the ring had become a blur. Her mother's sister had taken her in, following the death of her parents, after a road accident, when she was nine. However, the sister's husband was bedridden with terminal cancer. This meant Avril had to spend lots of time helping her aunt look after him. While her husband was in bed, her aunt was having an affair with another man, so when her husband finally died, the lover moved in. He did not like Avril being around and constantly shouted at her for virtually nothing. This naturally upset Avril. Her schoolwork was affected. She had no friends, and no one to turn to for help. All she could do was answer back in a vain attempt to defend her actions. This made matters even worse within the family, and just after eleven one evening, Avril woke, after being shaken, to find Beacher and another man stood by the side of the bed. They dragged her out of bed, down the stairs, to be thrown in the back of a van parked outside. That was the last she saw of her aunt.

Her life completely changed, Beacher had not taken her as a child needing to complete her education; he had other ideas. She had been taken to a brothel. Her job was to look after clients waiting to go with girls. After the brothel closed, Beacher would take her to his bed, where she was taught how to keep a man happy. Refusal in doing anything demanded of her, Beacher would have her held face down over the side of a table; her knickers pulled clear of her bottom, to be thrashed with a slipper. After two punishments like that, Avril did anything she was told and was soon sent to the paedophile ring.

In Avril's mind, Théo was the worse man they had forced her on. He looked at her more as a plaything with no feelings, rather than a human being. The only clothes he had provided were from a magazine that specialised in sexy bedroom wear, role-playing clothing such as nurses' uniforms. The dominant theme of such garments, besides being poorly made and easily damaged, was short, skimpy and often see-through. With her not allowed to have a television, read newspapers, all she had was books, many in a language she couldn't understand, besides spending most of her time, when she wasn't cleaning, in his bedroom. There he would have her role-play, not that she understood why she had to play such silly games. During these games, more often than not, she would be told she had been a naughty girl that day, so he would bend over his knees for a gentle spanking. Gentle, '*that was a laugh*,' she thought, he would become enthusiastic, hitting harder, enjoying her screams. Even with all this abuse, Avril had no option but to put up with it. What else could she do? She had no money, no idea what country they were in, or the nerve to leave the house dressed as she was. The only positive in her life, if there was a positive, was that she had two months left with him before moving to another man. What would happen to her then, she had no idea, but he could not be worse than what she had already experienced with Théo, or so Avril hoped.

Dawdling as usual in finishing tidying up, she eventually went through to the bathroom, clipped her long hair back before washing herself down. There was no use for condoms, after being sterilised when she was first taken. Almost glad they had done it, she would have hated carrying a baby from any of the men she had lived with. Avril pulled the new nighty over her head. It hardly covered her bottom, yet what did that matter, she would not be wearing it for long. Now ready she went through to the bedroom.

"Ah, you're here at last," he said, sitting on the side of the bed naked. "Come and sit on my knee and tell me how much you love to be with me while I hold you."

Avril smiled inwardly. At least it was not a spanking night, if he wanted her on his knee. "Yes, Papa," she answered with a smile, adding a baby tone to her speech.

Théo, after kissing and fondling her, pushed her out of the way, allowing him to move further onto the bed, laying down urging her to get astride of him.

Avril climbed on top. It did not bother her, all part of his ritual, knowing after finishing, he would want to sleep, making her night easy.

Théo was gasping, demanding she worked harder, but his wriggling about meant she could not keep him inside her. Just at that moment, when he was really getting frustrated and annoyed, the doorbell rang. She stopped, pulling him out of her, not sure, what he wanted to do.

"Don't fucking stop, they'll go away," he shouted at her.

However, the knocking persisted, putting him off. He pushed her away.

"We can't shag with all this noise going on. It is probably the grocer for his money. Said he might call. Go and tell him I will be there shortly, while I dress."

"Excuse me, if you haven't noticed, I'm in a see-through nighty with no knickers. It would embarrass me answering the door."

"Stupid girl, I don't expect you to answer the door looking like that. Collect your dressing gown and only open the top part of the door. Now go while I pull my pants on."

Avril sighed inwardly. Climbing off the bed, she ran through to her bedroom, slipping on what Théo considered a dressing gown. Although in reality it was a cheap thin silk jacket, finishing at her bottom, with no buttons or even a belt to keep it closed. Pulling on knickers, before going to the front door, she slipped the catch to open the top of the split door.

Marcel was standing there, although Avril did not know him. He looked at the girl, the gown opening revealing how little she had on. He sighed inwardly. Who in their right mind would risk sending a young girl dressed as she was, to answer the door?

"Sorry for the delay in answering. I was in my bedroom. Can I help you?"

"Where's Théo?"

"Who shall I say wants him?"

"Just fetch him, and next time, wear decent clothes to answer the door."

She looked at him, embarrassed, at the same time pulling the dressing gown tight around her. "Sorry, I panicked with your constant banging on the door. I'll find him," she mumbled before turning back into the house to get Théo. He was still in the bedroom, partly dressed.

"Who is it?"

"He wouldn't say, just asked for you by name."

"I hope you shut the door while you came to find me?"

She looked at him with her enormous eyes. "No, Papa, I didn't think. I'll do it now." Then, before he could say anything, she ran back to the front door. It was still open at the top, but the man was no longer there. Avril, confused as to why he hadn't waited, shut the door and went back into the bedroom to tell Théo he was gone.

"What do you mean, gone? I thought you said he was asking for me. Now he goes, without even waiting to talk to me. Did you insult him and I'm going to get grief?"

"No, Papa, although he complained I'd not dressed appropriately to answer the door."

"Sometimes, Avril, I think you are completely stupid. It must have been the grocer wanting his money. So what did you do, open the dressing gown showing off your tits and embarrassing him?"

She looked scared. "The dressing gown did open, Papa. I am sorry, but it has no buttons or even a cord to keep it shut. I did not mean it to; it was difficult to open the door at the same time as stopping the dressing gown flapping. The door sticks and needs a good pull with both hands."

"I think you're lying and wanted him to see all you've got. Get the dressing gown off, remove the knickers, and bend over the side of the bed. With a few slaps on your bottom, maybe next time you'll not be so stupid."

Tears were coming to her eyes. "Please, Papa, I meant nothing. Let us just finish what we were doing. I'll work extra hard and really make you come."

Théo was having none of it. She would do that anyway before the night was out, but he could not let her believe she could manipulate him, or have him change his mind by begging. It was important to stamp his authority on every aspect of her life.

He quickly grabbed her hair, dragged her to the bed, pushing her face down over his knees as he sat down on the edge of the bed. "When I tell you to do something you do it," he shouted at her, at the same time ripping her knickers clear of her bottom and laying into her. She was screaming, begging him to stop. Finally he did, pushing her off his knees, demanding she undressed quickly and knelt between his legs.

With tears running down her face, Avril quickly did as he asked, while he stood and unzipped himself before sitting back down on the side of the bed. She knew what he wanted, but with her bottom still stinging, this was better than bending her over the side of the bed, or getting astride him.

She was on her knees in front of Théo, holding his penis in her hands, when Marcel walked into the bedroom. She let go, staring at him in obvious surprise, as well as being shocked he had not left as she believed, but let himself in. She knew Théo would make her pay for it by taking the whip to her later.

"That's harsh, Théo, punishing the girl for leaving the door open. How many people slam the door in a visitor's face while they find the person they want? In my mind you should be punished for sending her to the door virtually naked, or more the point she may as well have been naked with what she was wearing and only wanted to find you, not stand there talking to me. As it is for the last few minutes, I have been waiting for you in the lounge. After all, I considered you would want to check the house. It would seem not, being more interested in punishing the girl before having her suck your cock. What sort of man are you?" Then he looked at Avril, still kneeling in front of Théo, not sure what to do. "Don't let my business with Théo stop you, Avril. In fact, I'm happy for you to continue, showing me at least one thing you've learnt over the time you've been with the ring to give pleasure to your owner."

However, Théo cut in before she could do anything. "Who are you to tell my girl what she should do, and why are you in my house? You can forget Avril doing anything for me with you watching. I'm not a peep show," Théo shouted at him, pushing Avril away, sending her sprawling.

"How remiss of me not introducing myself; the name's Marcel, a contract killer working for Beacher. You and I need to talk, Théo. You've not been very helpful in the recall of Avril, so I understand."

Théo turned to Avril. "Get some bloody clothes on and wait in the lounge. I'll sort you out later."

Avril scooped up her clothes and quickly left. Today was fast becoming a nightmare, with even more punishment to come for letting Marcel into the house.

"Why does Beacher want her back? I've two months yet?" Théo demanded, after Avril left the room.

"He's pissed off, particularly after you were told by Virgilio that her remaining with you could pull the entire ring down, besides the possibility of Beacher himself being targeted."

Théo frowned. "I cannot see how Avril remaining here carries any risk. It is true Virgilio asked for Avril back, but only because he suspected Blake's death may backfire on us all. I asked him how that was possible, but he did not elaborate. Because of that, I told him I was keeping Avril until I returned her to the pool in two months."

"Then it seems like poor communication between you all. For your information, Liberty walked out of Blake's house to be picked up by Unit T, meaning Karen Harris has her. Liberty knows enough to bring the entire circle down and point to the supply of the girls towards Beacher. If Harris walks into this house and Avril's still here, you go down for at least ten years and Unit T takes everything you own. If you believe Harris wouldn't, you only have to look at the size of LBNF and the fact that Harris is worth close to a billion. Where do you think it all came from? People like you, Théo. Harris will come, that is certain."

"Virgilio never told me Unit T was involved. He just said Beacher wanted Avril back. Then something is not right. It's well known Harris resigned her command of Unit T, so why would she still be around?"

Marcel smiled. "Why Harris is back in control of

Unit T does not matter, she is, and we all know what she was like when last in charge."

"I've already told Avril we're going away tomorrow. But now I am aware Unit T is involved, as well as Harris, I have a place to hide Avril and believe me; she'll be very safe and not found."

"Why are you insisting on hanging on to her, Théo? She's due to leave you in a couple of months anyway and Harris's operation could go on way longer than that, before it all settles back down. Unless, that is, you have an idea to hold on to her beyond that time?"

He shrugged indifferently. "Sometimes a girl comes along who makes a powerful impression and you don't want to lose her. Avril is one of those girls, she is beautiful and developing into a nice girl, happy to do anything you want of her without complaint. She's with the ring for another year, so I intend to keep her until she's sixteen."

"I'd like to see if she'd agree to remain here beyond her six months, when she's punished for nothing."

"It is clear you don't understand what it takes to keep a child under control. She is like a caged animal, constantly probing the captor for weakness, all the time using psychological means to better her position. If you don't keep the pressure on her, she will turn on you, the same as Blake found."

"What the fuck are you going on about? She's still a child," Marcel asked, confused.

"Perhaps, but she is constantly learning, leading her captor into a false sense of security, all the while attempting to take control. They bide their time, but they will strike back if they see even a slight advantage. That is why the circle will not leave a girl beyond six months with any of us, to prevent them getting too comfortable. Then the reason they go at sixteen, they are stronger, their owner, like me in their fifties is so much weaker, making them vulnerable, particularly if she gets hold of a weapon."

"And you still want to hold on to Avril?"

He shrugged. "She's different, and I know how to control her, so yes, I will have another year out of her and maybe even longer."

Marcel glanced at his watch. "Well, it's been an interesting conversation and I admit an eye-opener in the way the ring operates. Then whoever told you they are uncontrollable over sixteen, because they are stronger, is talking a load of shit. Avril is with people like you until she attains an age where she can fetch Beacher top money. As well as gaining valuable experience, being submissive and knowing her place, a hundred grand would not buy her now. In fact, she could be worth closer to a hundred and fifty to the right buyer, along with the prestige for Beacher among big money clients, knowing he can supply the best. So she is going nowhere with you. She comes with me."

"No, she stays. I have already paid for the next two months and I intend to keep her. Beyond that, I'll negotiate with Beacher directly, so tell him that."

Marcel allowed a hint of a smile to cross his face, as he pulled out his gun with the silencer screwed on, from his jacket pocket. "Sorry, Théo, you aren't listening. I told you when I came in, I was a contract killer. I am not here to waste time listening to your arguments about why she cannot leave. Beacher's already paid me for your demise, so you can go to your maker knowing I will look after Avril by finding her a nice man to replace you." Then he pointed the gun and fired. Théo fell back on the bed, gasping for breath. Marcel finished by putting a bullet in his head, and then left the bedroom, shutting the door.

Going through to the lounge, he found Avril sitting on one of the easy chairs.

"I thought you may like a cold drink before you go. It's out of the fridge," she told him, pointing to a can of beer on the side table. "Is Papa still mad at me?"

"Thank you," he said, picking up the drink and taking a large gulp. "That was very welcome. As for Théo, he can be as mad as he wants, but it means nothing. I am here to take you away. Your time with Théo has ended. He is not happy. In fact, I have left him blubbering like a child in his bedroom. Have you any outdoor clothes?"

"Not really. I have a dress except its short. I keep growing out of my clothes."

"That will have to do until I can get you to a store." Pulling out a carrier bag from his pocket, he handed it to her. "If you have any personal items you want to take with you, and they fit in this bag, take them. Sort yourself out, we leave in five minutes."

Avril was back in minutes. He checked in the bag. There were only knickers, a toothbrush, along with a brush for her hair.

"Is this it?"

She looked down. "I have nothing. The only presents you get are items to please your owner. Beyond that, you are worthless."

"It's the way of the world, Avril. Let's go."

"Shouldn't I be saying goodbye, not that I liked him, but it seems wrong not to."

"Forget him. Let him stew in his own self-pity. He had been told you needed to go back, but ignored the instruction. Now it has happened. He's pissed off."

They left the house, walking the short distance to Marcel's car. Opening the back door, he told her to get in.

As she climbed in, her eyes lit up. "Liberty, it's been a long time," she gasped, seeing her sitting there, before giving her a hug.

"It's fantastic to see you, Avril. God, you've grown."

"I have, what about you? I love the hair."

By now, Marcel had climbed into the driver's seat

and looked back. "You know each other?"

"Yes, we've met a few times at an exchange, as well as some of the party weekends when the men bring their current girl. Not that you get to talk to each other much."

"Well, you can talk now, but I don't want to hear you telling each other what has happened recently, particularly you, Liberty."

"I understand."

Chapter 12

During the drive back to Paris, the girls chatted. More about the different houses, they had been taken, as well as laughing about the way their so-called owners handled a girl. Marcel listened. This was the first time he had heard about the life they lived, looked at from their perspective. In their world, these men were nothing, something to laugh at, in the pathetic way they treated the girls. He could understand to a degree, with no access to a television, radio or internet, their life was repetitious, lonely. The only conversation with others would be what their owner has said or done to them. Arriving back at the motel, he parked, taking them both to the room.

"Are you hungry?" Marcel asked.

They shook their heads.

"In that case, get yourselves to bed. Use the double bed; I'll use the single. I am going out for a short time. If the house phone rings, ignore it. The door will be locked so you don't get unwelcome visitors. Now, sort yourselves out."

After he left and they heard the deadlock click, both girls quickly washed and went to bed. They lay together in the dim light.

"What will happen to us, Liberty?"

"I'm not sure, but I don't believe he's going to keep us. Probably send us to other men."

"I've had enough, constantly walking around partially naked, shagged at the man's whim."

"What can we do about it, Avril? You know he carries a gun?"

"No, I didn't, but I was sure I heard two thuds from the bedroom when Théo sent me out. Then Marcel would not let me go in and say goodbye. I would have probably spit in Théo's face, but Marcel told me he was upset and did not want to see me leave. That was not like Théo. I think Marcel shot him. After all, he told Théo he was a contract killer. What that means I'm not sure, but it seems logical with the killer in his words Théo's dead." She sighed, "I'll not lose any sleep over it, at least no other girl will have to go through what I did with him."

They both fell silent for a time.

"I don't want more years of this life, Liberty. I'm tired; I just want to lie down never to wake, if my future is to be raped day after day, with no love, no words of comfort apart from the *'you were a good shag'* comment."

Avril offered her a hand, Liberty grasped hold of it.

"Marcel didn't want me to mention what happened in the last few days, but it started with me killing Blake, the man who I was currently with. It was not intentional, more an accident, but I walked out free. It felt good, Avril. For the first time, I ran down a beach, sand on my feet and paddled in the warm sea. I found help from a charity and was going to live a life free of owners, but Beacher sent Marcel and he killed a man before bringing me back."

"God, Liberty, it must have been terrifying for you?"

"I suppose, but the same as you, I don't want to go back to my past life with another Blake. If we don't want that, we will not have much time to plan an escape. Are you with me?"

"I am, but on one condition."

"What?"

"Whatever we do, if it goes wrong, I don't want to live. I'll not go back, Liberty."

"Neither do I. We're free, or this is the end for both of us."

Avril let go of Liberty's hand and put her arms around her. The girls held each other tight for a time. While they had decided to attempt an escape; both knew talk was cheap, only actions would secure their freedom.

It was time to plan.

***

Marcel awoke to find the girls already up. Avril was combing her hair, Liberty sitting in an easy chair, reading a magazine left on the coffee table.

"Good morning girls. You are up early. Have you both showered?"

Liberty spoke for them both. "Good morning, we're used to getting up early and yes, the bathroom's yours. We shared the shower to wash each other's hair. One disadvantage of having long hair is washing and drying it yourself."

"Yes, I can understand that. Give me ten minutes, and then we'll find somewhere to eat and more suitable clothes for you, Avril."

"Thank you, I'd like something like Liberty's wearing, please."

"No problem," he came back at her, walking through to the bathroom, wearing only his underpants.

The girls looked at each other, a hint of a smile on their faces, waiting for the sound of the shower running. As soon as that happened, Avril went over to Marcel's clothes and searched the pockets. She pulled out a gun, a wallet with money inside and a few coins as well as the keys to the car, and a tagged single key for the door of the room. She glanced at Liberty. "Time we weren't here, I think."

"Let's go," Liberty answered with a wicked grin. "I think we should make it a little more difficult for him to follow immediately. We take his clothes, car keys and mobile, besides locking the door."

In less than a minute, they left the room.

Marcel came out of the bathroom to find the girls gone. "Shit, the sneaky bastards. They will pay for this," he said aloud, at the same time looking around the room for his clothes. Everything had gone. Although annoyed, he could not help smiling. These girls were far smarter than he had given them credit, with a well-planned exit and taking his clothes, delaying him that bit longer. But they would not get far. He was certain of that. Then it was punishment time, and one both girls would not forget. Determined to get after them as quickly as he could, and with the door having a mortise lock not a catch, he ended up smashing a chair through the window and climbing out. Still in his underpants, he banged on the next door, getting no answer. It took three more doors before a man opened one.

"Yes?" he asked, somewhat surprised to see a man stood outside in his underwear.

Marcel said nothing, just pushed past, ignoring a woman in bed, and started pulling out clothes from a suitcase on the floor.

The man came after him, grabbing his arm. "What the hell do you think you're doing?"

"What does it look like? I want fucking clothes. Keep out of my way, or you're dead," Marcel shouted back.

The man was having none of it. They began struggling. In fact, Marcel was getting the upper hand before something hard hit him on the back of the head. He staggered around the room, completely disorientated. The man turned to see his wife holding the brass bedside lamp in her hand and he pushed Marcel out of the room, slamming the door in his face. His wife put the lamp back on the bedside table before calling reception. When they answered, she told them there was a lunatic at large and to call the police. However, while the receptionist was calling the police, neither the people in the room, nor the receptionist, knew the police were already on their way.

Within minutes of the confrontation between the man and Marcel, three cars, with their sirens going, screeched in to the motel carpark, police with guns piling out. Marcel, still dazed, was holding onto a post, trying to pull himself together and decide what to do next. He was soon overpowered and taken to a police car, while other police ran to the reception, one scrabbling around behind the vending machines.

"What is this all about?" Marcel objected. "I've been robbed and those idiots in that room, when I asked for help, attacked me."

The two who had detained him said nothing, but a senior officer came up to the open door of the car.

"Have you caught the robber?" Marcel asked, still trying to play the injured party.

"We will sort it at the station, Monsieur. What is your name?"

"The name's Holstein. What about the people who robbed me, have you found them?"

"That is Marcel Holstein?" the officer asked, ignoring Marcel's question.

"Correct."

"Then you are the person a caller to the station claimed had killed a certain Théo Deschamps in the town of Chartres and who was hiding out in this motel. The caller also gave us the location of the weapon. We have just retrieved it from behind the vending machines in front of the office, where they said you had hidden it. You can understand these are serious charges, which need looking into, as well as your claim of being robbed."

Marcel went cold; surely such naive girls could not have planned to set him up and call the police, could they? Locked up for years, would they know how? Then Liberty, a girl who spent hours reading books, just what sort of books did she read, and was she the instigator of their plan? He was kicking himself for not taking more notice of Théo's warning on how manipulative the girls could be, leading to underestimating their abilities. The girls, this morning, had taken him in completely, only to join forces and escape besides being bright enough to leave a trail to the weapon for forensics. He shook his head slowly. As a contract killer, you accept the possibility of being killed, or arrested, both a hazard of the job. Except out of all the violent people, he had faced in the past, to be taken down so simply by two young girls hardly out of nappies, if it ever got out, he would never live that down.

***

Liberty and Avril, in fact, had not gone very far, after leaving the motel room; watching Marcel being taken away. They had considered, after Marcel found them gone, as soon as he got his car going, with perhaps a spare key they did not find, he would be searching the roads. Then as Marcel surmised, Liberty had read a great deal of crime books, which Blake loved, and if the books were to be believed, a call to the police reporting finding a gun would bring them out, as well as telling them someone had been shot and could be dead, although they were not completely sure if Théo had died. The gun they found in Marcel's pocket, she had hidden behind the vending machines while purchasing a can of coke with coins they had taken, before she ran back to their hiding place. Added to this, although Avril knew the name of the man she lived with, she did not know the area. However, for Liberty, that was not a problem. During their drive to the house, Marcel had used the satellite navigation inside the car. Such a clever device fascinated Liberty, when it directed them to Chartres, as well as the street Théo lived on. She also gave the name on the board outside the reception of the motel they were staying, conveying everything she knew to the police. There was another advantage in Liberty calling. She could speak French and could explain clearly all they had planned to tell the police, ironically using Marcel's own mobile to dial the emergency services to report him.

After cutting the call, they sat and waited. If the police were quick, with Marcel delayed in sorting clothing to wear, before getting into the car, they could be here before he left. All they could hope, is the police would believe the caller sufficiently to take Marcel away, giving them plenty of time to move on without fear of being followed.

"I can't believe we are free, Liberty. You're so clever," Avril said, after the police had left with Marcel.

"Maybe, but this is only the beginning. We have to survive. That will not be easy."

Avril grasped her hand. "I don't care if it's only hours, just to walk down the road once in my life free, is like you wanting to run your feet through the sand."

"You're right; there is one other thing we must do to prove to ourselves we are free. That is to revert to our original names. I hate Liberty, my name's Zoey Parsons. Do you remember yours?"

"Of course, I'm Charlotte Lucas, and like you, I want to be called by my real name from now on."

"Come on, first we need a shop to get you a pair of jeans, a top and trainers. At present you stick out like a sore thumb, not ideal to melt into the background."

"I don't suppose you can drive with all your skills? After all, we have the key to Marcel's car and they seemed to have ignored it," Charlotte asked.

Zoey laughed. "Good idea if you want to die. The books Blake gave me did not include instructions on how to drive. As it is, the shops are not far, we passed them coming here, then we will sort out a bus, or train, to move well away from this area. Maybe go to the coast."

Chapter 13

Jasmin and Karen were inside her office at home. Both knew Unit T's intelligence unit could not help in finding Zoey, or the man Beacher. This needed Karen's underground network. A private army of informers and covert operators entrenched in drug and human trafficking gangs. Karen controlled these operators herself. Why did she have such an operation after leaving Unit T? In the past, Unit T was plagued with informers, resulting in the deaths of the people working out in the field. The only way she could curtail leaks in information, was not to allow contacts and covert operators to go through the intelligence unit of Unit T. Operating outside Unit T, the operation was funded by a slush fund, which Karen had amassed during many of her own covert operations against the cartels. When she left Unit T, the American CIA approached her to work for them. She accepted and continued funding her own operation with their money. They even loaned her an aircraft, which she still used. Now back in command of Unit T, she did not consider there being any conflict of interest with the CIA. They were more interested in the drug cartels where Unit T was not. That suited Karen; often both crimes ran hand in hand, enabling her now to spread investigations wearing both hats. Before originally stepping down from command of Unit T, she would have walked away if drugs were involved, which was not part of their remit.

Karen put the phone handset down after calling yet another leader of an informer group and sighed. "It has become a waiting game, Jasmin, while my informers do their job. Zoey will not get far without being spotted."

"Then we have time to eat."

They walked through to the dining room. Maria, Karen's housekeeper, came out from the kitchen. "I suspected that dinner tonight would be a little flexible time wise, so I've made a hotpot. Is that alright, or would you prefer an alternative, Lady Harris?" she asked.

Maria always called Karen by her civilian title. Karen was fine with that, when out of the military camp.

"Of course, I love hotpot, its miss fussy here, being more into posh food. Isn't that right, Jasmin?" she mocked.

"Not at all, Maria's cooking is always fantastic. Bring it on."

Maria smiled to herself. She knew these girls often bantered like this, coming from uniquely different backgrounds. Jasmin educated at a private school where Karen attended a public, yet they were still obviously best friends and would do anything for each other.

While waiting for the sweet, Karen's main phone rang. She went over to the side desk and picked up the handset.

"I hope I'm not intruding on your evening, Karen?" Charles Lawson, head of the intelligence unit in Unit T, asked. "Except we have important information from the Paris police, I believe you should be aware of."

"No, that's fine. What have they called for?"

He explained to Karen about the strange capture and arrest of Marcel, as well as conformation that Théo Deschamps, a man suspected of being part of the paedophile ring they were investigating, was dead.

"This is looking like there's a cleanup in operation. What else have they said?" Karen asked.

"Police confirmed the gun retrieved at the motel, was the weapon used to kill Deschamps. But that is not all. According to the CCTV at the motel, Marcel was staying at the motel with two young girls. We received a still from the recording and one is Zoey."

"That's a turn up for the books. Do we know who the other girl is?"

"Not as yet. We are currently running the new girl's

photo through our database of missing persons. Looking at her on the CCTV, she's probably younger than Zoey, so her parents will have reported her missing."

"Are the police looking for them?"

"They are, but as yet, there have been no sightings. CCTV showed Zoey and the other girl leaving the grounds of the motel, wearing the same clothing they arrived in the night before. The girl with Zoey being distinctive in what she was wearing. A short and flimsy dress and looking at the photo, something a girl would wear indoors, not on the street. Zoey is wearing the jeans she purchased at our shop. I am not sure how all this fits together, but at this stage, I am assuming, the girl with Zoey, had been living with Deschamps and was collected from there by Marcel. Not that he is saying anything. As for what she was wearing when she left the motel room, I don't believe she had any other clothes with her."

Karen thought for a moment. "Can you request a comparison ballistics report on the bullets retrieved from Rolando Christopher and also photos of this man Marcel? Our own CCTV will confirm if it was Marcel who entered the camp and shot Rolando, if ballistics gives us a match on the gun?"

"I suspected you would require that information, so I have it in hand. What is our next move?"

"We need both girls' cooperation. They are key to this entire paedophile ring and even with the initial information we obtained from Zoey, before being taken, we know Beacher Marinez was the supplier. The girls must have gone somewhere after leaving the motel, leaving a trail. People could not help noticing two attractive young girls, particularly the way you say one is dressed, so they will stand out. In order to blend in, I also think their first priority will be for the girl with Zoey to find something more practical to wear. That means a local clothes shop or market. Hopefully, such locations will have security cameras, so at least we will know what she purchased and how she will look. Inform the Paris authorities that this has become a Unit T led investigation; they must not approach the girls without our sanction. They should only report confirmed sightings to us. Ask the police to visit all shops and premises in the area, and view their CCTV at around the time they took away Marcel from the motel. They are looking for sightings of the girls. Let us see if we can get an idea where they are heading. Also, contact shelters in the Paris area, as well as check out railway stations and bus terminals. We must assume they have money, probably stolen from Marcel. I will alert my contacts on the streets. If Zoey is true to form, she'll get out the area as fast as she did last time, this time will be no different, it's likely she'll head back to Spain, or to the coast of France. Both areas would be easier to hook up with people their own age on holiday, helping them to hide."

"I'll get on it right away. They cannot avoid us for long, Karen."

"Let's hope not. Beacher will soon know Marcel has been arrested, and with the police also not having the girls collected by Marcel, he will soon figure out they are on the run. You can be certain he will be looking for them, the same as us."

After cutting the call, Karen went back to her dinner, telling Jasmin what had happened.

Jasmin grinned. "Why does this Zoey remind me so much of you? In fact, it's showing that she even thinks like you."

"She's smart. I will give her that, but you and I know she is playing a very dangerous game by not turning herself in. People like Beacher will kill her. His entire business is at risk while those girls are free."

"True, but you can't blame her for not attempting to

get back in touch with Unit T. We did a pretty crap job of keeping her safe. Where she will head would depend on how much money she took out of Marcel's wallet. We also know Zoey can speak several languages, which includes French. I'd plum for your idea that she'd go south, after all two young girls thumbing a lift would have little trouble in someone picking them up."

"Then first thing we fly down to Nice. Maybe call in on Sir Peter; I've not seen him for ages."

Sir Peter Parker met Karen after she was first abducted. He was with the Metropolitan police in a department that dealt in human trafficking. When Unit T formed, he became the liaison officer between them and the British government. He got on well with Karen until he retired; now he lived just outside Cannes.

"It's premature, Karen, unless it is your intention to sit around on the beach? Remember, you are now the commander, not advisor. You can hardly wonder off on a whim."

She smiled. "What whim, I've got a lead that needs looking into."

"Oh, come on, that's all in your head. You are needed here, Karen, just accept it. I will go to Nice. You get in touch with any street people you have in the south and keep me in the loop. For both of us to go, you know as well as me, it is too much of a flyer to assume they will head in that direction. The girls could head to Spain."

"I suppose, except I'll be here and you'll be sunning yourself on the beach, or posing in some bar or cafe."

Why not, it is what girls do at my age. I hope you were not expecting me to be sitting in my bedroom, waiting for your call, because that will not happen. Seriously, I will always be a call away and available. Then I have an advantage, at least I know Zoey, and will immediately recognise her. If she is in the area, she won't be talking to a stranger."

***

The following day, with Jasmin on her way, Karen had gone to her office inside the camp. Charles Lawson from the intelligence unit had requested a meeting to update her. He was already waiting, but Karen, being tied up with camp business, had only just become free. He came through.

"Sorry about the delay, Charles. I had forgotten just how much work there was running the camp. Pour yourself a coffee and would you top mine up please?"

He filled the cups and took a seat opposite her. Just at that moment, a mobile, Karen kept for informers to contact her, rang.

"I must answer this," Karen told him.

"Do you want me to step out?" he asked.

She shook her head and answered the call. Listening to what was being said. She thanked the caller and cut it.

"Right, how far have your investigations got?" she asked.

"You were correct; the girls were caught on security cameras in a shop purchasing a cheap pair of jeans, a top and a jumper, along with trainers. They went directly to the railway station. Five different cameras on businesses recorded them walking past their premises. We lost the girls in the station, so we were unable to determine what train they took."

"You did well to get that far, but I believe I know where they are heading. I circulated Zoey's photo to several contacts in Paris and the call I have just taken was from one of them. She has been told by a man, who virtually lives in the station that a girl who matched Zoey's description, along with another, had been hanging around. When an announcement came for Lyon, they headed off to the platform the train was due to depart from. I do not believe Lyon is their final destination. I think they are short of money and could only afford tickets as far as Lyon, Compared to Paris, it is a far more difficult location not to be noticed. With that in mind, I think they are heading south. It makes logical sense. Once in the holiday areas, there are plenty of people around their age, making it easier to blend in."

Charles shook his head. "Do you really need us, Karen?"

"In the position we are in, I need everyone. You should understand, Charles, street people are a valuable resource. Most sit around all day weighing up who is likely to give a few coins. The advantage of my network, I am able to get a photo to these people within a defined area through local contacts, then for a few euros, they become my eyes and ears. Unit T will come in when we decide the girls need to be collected."

"So you're going to let them run and not pull the girls in after you've located them?"

Karen took a sip of her coffee, and then looked at him. "Look at the situation from their perspective. Since the age of eleven, the ring has locked these girls up, to provide sex to men a great deal older. To survive such an ordeal, is very unusual. Most girls of that age, taken into the sex industry, fall by the wayside, turning to drugs to get through the day, or end up dead. This paedophile ring seems to have been different in the way they looked after their girls, as the survival rate seems very high. When I met Zoey, it was obvious she had become a very competent young woman, educated herself to a degree, as well as learning to speak many languages. I think the girl with her is similar. The information Zoey has already given us is important, going forward, we have enough to carry on our own investigations, so they deserve a little freedom for the moment, giving them time to adjust before they are collected. Providing we can watch and keep them safe, I'm fine with that."

"If that is your intention, I agree. Can we turn to Marcel? Numbers called from the mobile the girls used to contact the police, we have tracked. I believe the mobile they used belonged to Marcel. One prevalent number that kept coming up belongs to Beacher Marinez. The location of that mobile is near the docks of Leixões, Portugal. Later next week there is a container ship arriving at that dock, and due to return to South America. When you talked to Zoey, she was adamant that when they turn sixteen they are killed. I do not believe it. In fact it's more likely they are shipped out of the EU to begin a similar life."

Karen thought for a moment. "You know, you could be right. A girl aged sixteen, experienced in looking after a man would be extremely valuable. It would not make any sense to kill her, but while she would always be a threat in the EU, not so, on the other side of the world. With Marinez's contacts, such girls could even be payment for a drug shipment coming the other way. Of the names Zoey gave us, have our teams come up with anything?"

"We have visited two, both had no girl. Fingerprints and DNA swabs from around the houses have been taken and confirmed two persons were living in the house. If the girls turn up, we'll have sufficient evidence to tie the men to at least two different girls."

"Then with the girls already gone, even Marcel collecting a girl, it is possible Zoey's escape was the catalyst to pull them all out, until they were sure Zoey couldn't point the finger at others still with a girl. Zoey did mention that they moved them around every few months," Karen suggested.

"I'd say it's more than possible, but rather than ship only the sixteen-year-olds, Marinez may decide to dump the lot held in the paedophile circle into South America, replacing them with a new batch later."

Karen nodded her head slightly. "With that possibility, Portugal will be the country Marinez will use to ship the girls out of Europe. It is time to send in surveillance and move a Dark Angel unit close enough to react. We will not use one of the C4 transport aircraft. So as not to panic Marinez, we'll use the service aircraft and mine to transport them to...," Karen hesitated while she checked the map, "Lisbon. Leixões is a three hour drive, so there would be little association for Marinez of our movements being directed towards him."

"Are you going to pull all the other girls out, if that is where they're all going?"

"Possibly, but it will depend on the Americans."

"Excuse me, where do they come in?"

"They may ask that the girls be allowed to continue on their journey and they will meet the ship at the other end. We have to accept they also have a problem both with trafficking and drugs supply. This could be a break they need to clear up their side."

"So we now work with other agencies?" he asked, obviously surprised by her statement.

"What I'm going to say is to enable you to do your job. No one else must know, at least for the time being. Unit T is to change going forward. My job, after relinquishing command of Unit T, was to work with other countries, as the EU representative, on both trafficking and drug supply. It was all very low-key and is already producing results. Zoey's escape, gave us an opportunity to break a major criminal gang supplying drugs into the EU. Their operation is far larger than the trafficking side. I will need to talk to both EU officials and the CIA as to the value of what we know. That will determine if we let the ship sail with the girls, providing we can confirm they are on board."

"Isn't this high-risk for the victims?"

Karen took a sip of her coffee. "Unfortunately, in

order to prevent more children being sucked into what is a horrendous life, even for an adult, it means we can lose a child. I have worked for years taking such criminal groups on, even during covert operations being taken myself. Over the years, you realise for the ones running it, this is all about business, and children, as well as young women have value. Children, by the age of sixteen, involved in a paedophile ring are extremely valuable taking years to replace. Believe me; they will be very safe and unconcerned in being locked up. Would a few days, or longer matter, experience tells me no. The girls will not be expecting anyone to be coming for them. They will carry on as usual, doing what their owners tell them to do."

He shook his head. "You know, the deeper I go into this vile crime, the more I loathe these people. Yet you seem to just let it roll over you."

Karen shrugged. "You'll get used to it, providing you keep in the back of your mind no matter how hard we try, we will lose victims, but we will also save victims. Then it's all worthwhile to see a child's face light up when brought out."

Chapter 14

Charlotte wondered around the clothes shop in awe. With so many clothes to choose from and different styles, she had no idea where to begin.

"I seem to have missed so much. The clothes are fantastic," she said to Zoey, who was also looking through the racks.

"Tell me about it. Those men owe us a great deal, taking away so many years of our life. But we need to move on. There is a rack at the back of the shop, which has jeans with sale prices. We can't afford anymore, everything seems so expensive."

"I know. I've seen the tags, but it has been fun looking at everything. Let's find a pair that fit me, then we'll go."

The store manager behind the counter looked at Zoey strangely, as she presented a pair of jeans and a jumper, along with trainers to her. "Your friend wants to keep the jeans, as well as the jumper on?" she asked. No one had wanted to do that before.

Zoey answered for Charlotte, speaking the language better. "Is it allowed, she can change outside if not? While we were at a party last night, someone stole most of our clothes from the hostel. My friend has nothing, apart from the dress she is wearing and not the sort of clothing to wear on the street. We even lost most of our money, leaving just enough to pay for these."

"What about food? You have enough for food?"

Zoey nodded her head. "It's tight, but we'll be okay. We're going to get our parents to send us money, so we can get home."

She looked at the price tags. "You're lucky. These clothes are on the list to be reduced further later this week. I'll put everything through at the lower cost," she lied, inwardly concerned with the girl's dilemma, but while she could not give the clothes away, she believed a further discount would help. "Your friend can use the changing room."

They left the shop, heading towards the railway station.

"Do you think they were cheaper, Zoey?"

"Certainly lower than the prices on the tags, then I thought they were very expensive anyway, but I'm so out of touch, I've no idea how much anything should cost these days."

They walked on, Zoey asking a woman where the railway station was. She seemed confused, as unknown to the girls, there were, in fact, a number of stations. The woman directed them to the closest. Once inside the station, they looked at the map on the wall, trying to decide where to go. Finally, they plumbed for the south coast, hoping they could mingle with holidaymakers, particularly the younger crowd. While this was a good plan, there was one problem. They only had enough money to get them as far as Lyon, but undeterred, they purchased the tickets. At least they would be out of Paris and more than halfway to the coast. They could always thumb a lift for the last part of the journey.

While on the train, Zoey told Charlotte of her time with Unit T.

"They sound really nice and wanting to help. So if Marcel actually drove you to Paris, the Unit T base you were in can't be that far away," Charlotte suggested.

"I never thought of that, but it wasn't exactly secure. Marcel just walked in."

"You have a point there," then Charlotte had an idea. "How about the charity, we could head there. Surely they wouldn't turn us away?"

Zoey grinned. "Probably not, but have you any idea

just how far away they are?"

Charlotte shook her head.

"It's got to be around fifteen hundred kilometres. If we could cadge lifts, it would take two or three days."

Charlotte sighed, becoming despondent. "Seriously, Zoey, how are we going to survive without help? We have little money left, as well as not having lived in the real world for years. Just how long will it be before we're picked up by someone like Beacher, and locked up again?"

"I don't know, so we have to make the most of our freedom. Already I have seen so much, I will not go back to being an old man's plaything. No matter what, I will fight for my freedom."

They both fell silent, deep in their own thoughts, gazing out of the window at a landscape neither girl had seen before.

"I never realised how much I've missed, if only being fields and trees," Charlotte commented, then she looked at Zoey. "You said Unit T came for you and even flew you to their camp."

"Yes, why do you ask?"

"Surely they would be in the telephone directory, or even the charity you said Karen ran? I cannot see a girl, already in trouble, having to make her own way to the coast of Spain. They must have offices or local contacts."

"I suppose they must. When we get to the coast and struggling to find a bed or feed ourselves, we will attempt to get in touch with LBNF. Maybe they can look after us better than Unit T, agreed?"

"I like that plan."

Already Charlotte felt better, unlike Zoey away from papa, the world terrified her, when out of the confines of the houses she had been locked away in for so long, the world seemed so big. In the railway station, they had sat on the floor in a corner of the main hall. Everyone seemed to be rushing around, as if knowing where he or she was going, completely oblivious of anyone else. Is this what the worlds like, when all they could rely on was a woman Zoey had met only once, fabulously rich, with her own aircraft and in charge of hundreds of people. Then Karen was like them, sold into slavery and again like them she escaped. Since then Karen had turned her life around, surely if she could, they could do the same.

***

"Charlotte, snap out of it, I said we're here, it's time to go," Zoey spoke to her, in a slightly raised voice, shaking her arm.

The journey to Lyon had been close to two hours, and Charlotte was effectively in her own world, indifferent to what was happening around her. This was usual, over the years with often only one man in the house and nothing to do, or anyone to talk to, apart from tidying, she often found solace in becoming detached from the reality of her life.

"Sorry, I was trying to take in what has happened to us over the last hours."

"Yes, I've had the same thoughts. It is all so strange. But at least I read books and had some understanding of the world outside the house. Anyway, let us get out of here. We've still a long way to go."

They came out of the station, ending up in a huge pedestrian shopping area, standing for a moment, gazing around.

"What do we do now? Where do we go?" Charlotte asked.

"I don't know. I expected a small high street, but this is something else. Anyway, according to the map at the Paris station, we need to find a road numbered A7. That is the one going south to the coast. We should ask around, but let me do the talking."

Walking up to a couple sitting on a bench eating, Zoey spoke to them in French.

"Hi, we're hitchhiking down to Marseille. I am told we need to get to the A7, maybe a fuel stop and cafe area. Do you know how we find such a place?"

They talked for a minute between themselves, and then the man looked at her. "You are best going to a truck stop and 24 hour petrol station." He pointed a direction to go. "Follow this road to the river. Do not cross the river there, turn left and follow the river until you reach Pont Pasteur Bridge. Over the bridge, there is a TankPool 24 petrol station directly in front of you, and close to the A7 entry road. Stand at the side of that road, you will easily get a lift. It's about an hour's walk from here."

They thanked him and set off. Finding the river easily and following it before crossing, as directed, over the bridge towards the petrol station in front of them. Zoey looked at signposts for the one to Marseille. Walking alongside the road for a short distance, they stopped and began thumbing for a lift. A few cars stopped, but none was going as far as the coast, suggesting they drop them off. Charlotte did not want them to be left out in the middle of nowhere. She really wanted a lorry so she would decline the offer. Many vehicles passed, until eventually one stopped for them.

"Where are you going?" a man, Zoey estimated to be in his late fifties, asked.

"We are trying to get to Marseille, but any part of the coast would be good," Zoey answered.

"I'm going to Nice, but I've a drop about five kilometres outside Marseille, if that's any use?"

"Great, thank you. In fact, Nice would be better for us."

They climbed in and were on their way.

"Is it a long way?" Zoey asked.

"My first stop outside Marseille is about four hours

with a break, then another two to Nice. I take my break in a couple of hours, stopping at a cafe. Anyway, I'm Denis, and you two are?"

"Zoey and my friend's Charlotte."

"Backpacking then?"

"That was the idea, but our backpacks were stolen on the train to Lyon. I've called mum, and she's planning for me to pick up money sometime tomorrow."

He sighed. "It's getting pretty bad when people will steal a girl's clothes. Have you both eaten?"

"No, I'll have money in the morning, so we'll be fine."

Denis pointed to the sleeping cabin behind the seats. On the bed was a plastic bag. "My wife insists on making me sandwiches. They are only cheese, but I rarely eat them. I prefer a hot meal when I stop. You are both welcome to have them. Otherwise, I give them the birds. I daren't take them back home."

"Thank you," Zoey said, reaching back and grabbing the bag. Inside were two thick slab sandwiches, which, like he said, contained cheese, yet again a thick slice.

"Your wife certainly looks after you. These are great." Then she changed her language to talk in Spanish, hoping Denis could not understand. "What do you think, Charlotte, is the sandwich alright for you?"

"It is, and I didn't realise how hungry I was."

"Where did you begin your journey?" Denis asked.

"Charlotte came to London, after looking at the sites we set off from there. We are going along the coast eventually to Gibraltar. I need to be home for college in September."

"That's quite a journey. May I ask how old you are?"

"Seventeen, but close to eighteen."

Denis could not believe they were that old. His own daughter had children that age, and these two did not look even sixteen. He suspected they might be runaways, with no luggage, and supposedly parents sending money, but how would they know where to send it? Then Charlotte had said nothing. Apart from answering Zoey, he assumed about the sandwich.

"My granddaughter is off to university this September," Denis commented.

"I'm not that bright. I was lucky to get a place in the local college," Zoey answered with a smile.

"But you speak French fluently. I could not even tell you were English. Then what was Charlotte speaking?"

"Spanish, but she's trying to learn English. I speak several languages, so I interpret for her. My French is good because both my parents came from Paris and settled in London. We would only speak French at home."

Zoey hoped she would be able to allay any doubts he had about who they were and where they came from. In fact, Charlotte could speak all the languages Zoey could, but was not good at French and may misunderstand what was being asked of her. Added to that, her voice, her mannerisms, while typical fourteen-year-old, Zoey knew she would struggle to pass for seventeen. So they had previously agreed she kept in the background, letting Zoey speak for them both.

They travelled on. Charlotte was asleep, Zoey leaning on her, dozing. Soon they turned onto a large car park area in front of a cafe.

"This is where I take a break." Denis glanced at his watch. "One hour only. My first drop is on a fixed time entry. I can't be late, or I'm stuck there all night."

"We'll be waiting here," Zoey told him.

They all climbed out of the lorry and after locking the door, he set off heading for the cafe, before stopping and looking back at them.

"Have you any money?"

Zoey shook her head.

"Come on, you should at least have a hot drink."

They followed him in, taking seats on the other side of the table.

"Denis, it's good to see you, the usual?" a woman with a pinny around her waist asked, welcoming him as she came up to the table.

"Yes please, Lili. Can you also give these two young ladies any drink they want?"

They both ordered tea, being used to drinking tea or coffee, with no fizzy drinks when they were locked up, so asking for what they knew.

Denis stood and went through to the toilets. Lili came back with the drinks. "Are you girls not eating?" she asked.

"No thank you, we've had a cheese sandwich in the lorry," Zoey answered for them.

She left, but caught Denis coming through from the toilets. They were out of sight of the table the girls were sitting at. "Who are the girls? They are certainly attractive, and getting lots of admiring glances from the lads, but both look very young."

"I don't know, I picked them up in Lyon thumbing a lift. I thought they looked very young and while I would never normally pick up hitchhikers, I couldn't leave them looking for a lift. It's not safe for such girls. Since travelling with them I suspect they may be runaways."

"Why do you suspect that?"

"Both have no luggage, no money and the way they speak it's as if they have little idea of the world around them. Then the blonde one does not even speak French. I think she's Spanish."

"Shouldn't you inform the gendarmerie of your suspicions?"

"I'm not sure, Lili. I have no idea why they may

110

be on the run, if they actually are. So I don't think it's my place to turn them in, unless they're asking for help."

"You're on your usual route, calling just outside Marseille?"

"I am, why?"

"If you have further doubts, I'd give the gendarmerie a call while you unload. Once you drop them off they could be at high-risk, being completely broke. Anyway, I will come through after your dinner and give them both a slice of pie. At least they will have eaten."

"Thanks, Lili."

When Denis returned, two local lads in their early twenties had moved to the table behind the girls, trying to talk to them. Both girls were ignoring their advances.

"Who are your friends, Grandpa?" one asked, when Denis sat down. "It's obvious you're far too old for them."

"And you as well, so clear off, or I'll have you removed."

The two lads moved away to a pool table, but did not take their eyes off the girls.

"Sorry about that. You always get the local so-called studs, believing they are god's gift to women. They're harmless."

"We're fine, it happens," Zoey answered.

Following his meal, Lili came through with three slices of pie. "I thought you'd like to join Denis in tasting one of my famous pies."

"Thank you, it looks really nice," Zoey, answered, then she reverted to Spanish. "The lady has given us a slice of pie each, Charlotte?"

She looked at Lili, "gracias."

"You're both very welcome," then she walked away.

After they finished the pie, the girls went to the rest room.

Denis was sipping his tea when a driver, he knew

well, came up to him.

"Antoine, how are you? I've not seen you around for quite a while?" Denis asked.

"Trouble with my leg, the doctors had me rest for nearly a month, but it's good now. I was going to come up earlier, but you had two young girls sitting with you."

"Yes, a couple of backpackers on their way south. I picked them up in Lyon. They had their bags stolen."

"How old are they?"

"Told me seventeen, why do you ask?"

"The blonde one looks nothing like seventeen, more like fifteen or even younger. Just be careful, Denis, they could be baiters."

Denis looked confused. "Baiters, what does that mean?"

"A few drivers have had a close thing picking up young girls with no bags or obvious way to support themselves. Baiters have handlers that look after them. Usually one girl is under fifteen. She only has to claim she has been molested and you're facing a long prison sentence under the new law. Most men faced with such punishment pay the handler big money for the girl to keep quiet and go away. Those two girls look very comfortable around men and not shy. Both being very attractive with an odd story that someone robbed them, yet they have not gone to the gendarmerie. If they had, the gendarmerie, because of their age and high-risk with having no visible means to support themselves, would have called in people who can help them out, or at least kept them until they'd clarified all was well with their parents and money sent."

"You're correct, it is a job for the gendarmerie and I thought it strange they hadn't gone there. One said she'd contacted her mother, and she was sending money."

"If that's the case, why are they on the road and not waiting at a bank for the money? Anyway, I could be wrong and they are what they claim. I'm just saying it does not sound right, Denis, so be careful. You've got a seventy-five thousand euro rig out there, don't risk it."

Antoine walked away, leaving Denis not sure what to do. He could hardly leave them, particularly with the local lads hanging around. Although if Antoine is correct, could he be heading directly into trouble? After all, Charlotte had said very little, could she really be far younger than she claimed, maybe under fifteen? Then if she talked, would he quickly realise just how young she really is? Was that why Zoey said she did not understand French? All these unanswered questions were running through his mind, only brought out of his thoughts when the girls returned.

"Right, I'll pay, and then it's time to get back on the road."

He went over to the counter.

Lili came up to him. "Ten euro is fine, Denis. The girl's food is on us."

"Thank you, Lili, but I may have a massive problem."

"Like what?"

He told her what Antoine said, finishing with, "I can't leave them here, Lili, particularly if Antoine is wrong, but do I risk losing my rig? It's all my wife and I have."

"I said you should have let me call the gendarmerie. But you could look at it in a different way. You have already travelled for two hours, brought them in here and neither has made any complaint. If a so-called minder were watching, he would hardly want to wait hours. He would have wanted the girls to make out they had been abused closer to Lyon. You have an hour left. Just take them to Marseille, and then tell them there's been a change of plan and you have to return to Lyon, or some other location bringing you back north."

"You're right, Lili, I'm all in a fluster and panicking. Within the hour, they will be gone."

113

After Denis left with the girls, Lili went outside to use her mobile telephone. Quickly, she dialled a number.

"It's Lili, I need to talk to Petar urgently," she said to the man who had answered. He told her to wait.

Petar Florescu, a Rumanian, aged thirty-three, was a pimp, with several girls working around Nice in the South of France. Added to this operation, he dealt in drugs supplying clubs, bars and small dealers selling to local addicts. He began as a moneylender, this operation becoming very useful once he moved into drugs, enabling him to launder the large amounts of cash through his other businesses. Lili had become involved with him when her husband left, leaving her with all the bills. Struggling to pay him off, he had suggested, if she saw any girls suitable for his business, particularly ones hitching rides on the lorries, there would be payments enabling Lili to reduce her debt.

Petar came on the phone. "What is it, Lili?"

"I've got information for you on two girls, so-called backpackers, but I think they're runaways. Aged fifteen to seventeen and both slim, long legged and very attractive. If I give you their route and where you can collect them, is my debt paid off?"

"A deal is likely. Where are they?"

"On a lorry bound for Marseille, your area. They arrive in an hour. The lorry driver will drop them off short of Marseille, and they are looking to head to the Nice area. I can text the lorries registration and route. Both you and I know they are worth a great deal of money."

"I'm not disputing their value. Text the info, if we can intercept and they are as you say, I will write your debt off. I can't be fairer than that."

"Thank you, Petar, I appreciate it. I'll send the details."

Chapter 15

Petar walked into another room. Two men were lounging about on easy chairs, watching a football match.

"Sorry lads, footballs off. It seems we have two girls hitching a lift on a lorry heading our way. I am told they claim to be backpackers, but my contact thinks they are runaways. Collect them," he said, handing one a piece of paper with the details of the destination.

"You want them here, or the house?" one man asked.

"Best go direct to the house. Call me when you get there. A word of warning, these girls could be valuable, so keep your cocks inside your pants. Otherwise, I'll cut the fuckers off. Now move."

After they left, his partner Sandu Macek, a Rumanian the same as him, and aged thirty, came into the room. "Where are they off?"

"Collection of two runaways aged around sixteen. We will see it they are suitable for our business, if not sell them on. Either way, it's a no-brainer."

"It is, and an excellent opportunity to replace two girls. Clients like to see a change. Anyway, Beacher has been on the phone. There's two hundred kilos of cocaine arriving later in the month. He has already placed a considerable amount and wanted to know our requirements. Apparently, after this shipment, it will be a delay of three months before he has more."

"Why's that?"

"Trouble among the cartels, back in South America, two of the larger drug cartels are fighting over a territory dispute. That is why he has had so much shipped. They're killing each other's men like it's going out of fashion."

Petar shrugged indifferently. "Fucking idiots, there are plenty of outlets to go around for everyone to make a bloody good living," he hesitated. "What's he asking?"

"Five thousand dollars a kilo, that's cheap, it's usually eight, so we're doing alright out of it."

"We'd better book twenty, before everyone panics and it all goes."

"I'll call him."

***

The drive to the industrial area just outside Marseille took just under fifty minutes from where Petar was based. Pavel Dragos and Alberto Popa, both in their twenties, had parked up in a position where they could see vehicles coming off the main road into the industrial area. With not knowing which warehouse the lorry was heading, they could only follow when the lorry came into the area.

Denis's lorry came off the main road into the industrial area, drawing to a halt alongside palisade fencing that had a small grass embankment in front.

Inside the cab, the girls were ready to get out. Denis had told them that his delivery was to a secure warehouse area and only the driver would be allowed in, passengers had to wait beyond the gates. They understood that and watched him set off rounding a bend a short distance further down the road, before settling down on the grass verge to wait his return.

With Pavel driving, they had followed the lorry, watching it draw up to allow the girls out. While he could have come up behind to take the two girls, it would require both of them to be out of the car. Deciding that would be too risky, with wanting both girls, he parked a little further down on the other side of the road. Armed with plastic tie wraps, in order to secure the girls hands behind them and around their ankles, preventing them from running, while one of them brought the car closer, the two men were quickly out of the car.

Zoey watched them climb out, before heading directly towards them. Already she had a bad feeling, when the only people around was them. "This doesn't look good, Charlotte. Let's go."

The girls, not hampered by heavy bags, were up and running. Both fit and determined to escape, if the possible, neither was hanging around.

Pavel and Alberto, not expecting them to make a run for it, gave chase. If they lost one, it would be better than both.

Charlotte was lagging Zoey as they ran alongside the palisade fencing that surrounded the large warehouses. The men were gaining as the girls rounded the corner. A short distance ahead of them was the entrance to the warehouse complex. There was also a security lodge between the entrance and exit, where vehicles entering, or leaving, would stop because of the barriers. Inside the lodge were at least four men.

Zoey realised, with their help, they may prevent them from being taken. "Head to the security lodge, Charlotte," Zoey shouted back to her.

Arriving first, Zoey began banging on the door, asking for help.

In fact, normally there would only be two guards, but it was a change of shift, so they were all there for the handover. Everyone turned in surprise, but one broke away coming to the door pulling it open. She burst inside, followed in seconds by Charlotte.

"Those men are chasing us. I think they want to hurt us. Can you help?" Zoey gasped, talking in perfect French.

All the security men looked towards Pavel and Alberto, who had also rounded the bend and suddenly stopped, realising where the girls had run. It was obvious, once inside the gatehouse, there was no chance of taking either of them. They turned to go back to the car. However, three of the security men burst out of the lodge, giving chase.

"Fuck, the bastards are after us now," Pavel shouted, as they both set off running to the car, yanking the doors open, with only seconds to spare, they drove off at high speed.

"That was close. What do we tell, Petar?" Alberto asked, still breathless from the run.

"We say the girls never arrived. He'll go berserk if he thought we'd fucked it up."

"You can say that again, so it's agreed the lorry never arrived. We'd better stop off for a drink to pass some time, before calling to ask what he wants us to do."

Soon, all the security men were back in the lodge.

"Have the men gone?" Zoey asked.

"They certainly have and won't be back," one answered. "The name's Joseph. Would you like a mug of coffee while you tell us what this is all about?"

Zoey spoke Spanish to Charlotte. "Do you want coffee, with or without sugar?"

"Without," Charlotte answered.

Then Zoey turned to Joseph. "Sorry Charlotte does not speak French. I am Zoey. We would both love a coffee, thank you, but no sugar. As for why we were on the banking, a lorry driver, called Denis, is taking us to Nice. He said we could not go inside, and to wait for him to come back out. We had no problem with that. After all, it's not cold. We were sitting there happily, when a car drove past, slowed and turned around before parking on the other side of the road. Both men climbed out of the car, heading directly towards us. Charlotte panicked and ran. I followed. They ran after us, that's when we realised we needed help. Charlotte's not as fast as me, so when I saw the lodge, I shouted for her to head for it."

Zoey hoped they would believe her explanation. After all, it sounded logical. There was no way there would be any suggestion that the men could be traffickers here to take them back. To mention anything like that would almost certainly have them calling the authorities.

"I can't understand Denis telling you to wait on the roadside. We could have looked after you. It is stupidity to leave two young girls by the side of the road, and it's asking for trouble. Anyway, you are more than welcome to wait inside here, until he is ready to leave. He can't go without you, as he has to stop at the barrier while we check his signed discharge docket."

Zoey thanked him and interpreted what he had said to Charlotte. They had to keep to the same story that she could not speak French, in case they talked to Denis.

"Tell me, Zoey, you both seem very young to be hitching, aren't your parents concerned?" Joseph asked.

"We're seventeen and backpacking down the coast through Spain to Gibraltar, then we go home, but on the train to Lyon, someone pinched our backpacks. Mum knows and is arranging for us to pick money up in Nice, after we called her to say we had a lift down to there."

"Then you're both from the UK?"

"No, we started there; I wanted to see the palace and other places. I live in Portugal and Charlotte's from Spain. We're pen friends."

The day staff left, leaving Joseph and another man. It was going dark when Denis's lorry came to the barrier. Joseph went out to sort the documents and talk to him. He knew Denis, with him being a regular driver for a business on the estate.

"How's the family, Joseph?" Denis asked, handing him the signed transfer documents.

"They're good and your wife?" he answered, checking through the papers.

"I'm looking forward to my retirement. It's getting so expensive to keep the rig, and it's biting into my income."

"We've all got the same problems. Everything is

going up. Anyway, your two passengers are in our lodge. You should not have left them at the side of the road. That attracted the attention of two men, and you have been longer than usual beside it getting dark. You should have at least called us to make sure they were safe."

Denis looked a little sheepish. "To tell you the truth, it was an error picking them up. A fellow driver suggested that they might be baiters. I did not know what baiters were, but apparently, they are underage girls used to compromise a man with sexual claims, followed by a demand for money. I have all my savings tied up in the rig. If I lose that, I have nothing."

"So you intended dumping the two girls at the side of the road, miles from public transport, no food and it fast going dark? Come on, Denis, if you planned to do that, you should have had the bloody guts to tell them. Not leave two vulnerable girls sat at the side of the road expecting you to return. By the time they realised you were not coming, they would have wasted hours when they could have tried to get another lift."

"You are correct; it was heartless and stupid of me. After all, they have been with me since Lyon and nothing has happened. Neither of them has even made any suggestions that could lead us to sexual contact. In fact, the girls are very pleasant, apart from seemingly being naive. I'd decided they were no threat to me."

"Very well, all your paperwork is good, I'll call them and you can get on your way. Just make sure, where you drop them off; they are close to transport and not in the middle of nowhere."

Chapter 16

For Denis, with his final delivery, not until six the following morning, he had taken advantage of this delay for his mandatory rest hours. This suited the girls, giving them somewhere to sleep. In fact, they slept in the back of the lorry, which was now more than half-empty after the first drop. On waking, they said goodbye to Denis, before making their way to the promenade, finding a row of seats facing out to sea, and sat down.

"This is something else, Zoey, coming from a small village with a few boats. I'm completely stunned."

"Yes, it's the same for me. We never lived on the coast, so when I escaped and walked on the beach for the first time in Portugal, it was magic. Now we are here. It's time we looked for work, if only to feed us."

"What do you suggest?"

She shrugged. "We'll not get anything better than a cafe, or bar looking for casuals. Let's walk round the streets and see what there is. There is bound to be a homeless shelter around, we should find that as well. Anyway, cafes will soon be setting up for the day, so let's speak to the owners."

***

By lunchtime, they had found no one who wanted help. However, one cafe owner gave them the address of a homeless shelter. They set off to find it. At least they may be able to secure a bed.

"We're not doing very well, are we? No jobs around and now considering living in a shelter, if they let us in," Charlotte commented.

"I suppose, but neither of us has been in this position before, so we have to start somewhere. Then if they give us a bed for a few nights, we'll have a base to look for work from. They may even have contacts looking for workers."

"What about languages? Do I pretend I only speak Spanish?"

"No point now, but it could have an advantage if they find we can speak several languages, maybe a shop or hotel would be more interested in us."

They found the shelter, but before going inside, they watched from a distance as people came out with bags.

"They must be the ones who stayed there last night. It is all men, Zoey. Are you sure this is the sort of place we should be asking for a bed?" Charlotte commented.

"If the alternative is sleeping on the street, then yes we should. We've handled old men long enough to know how to look after ourselves."

"True, but can we wait till they have all gone."

Once everyone had left, the girls walked up to the door. A taped sheet of paper on the door read, '*Come in, all are welcome*'. Trying the door and finding it locked, Zoey pressed the bell.

A female voice came over a small speaker by the side of the door. "The door's open," she told them, followed by a loud click from the door.

Pushing it open and going inside, they found themselves in a large open area.

A woman came out of a room, walking over to them. "If you are looking for a dinner, we don't open until one."

"We came for advice," Zoey began. "We've no money, nowhere to stay and a cafe owner we asked if he had any jobs available, suggested we come here. Can you help us, please?"

"I'm sorry; while we are a charity we have many coming for help. We cannot afford to hand money out, or give anything free. We offer a lunch for a euro and a bed for two euro. That is all I'm allowed to offer."

"We're not asking for anything for free, we'll work, we just need a chance, or a direction to go," Zoey said.

"If you can't help us that way, can you call Beacher Marinez? He owns us. He will come," Charlotte, added to the conversation.

The woman was appalled at the suggestion. "I can hardly ring up a man and ask him to take back two children who claim to be owned by him. May I ask how old you both are, and why you are asking for help, beyond being broke? I am in contact with other charities that may be able to offer assistance."

"I'm Zoey Parsons and fifteen, my friend's Charlotte Lucas, aged fourteen. We escaped from our abductors two days back and have tried all morning to find a job, just to eat, but no one wants us. They say we are too young and should go home. We don't have a home and don't know what to do, apart from what Charlotte suggested; go back to our owner."

While the lady had heard many stories, most were lying, to make her feel sorry for that person and hand money out, so she would stand away and not become emotionally involved, following the rules of the charity. Yet these two girls were obviously not on drugs, and while their claim to have been abducted may or may not be true, she had no way to check out such a claim. Even if what they claimed were lies, she had a concern over their ages. They would be at high-risk on the streets. Something needed to be done, that was certain.

"As I said, I will make a few phone calls to charities in the area who deal with girls of your age. Go through to our cafe and get a drink, while I see what they can do for you."

"Thank you, we could help in the cafe to pay for our drinks," Zoey offered.

"Very well, ask the girls working in there if they want anything doing."

Returning to her office, she dialled a local number

from the book. "Hi John, it's Germaine from the Church Alliance Centre."

"Hi, Germaine, I assume you've called with a problem?"

"Yes, I've two girls, aged fourteen and fifteen, just come in. They need help, John. I cannot help them, nor could I offer them a bed. We run mixed dormitories. With recent changes in the law regarding minors, placing them in such an environment, particularly with one under fifteen, would be high-risk. If another person high on drugs interfered with the child, that person could face a prison sentence. We could never risk putting vulnerable people in such a position. Can your charity do anything?"

"We have the same problem, Germaine. In fact, between you and me, since the law changed, our directors are so nervous, if a young person comes to the shelter, we've been told to turn them away."

"That's harsh. We are supposed to be open for everyone."

"Maybe, but I can't mix, and like you, we don't have the luxury of keeping an area for children, just in case one turns up. Why not call LBNF, they are the only charity I know, who have the facilities to look after minors?"

"Aren't they in Spain?"

"True, their major complexes are there, but they operate across the EU. In fact, they are part funded by the EU, so you can be sure they will have local connections."

"I wish it funded us that way. How did they manage that?"

"Set up and still headed by Karen Harris. Need I say more?"

"Not really. That says it all."

"Do you want the number?"

"Yes please. Is there anyone I should ask for?"

"I can't help you with that, I have never called. All

I have is a number to call, but they are bound to want information about the girls before they will help."

Armed with the number, Germaine made the call.

"Good morning, LBNF."

"Who do I talk to regarding two underage girls coming into our shelter looking for help?" Germaine asked.

"Are you calling on a code red?"

"Excuse me, what is that?"

"Are the children at imminent risk and need protection?"

"No, they are fine."

"Then it is okay to talk to me. May I have your name and location?"

"Germaine Allard from the Church Alliance Centre in Nice."

Germaine could hear typing. "Is this Nice in France, and do you have authority to speak for the shelter?"

"Yes, I'm the manager, but I dialled the code for France and you're asking if Nice is in France. Have I dialled the wrong number in error and you're somewhere else in the world?"

"You are calling us on an advertised local telephone number for all European countries, they, like yours, are redirected to LBNF's call centre. This is a twenty-four hour seven day a week live personnel answering service for advice and help, as well as to route a code red emergency. We are not based in Europe. My computer was displaying several towns and villages called Nice across Europe. I just needed to be certain where you are located, in order to give advice available local to you."

"I'm sorry, I didn't realise. Of course, you would need our exact location."

"That is fine. May I have the full names of the girls and their ages?"

"Zoey Parsons, she's fifteen and Charlotte Lawton,

who's fourteen."

"Can I confirm you said Zoey Parsons?"

"Yes."

"Thank you, please hold."

Germaine waited, listening to music. She had never contacted them in the past and was already wondering just how large the charity was to have a twenty-four hour call centre. Then where was the major operations centre located, if not in Europe? She also noticed a distinct change in tone when she had to confirm Zoey's name. Why was that? Do they know her?"

Soon the girl came back to her. "Sorry for the delay. We class the girls, in view of their ages, as at risk. Can they remain in the shelter until our local agent arrives?"

"How long will that be? We only offer dormitory accommodation. There are no facilities in the shelter for children staying overnight."

"We are aware of what is offered by the Church Alliance. We will take the girls to one of our own facilities. My computer is showing a maximum of two and a half hours before we can get to you."

"That's fine. We will provide dinner and find a few jobs to keep them busy."

"If there is a cost in that, inform our agent who will reimburse your charity. Can you make a note of our reference number? The agent will have identification with them and this reference number. Please ask to see it, and contact us directly, giving our reference number if you have any other concerns."

Germaine sat for a short time after she finished the call. It had surprised her how well set up the charity was. Easy to contact, with no hassle, or long explanations needed. They even had information on the shelter. Although thinking about it, with Karen Harris being involved and her connections with Unit T, was the time they kept her on hold used to find out about the Church Alliance, or getting permission to actually come to the shelter for the girls? Then Zoey had not been mentioned again. Had they mixed her up with perhaps another girl they had an interest in? She sighed. No one would ever tell her, but at least the girls would be taken away. Children hanging around were not what she wanted. In particular, very attractive girls, who she suspected were streetwise and knew how to play up to men. She went through to the dining room. A queue was forming waiting to go inside. Zoey and Charlotte were standing behind the counter, ready to help serve. She smiled to herself. It would seem these girls were not afraid to work. She called Zoey over.

"I'm afraid none of the local shelters can take you, but only because they don't have separate facilities, insisted on by the authorities, for a young person. I have been in contact with LBNF. Their agent is on the way to see you both. They have the facilities, so you will have somewhere to sleep tonight."

"Thank you for your help."

"You're welcome. When it gets a little quieter, both of you break off and have your dinners. They don't expect to be here for at least two hours."

"Where are they coming from?"

She shrugged. "Who knows? We know very little about how they operate, apart from the fact they are one of the largest charities in Europe with resources that dwarf charities like us."

Zoey, of course, knew all about LBNF, after talking to Jasmin and Karen, as well as reading a magazine published by the charity, but decided not to volunteer the information. She also had little confidence they could keep her safe, yet realistically it was becoming obvious that because of their ages, this shelter and others around here would not take them, leaving only LBNF, or the street.

However, she detected a hint of annoyance in Germaine's tone.

"You don't give the impression you rate them very highly. Why is that?"

"I admire what they do, but that is so specialist, it closes the doors on the vast majority of the homeless, leaving small places like us struggling to cope. Although to be fair, Karen Harris, the founder of the charity, provides grants from her own pocket. That is tiny compared to her true worth and LBNF. Take our food programme. Even with the contribution of a euro, it still costs the church nearly ten thousand euro a year. Karen claims she helps charities like ours, but she could do more, in fact, a lot more than she does. Read about her in the press, she earns close to fifty million a year just in interest and rents, yet her grants are around five million. What is she doing with all the rest? She has no need of it, apart from the purchase of large fancy houses across the world, or more property for LBNF, which she can rent back to them. She should come and see what we do, how we are struggling, and maybe she'll divert some funds from LBNF to charities like us."

Zoey looked at the queue growing, seeing a reason to get away from Germaine. She'd had enough of the woman's whining. Karen was not a business; no one was helping her, it was her own personal money she was using. Then, reading the LBNF magazine, she donates far more than what Germaine was suggesting. "I really don't understand. I suppose on the face of it, she should, but what do I know? Thank you for allowing us to have a dinner; we really appreciate your help."

**

In fact, the delay at LBNF during Germaine's call came about when the girl in the call centre keyed in Zoey's name, it came up with a red flag at the side showing Unit T was to be contacted immediately. They notified Unit T, who told them to tell the shelter someone would come, after talking to Karen. Karen in turn called Jasmin.

"Hi, have you any info yet?" a sleepy Jasmin answered.

"Don't tell me you're still in bed?"

"No, sat by the pool with a coffee. Mind you, my night out turned out to be a late night, so I'm taking it easy this morning."

"Well, it's time to work. LBNF has contacted us to say Zoey's name pinged on their computer as a girl of interest to us. She and the other girl have turned up at a shelter in Nice. Get yourself down there."

"No problems. Am I there as LBNF, and are they going to Torre del Mar?"

"Let me consider that while you hook up with them. I am leaning towards them being placed with a housemother. Zoey is unlikely to have much confidence in Unit T. They will become our guinea pigs. I want to see who, if anyone, attempts to snatch them back after the last man failed."

"I assume you're sending surveillance and military backup?"

"Why, I have you?" Karen asked cuttingly.

"Yes, like I'm going to be everything all in one and never sleeping."

"Oh you poor person, I'd better send help before you cry. Seriously, if I decide to run with my thoughts, I will put in place everything to watch them. It's bloody embarrassing that we can't even look after one girl inside the camp, and now we've two."

"I agree, but we are also aware of the risks involved in looking after Zoey, caused, I suspect, by an anxious paedophile ring. We must stick to her like glue."

"We will. I also need a photo of the other girl and find out where she was born and lived until they snatched her. The photos from the motel and the shop are not good enough. I need a frontal, and then maybe we can identify her. Someone must have reported her missing, if only the school."

"Maybe, maybe not, Zoey was never on a list of missing children."

"Good point, but we have to be sure either way. How long would it take to get to the shelter?"

"Which one is it?"

"The Church Alliance, in Nice."

"Give me a moment." Jasmin keyed in the details on her phone and looked at the map. "It's suggesting an hour's drive from Cannes; I'll need to change before I leave. The girls are safe, I assume?"

"Yes."

"Then an hour and half should see me there, maybe quicker if the traffic's okay."

"That's fine. It's well within our expected time of arrival given to the shelter."

Chapter 17

Petar had listened to the lads on the phone and called Lili. "I don't like being given shit information. It's cost me time and money, so I've added it to your debt," he began, as soon as she answered. "Who is the driver and where else is he going?"

"He's called Denis and always goes on the same route. He has done it for the last year. To miss him would be impossible, with a time slot he cannot change. So even if he were alone, your men would not have missed the lorry. Then it is one of those secure warehouses, so the girls could not go in with him, they would have waited outside. With nothing around the warehouses like shops or a cafe, the girls would have probably sat on the banking waiting for him. From that drop, he goes on to Nice, sleeps in the cab overnight and delivers first thing, when they open at six thirty. It is not fair to make me pay. I can only tell you what is happening. It's more likely to be your people not telling you the truth."

"Suggest that and once they know you're accusing them of being incompetent, you can expect a visit and it wouldn't be pleasant. Where about in Nice, is his next drop?"

"I'll have to check with one of the other girls and text you."

"See you do. If we miss him this time, you're in the shit," then he cut the call.

Sandu came through into the lounge, just as Petar finished on the phone. "Were you on to the lads? Have they got the girls?"

"No, we've not got them. According to the lads, the lorry never arrived, but according to Lili, they are taking the piss. The driver has been doing the same run for a year with a tight time slot for entry into a secure warehouse. He can't be late, or just not turn up."

"So did they claim the lorry never came, or the girl's never got off?"

"They claimed it never arrived. If that is true and he missed the slot, his next drop is here in Nice. I think we need to have words with this driver and find out where he dropped them."

"I agree, but we go ourselves and if he was at the other drop, leaving the girls outside, Pavel and Alberto had better have a bloody good excuse why they couldn't collect a couple of kids."

***

Early the following morning, armed with the final location for Denis, Petar and Sandu were waiting when his lorry joined a small queue at the entrance of the warehouse complex.

He had just turned off his engine when Petar pulled open the passenger door and climbed inside.

"Who the hell are you?" Denis demanded.

"Your worse fucking nightmare, unless you answer my questions?"

"Like what?"

"Lili told us you'd picked up two backpackers."

"I did in Lyon, but they've gone."

"What do you mean, gone? When did this happen?"

"About half an hour back, if they had come here, they would have been waiting around for at least an hour and they wanted to move on. To tell you the truth, I was nervous carrying them. Apparently there are minders using young girls to bait drivers," he hesitated. "You aren't their minders, are you?"

"No. But they did a runner and we want them back. Why didn't you go to the warehouse in Marseilles?"

"I always go. Why do you ask?"

"Then where did you leave the girls?"

Outside, sat on the bank. Apparently two men tried to approach them and they ran, ending up in the security lodge," then he realised something. "Were you the men?"

"Not us; two of my lads."

"Then why didn't they wait for me to come out and say so? They could have taken them back. Like I said, I was nervous about the girls being in my cab."

At that moment, the gates opened and the queue began to move slowly to the security gate, where documents were being checked.

"You need to get out of the cab, otherwise security will tell you to. If you want any further information, wait till I come out."

"We've heard enough. Where did you drop them?"

"Off the M6098, close to the Fontaine Du Soleil. I shouldn't have stopped, but it was only for a minute."

"If you pick up anymore, you tell Lili, then keep hold of them," Petar demanded and began climbing out of the cab.

"I'll not be doing that again, that's for certain. Particularly girls obviously under age," he shouted back at him.

Denis was more than annoyed at Lili. He had trusted her, yet she let him down and risked the girls lives and maybe his own. Then while he told them where they had been dropped, that was not quite true. They had been dropped nowhere near.

***

"I'll fucking kill them, both girls in their hands, and they let them escape. Any fool with a minuscule of sense would know not to allow them to run towards the main gate. All they had to do was come up between them and the security lodge, forcing the girls to run the other way," Petar said with obvious annoyance.

Sandu shook his head. "The problem is, they will

133

know someone is after them, so could that experience force them to contact LBNF and safety?"

"Who knows, then why are they backpacking, or are they on the run for some other reason? We should cruise the streets and see if we can find them. Two girls walking around at this time of the morning can't be that difficult to find."

For a good two hours, they drove slowly around, even stopping and asking the cafe owners, they knew, if they had seen the girls. Virtually giving up, Petar had drawn up outside another cafe where the owner was putting out his chairs.

"Ivo, do you have a minute?" Sandu called, after winding down his window.

Ivo came over. "Not seen you around lately. When are you coming in for a dinner?" he asked.

"Soon, Ivo, we've been busy. The reason we stopped, we are looking for two girls, aged around seventeen. You've not seen them, have you?"

"Blonde are they, and both very attractive?"

"Yes, that's them?"

"More than seen them, I spoke to them. They were looking for casual work. Told me they needed work to pay for a bed for the night. Looking at them, they would be wasting their time in a cafe, when they could earn a hundred times that laid on their backs. Not that I suggested it, just told them I had no work."

"Where did they go?"

"Probably the Church Alliance Shelter, that's after I suggested they would get a bed there for the night. Shelters never turn away minors; most would be able to find them somewhere. But I had not put either of them at over sixteen, one even younger. Employ them and the gendarmerie walk in, I would be facing heavy fines. Why are you looking for them?"

"They belong to us and are not as young as you think. As I said, both are seventeen. When we get them back, if you want one for the night, you can have her."

"I'll hold you to that."

Petar put the car in gear and set off towards the shelter.

Ivo watched them go. *'Seventeen, my backside,'* he mumbled. If they didn't mind spending time behind bars for touching a child he reckoned to be fourteen or fifteen, he did. They could keep them. He'd not be taking up their offer. Then he carried on setting out his tables.

"We may be lucky and they are hanging about outside, not knowing it doesn't open till early evening," Petar suggested, as they headed for the shelter.

"For a bed, yes, but the door will be open to let the overnights out and it also opens for dinner. If they're not there, what do we do then?"

"We stay around for a while to see if they turn up. I will not trust Pavel or Alberto to do that, but if the girls are inside, they can get them out."

Driving down the road to where the entrance to the shelter was located, they could see people coming out. However, with most of the other entrances on the street being office accommodation apart from two small cafes, there was little in the way of places to stand around without attracting attention. Even the parking was bad, with all the places already taken.

"We'll spend an hour in a cafe. It's a good location to watch if they come," Petar suggested, parking the car on another road.

They wondered back and had only been in the cafe for half an hour, when they saw the two girls go into the shelter.

"I don't know how we missed those two walking around the streets, both are very attractive. But as Ivo surmised, very young," Sandu commented.

Petar grinned. "The younger the better in my book, they will fetch good money. Call Pavel and Alberto, have them go into the shelter and pull them out. Even they can't mess that up, particularly with us watching."

Chapter 18

Pavel entered the shelter, followed by Alberto. They looked around before heading to the dining room. Inside, a large number of people were sitting on bench seats at tables, eating. Behind a serving table, Zoey and Charlotte stood there talking to each other.

Pavel grinned, walking directly up to them. "Believed you could get away from us, did you?" he began, and then opened his jacket to reveal a gun. "You leave with us, one of two ways. Come quietly and no one gets hurt. Object and we will begin shooting and drag you out. Do you want people to die for you?"

Charlotte looked at Zoey talking in German, not the French Pavel expected. "What do you say? Do we go quietly and scatter in both directions outside, or tell them to get lost?"

"Let's confuse them first and speak German," Zoey said, and then grinned. "It's fun to see what they do."

Pavel had listened to their conversation, quickly realising that maybe they did not understand French. He turned to Alberto. "What the fuck are they speaking?"

"Could be German, these girls are not French as Petar said they were. I will try Italian. Maybe they understand that?"

"Listen, you little fuckers, come with us, or we'll turn this room into a bloodbath," Alberto demanded, talking to them in Italian.

Of course, both girls understood Italian and French. They just looked at each other with a hint of a smile. Then Charlotte tilted one of the large pans, still on the serving table, towards them, so they could see it was empty.

"All gone," Zoey said in very broken French, before laying the pan back down, and opening both her hands in a gesture. "Sorry."

"The stupid fucker believes we want dinner," Alberto said in frustration.

Pavel realised that maybe at least one could understand a little French. "You," he said, pointing at Zoey, "come with us."

"No, no, we work for dinner," she objected.

"You come now, forget dinner," he shouted at her, getting more frustrated.

People had stopped eating, attracted by the increasingly raised voices at the serving table.

"You two, fuck off. Can't you see there is no food left?" a man shouted out.

Then another shouted, "Yes fuck off," followed by others shouting the same.

Alberto had enough. He pulled his gun and let off two shots over the heads of the diners. While he hoped it would shut everyone up, it had the reverse effect. Everyone panicked. They threw empty plates at him. Benches were upturning, as people attempted to get out, some even climbing over the tables, heading for the exit. All that did was to cause chaos as nearly sixty people attempted to get through a single door.

Germaine, inside her office, heard the gunshots, followed by the commotion. She stormed out into the entrance hall to find men breaking through the door, heading for the entrance and safety.

"What's going on?" she shouted at one man, after grabbing him by his jacket.

"There's a bloody madman inside firing a gun. You need to get out."

She stood dumbfounded, watching until everyone had left. Then she went into the dining room. Both men had pocketed their guns and were dragging Zoey and Charlotte out from behind the serving counter, by their hair.

"What are you doing? Leave the girls alone,"

Germaine shouted at the two men.

"Fuck off, they are coming with us. Try to stop us and I'll put a bullet in your head," Alberto shouted back. He was still keeping hold of Charlotte's hair, dragging her after him, towards Germaine and the main entrance.

Germaine realised there was nothing she could do to stop them, faced with a gun, she backed away to let them pass. Pavel followed him, dragging Zoey.

Once out on the street, Alberto hesitated, waiting for Pavel to catch up. However, what Alberto had not noticed when he grabbed hold of Charlotte; she still had hold of a fork when he dragged her out.

Charlotte decided this could be her only opportunity to break away and run. Kicking Alberto in the shin caused him to let go of her hair for a moment, at the same time cursing. After all, it was painful. Charlotte had not finished, as he bent forward, she brought the hand up which gripped the fork, stabbing him under his chin. Although not life-threatening nor disabling, it was sufficiently painful for him to grab the fork from her hand. That's all Charlotte needed to break away and run.

Zoey saw her go, glad at least she had escaped. Although her fate was not so good, being dragged down the street and bundled into the back of a van, the door slammed shut. Even inside the back, she could hear the screams of sirens as police cars bore down into the area.

The senior inspector in charge had closed the roads all around, believing he was dealing with a terrorist attack, and with France's experience of such attacks, they had in place a well thought out plan of action to contain such a threat.

Pavel was sitting in the driver's seat, with Alberto at his side.

"I'll kill that girl for nearly ripping my throat out with that fucking fork," Alberto commented, holding a not so clean rag he found in the van, up to his throat.

"What were you thinking, pulling a fucking gun out and firing it? What the fuck are we going to do now, the fucking gendarmerie are everywhere. They're bound to want to search the van."

"Then we bail, if we can't get her out. I'm not going down for being caught with a young girl in the back."

Pavel thought for a moment. "You're right, let's go."

Both vacated the van and ran. Stopped further down the street at a police cordon, Pavel claimed the scramble away from the gunmen had injured his friend and he needed medical help. The gendarmerie let them through and they disappeared into the enlarging crowd of onlookers.

In the cafe, Petar sighed. "Looks like the lads have fucked up once again. We may as well go. There'll be no chance of catching either girl now."

They paid the bill and left the cafe.

***

Jasmin finding the road blocked, parked up, and after showing her Unit T ID to the gendarmerie at the cordon, they let her through, meeting the officer in charge outside the shelter.

"Jasmin Dlamini, Unit T. What happened?"

"Two men tried to snatch two girls. One man used a gun to cause panic. We know one girl escaped, but we found the other in the back of a van one street away. Witnesses told police they had seen a girl bundled into the back, which directed us there. The driver and passenger have disappeared."

"Are you searching for the girl who escaped?"

"We are. What is your interest?"

"I have been sent to collect them. One is fourteen, the other fifteen, and we deemed them to be at high-risk. We will take charge of the girl you've found."

"I understand from our station, this girl's wanted

by the Portuguese police on a murder charge, so she must remain with us."

"Unit T is aware of the claim by the Portuguese, which we're looking into. If she has committed a crime, we will pass her across to the authorities. In the meantime, in view of what has transpired today, this is an attempted abduction of a minor and comes under the remit of Unit T. EU law pertaining to victims of human trafficking requires a victim to be placed under the protection of Unit T. No EU country has the authority to override Unit T."

The officer knew the power of Unit T across all EU countries, and Jasmin was correct. They could not hold a victim of human trafficking. That was unless the crime she had supposedly committed was actually in France. Then there may be an argument.

"Personally, I'm happy for Unit T to take responsibility for the girl. She should not be in a police cell. I haven't the authority to hand her over to you, so I'll make our people aware of Unit T's involvement and request clearance. She's currently in the shelter under guard."

"That's fine. Inform them I'm here under direct orders from Colonel Karen Harris, currently the commander of Unit T, to collect the girls."

He looked at her for a moment. "She's taken back command?"

"She has, less than a week ago, but only temporary until a new commander arrives."

He smiled. "I met her once, a really pleasant girl, but between you and me, there is no way Karen will relinquish control of Unit T. It's her life and we all need her there."

Jasmin smiled. "You may be correct in that analysis. I'll talk to Zoey, while you sort out her release to us."

"Then you know the girl's name?"

"I do. In fact, we know quite a lot about her. It's the

girl who escaped we haven't seen before."

Going into the shelter and through to the office, Jasmin introduced herself to Germaine, who she found with her head in her hands.

Germaine glanced at Jasmin's ID, giving her a weak smile. "Thank god you have turned up. Is this the norm for Unit T, when you collect children?"

"Not quite, but we have our moments. Never turn one away, always call us."

"I'm not sure what I'm going to tell the church wardens. We've so much damage, with broken chairs, crockery and even the doors come off its hinges, repair costs will really impact on what we can offer."

"Don't worry about it. Once you had contacted LBNF, the girls became our responsibility. We will cover the cost of any damage. If you telephone our call centre, they will fill in a damage form over the phone, passing the claim across to Karen for sanction. Once you have a final quote, let them know and they will send payment to your bank."

"She'll really do that?"

"Of course, Karen would not allow a charity, which can ill-afford repairs, to be out of pocket."

"Will you thank her for us?"

"I will. Now I need to speak to Zoey."

Jasmin went through to the dining room to find Zoey eating her dinner.

"You always seem to cause me problems, Zoey, as well as costing Karen money," Jasmin said, as she approached her.

Zoey looked up, a beam spread across her face. "Jasmin, what are you doing here?"

Jasmin looked around at the devastation. "Judging by the damage you and your new friend have caused, it's a good job I am. In fact, there was me, sat in Cannes sunbathing, with fresh coffee at my side after a wild night, when Karen contacted me to come and collect you and another girl she said was called Charlotte, but she seems to have done a runner."

"Wow, I wish I could have been in Cannes with you, but I'm afraid you're a bit late. I'm on my way to prison. According to the senior officer, I will be charged with murder. It's cool. At least I'll be safe."

"He's talking rubbish. It will be Karen who decides what happens to you, not a local officer, or even the French authorities?"

"Karen's that powerful?"

"You'd better believe it. Anyway, how do I get a coffee around here? I've been on the road for ages because of traffic."

"I'll fetch one. Do you take sugar?"

"Yeah, like I'm going to add pounds to my weight. No milk either."

Zoey was quickly back, taking the seat opposite. "What will happen to Charlotte when they find her?"

"We will take her in. Does she have a family?"

"I don't think so; well she does in a way. Her parents died in a car accident and she went to live with a relative. She believes the relative sold her to Beacher the same as me. Apparently, the new partner did not want her around. So she'd not want to go back to them."

"If they have, then Karen will destroy them. As for Charlotte, she'll go to LBNF, probably staying at one of the complex's where she'll go to school, or if she prefers in view of her age, she could decide to be adopted and live more of a family life."

Zoey shook her head. "Charlotte wouldn't trust any family looking after her wellbeing. She will want to remain, like me, in the complex. Unless, that is, I'm sent back to Portugal to stand trial."

"Forget Portugal, Zoey, we know all about Blake Fellows' death. In fact, I spoke to Karen about what was going on in that respect. She was not concerned. Your actions, in her view, were self-defence. Yes, you panicked, but that was understandable. The man was part of a paedophile ring and you were terrified of what they would do to you if you had stayed around, or even called the police. After all, you knew of at least two in the ring who were senior police officers. So trust in them would not have been high. Of course, they will want to interview you about what actually transpired, probably at Unit T's camp, but Karen will be there."

"You make it all sound so simple, as if Karen is the law. That can't be so, can it?"

"She's not the law, but Karen's been looking after girls like you for fifteen years. She knows what she can do and how far she can go. If you knew my background, believe me, yours is nothing, yet Karen was able to wipe the slate clean for me. That is some going, I can tell you. Then, if there is a problem, she has access to the finest legal brains in Europe. You'll be fine."

At that moment, the senior officer Jasmin had been talking to earlier, came in to the room, walking over to them both.

"I have permission to pass the responsibility of Zoey and the other girl, once she's found, over to Unit T. As their on-site representative, she is now your responsibility. Do you need our help?"

"No, I'll be fine."

"Then you can leave as soon as you want. Send my regards to Karen for me and welcome her back."

"I'll do that. You never know you could meet her again."

He nodded and walked away.

"God, does everyone know Karen?" Zoey asked.

"They like to think they do. Many only ever meet her once during some investigation or official do, but when you are talking about a girl, the world knows and holds in high regard, it's like a personal boost to claim you've met, and know her that little better than the average person."

"Yes, Karen is certainly strange in the way she talks and acts, but you do feel relaxed in her presence and I suppose believe you understand her way of thinking. But you don't do you?"

"No, at times, she even manages to surprise me."

"Can I tell you what Charlotte and I had agreed if we got split up?" Zoey asked.

"Course you can, that's what I'm here for."

"We would make our way to the Cathedral of Saint-Nicolas. She will try to get there if she can."

"Then that is where we will go."

Chapter 19

When Charlotte ran away from Alberto, she had no idea where she was heading, only that she must get as far away as she could, before he came after her. However, she had not gone a hundred yards when a man came out of a narrow passage and grasped her arm.

"Come with me. They will find you if you stay on the main roads." Sensing her hesitance, he finished in a softer, more comforting voice. "Don't be afraid, we look after our own,"

With this reassurance and recognising him as a man from the dining room she had handed a dinner to, Charlotte turned to follow him down the narrow passage. He did not run, more hurried, darting down more back alleys until finally going through the back door of a dilapidated building. It was dark, smelt musty and damp.

As soon as she had become used to the dark and looked around, she could see there were two more men sitting down on old mattress's leaning against the back wall. Both she recognised from the shelter.

"I'm Pons, that is Erec," nodding towards one of the men. "The one with the beard is Fernand, but we call him Fern. What do we call you?"

"My owner called me Avril, but my real name is Charlotte Lucas."

"What do you prefer?" Pons asked.

"People will be looking for an Avril, so Charlotte would be the best."

"Then we will know you as Charlotte. Sit yourself down; would you like an apple? We have little else."

"If you are sure, I was just about to have my dinner, when those men came in, so an apple would be appreciated, but I don't want to take anyone's food."

"We've all eaten. You're welcome to the apple."

Fern passed it across. She thanked him and after sitting down, began eating.

"Tell us, why did those men want you?" Fern asked.

"I don't know. I think my owner sent them to take me back. That was the second time they have tried."

Erec frowned. "What is this word owner? Who is this person you are talking about, you don't look old enough to be married."

She shook her head. "I'm not married, thank you very much. After all, I am only fourteen. My parents sold me to a man called Beacher, so he owns me now. He passed me to a paedophile ring where I lived with different men. I escaped with the girl that was with me in the shelter. We were not allowed to stay there, we are too young, so a charity called LBNF was coming, hopefully to give us a home."

"That's Karen Harris's charity. It's what they do," Pons commented.

"You know her?" Charlotte asked, surprised.

He laughed. "We all know about her, Charlotte. For years, we would often see her walking through areas where rough sleepers congregate. She would be looking for girls and boys your age, offering them a place of safety. You've met her, haven't you, Fern?"

"Many years back. A slip of a girl you would never expect to be out in dangerous areas, particularly for women, at night, but those with bad intentions would not go near her. It was always said she was a trained combat soldier, carried weapons and knew how to use them. Often in winter, she would stand warming herself around the oil drum and talk to us. No airs and graces with that girl, never looked down at anyone, even though she was worth millions."

"Does she still do that?" Charlotte asked.

Fern shrugged. "Who knows, there were so many

criminal groups destroyed by her, it was becoming more and more dangerous for Karen to be out on the streets alone. Mind you, that girl had no fear of such people, so she probably does."

"I'd arrange with Zoey, the other girl, if we got split up to meet at the Saint Nicholas Cathedral. She could not manage to escape, so I can't see her going there. How would I get in touch with LBNF?"

They all looked at each other. Fern answered. "We have no idea. For us, it would never come up. One of us could ask Germaine at the shelter."

Charlotte shook her head. "I don't think that's a good idea. Someone must have told those two men I was there, and only she knew who we were."

"She has a point, Fern," Pons said.

"Maybe, but Charlotte has to eat. We can't find enough food for her to hide out until those men go away."

They all fell silent, trying to think of how Charlotte could survive.

"It's obvious," Erec said. "I will take her to the Central Police Station in Des Freres. They are open twenty-four hours and will know how to contact LBNF."

"I'm not sure. Two of my owners were senior police officers. What if one is there, and he recognises me?"

"If he does, so what, point him out to others in the station? He'll not be alone, they'll crucify him, taking a child to his bed," Fern told her.

"I suppose you are right. If you give me a map, I could find it myself," Charlotte volunteered.

"No, Charlotte, I will make sure you get there. I know all the back routes. Besides, it is a change to help someone. Life on the street is no fun," Erec said.

"Very well, thank you for offering, Erec."

"Come on, let's go," Erec told her.

Saying goodbye to Fern and Pons, Charlotte left

with Erec.

The two of them went down streets and passages, before Erec turned down yet another narrow street. Stopping half way down, knocking on a door.

"Is this the police station?" she asked, confused.

"No, that is only minutes away; I just need to collect something from this house."

The door opened, and a man looked at Erec. "You're here to pay?"

"I am, Pascal, with something that's worth a lot of money," he came back at him, at the same time grasping Charlotte's arm pulling her forward in front of the man. "Petar is trying to find her, but she belongs to Beacher who sold her on to a paedophile ring four years back. You should offer her back to Beacher. She's worth a fucking fortune."

"Excuse me, you said you were taking me to the police, not selling me on," Charlotte cut in.

Erec looked at her. "Get real; on the street you exist, you don't live; that is for the lucky people with a job and somewhere to sleep. We have to take every opportunity to make enough to survive. As for you, look on the bright side. You'll have a bed and regular food, we don't." Then he looked back at Pascal. "Well, do you want her?"

"I'll write your debt off in exchange for the girl."

Erec frowned. "I only owe just under a hundred euro. She's worth thousands."

Pascal shrugged with indifference. "Then sell her yourself and bring me your money. If I had her, I'd need to contact them, hold on to her and it's uncertain they will even want to pay anything."

"I'll take five bags of skunk and you clear my debt," Erec said, resigned that he would get very little.

"Deal, bring her in and I'll fetch your payment."

They dragged Charlotte into the house and pushed

her into a downstairs room. The door was slammed shut and locked. The only window had bars on the outside, but the window was also screwed shut.

After Erec had gone, Pascal called Javier. He knew him to talk to, with buying drugs from him.

"What do you want, Pascal?" Javier asked.

"Word on the street, is you're looking for a girl who escaped a paedophile ring?"

"Why, do you have information, as to where she is?"

"I believe I can secure her for you, for a price. It would cost me."

"Hold on."

Javier muted the telephone and walked through to another lounge to talk to Beacher. "Pascal's on from Nice, claims he has the girl from Spartes paedophile ring. He's after payment if we want her back."

"There is something not right. Of the two girls still missing from Spartes, according to Marcel, one is still with Unit T, the other he was supposed to collect. The police caught him and we have heard nothing about what happened to that girl. I assumed the police have her."

"Could she have escaped from Marcel before he was arrested and not been taken by the police, but made her way to Nice?"

"Anything's possible, but if she is, she's fourteen, and has been locked up for close on four years. How much would she know about the modern world? Would she have been bright enough to get down to Nice without being picked up by the authorities? I doubt that very much. Ask Pascal for her name. Also, her age, what she looks like and why he believes she has come from the Spartes ring. Don't say I'm available as yet."

Javier talked to Pascal before cutting the call. "He's coming back to me with her age, but said her name was Charlotte, very attractive with blonde shoulder-length hair.

Said a druggy living on the streets, brought her to him."

Beacher frowned, "I can't remember sending a girl to Spartes of that name, unless," he hesitated. "The fucker has reverted to her original name. Give me a minute."

He went to his safe and took out a book, flipping through pages. "Found it. We had an eleven-year-old blonde-haired girl called Charlotte Lucas, paid the relatives three thousand euro for her. The ring would have known her as Avril. Avril is also the name of a girl Marcel was to collect. The point is, is this a setup and the girl's bait? After all, if the police had her, they will know about Spartes, but maybe they are trying to get at the supplier, us."

Javier shook his head. "I don't believe the police would risk a young girl, but Unit T would."

"You're right, with Harris back in command; she'd sacrifice one girl to bring us down."

At that moment the telephone rang, Javier answered.

"It's Pascal. I have checked with the girl. Claims she's fourteen and wants to come back to Beacher. She is scared and tired of running. Told me Beacher would know her as Avril, her owner was a Théo Deschamps, but thinks he's dead, killed by a man called Marcel."

"We know the girl. I will get back to you. Do nothing until you hear from us."

Javier looked at Beacher. "It is Avril, Pascal says she's scared and wants to come back to you. What do we do?"

"I would not want to risk her with the other girls, in case she is a plant. Having said that, she is valuable, so I could place her, but should we take the risk, or do we forget the girl? After all, she's already earned us plenty?"

"I think we should take her, but on conditions. Nothing must be able to come back to us, meaning Pascal has outlived his usefulness. We must also eliminate the one who brought her to Pascal. We'll send her to Jacqueline for a short time and see what happens, police or Unit T wise that is."

Beacher thought for a short time. "Pascal and the man off the street, I agree. Leaving her with Jacqueline is a risk, but if Harris is watching her and moves on Jacqueline. She'll claim the girl wanted help, and she gave her a roof over her head."

"To do that, she can't risk putting her to work."

"She'd better not; otherwise she faces prison for touching a fourteen-year-old. Besides, once it's apparent Harris, or the police, aren't watching Avril, I want her back to sell on at the top price, so I don't want a girl who's been prostituting and bruised."

Chapter 20

Ramiz Shaban, an Albanian worked for Beacher as an enforcer to extract payment from dealers Beacher supplied. His territory was the South of France, today Ramiz was on his way to collect Avril from Pascal. Arriving at Pascal's house, Ramiz knocked on the door.

Pascal opened the door. "Yes?"

"I'm from Beacher. You have something for him?"

"I do, come in."

They both went through to the back room.

"Drink?" Pascal asked.

"Beer's good. Where is the girl?"

"Upstairs, ready to leave with you. I have fed her. Javier called, and we agreed payment of one kilo of heroin. Have you got it?" handing him a can of beer.

Ramiz opened the can and took a long drink. "Once I've seen the girl, then we deal."

Going upstairs, they entered the room Pascal had moved Charlotte in; she was sitting on the side of the bed.

"I'm told you want to return to Beacher. Is that true?"

"Yes, I can't cope, and just want to be looked after by someone I know. Beacher always promised to look after me."

"What name did he know you by, and who were you with?"

"I was with the Spartes ring, they knew me as Avril."

"What is your age?"

"Fourteen,"

"How did you get here?"

"By train and lorry with another girl, but we split up."

He nodded, and then turned to Pascal. "I am happy this girl is Avril. We should go downstairs."

Leaving Charlotte in her room, they went back to the

lounge.

"You have my payment?" Pascal asked, closing the lounge door.

"Yes, it's inside the bag. Tell me, who brought Avril?"

"Erec, he's on drugs and buys off me, along with Fern and Pons. They hang out in the old print works. Why do you want to know?"

Ramiz shrugged. "Just in case Beacher asks, you know what he's like, wanting to know everything, so it's best to have a complete picture."

Pascal did not answer; he had his back to him after placing the bag Ramiz had brought onto the table, before pulling out the heroin wrapped in cling film.

Seconds later, Ramiz was up behind Pascal, he yanked his head back, and slit his throat. It was so fast Pascal did not even have time to prevent him. He just sank to the floor.

Ramiz replaced the heroin into the bag, wiped his knife on the clothes of Pascal and left the lounge, going upstairs to Charlotte.

"Pascal and I have agreed for you to come with me. But before that happens, with only your word as to where you've been, I intend to check you have no device on your body placed by the police, or Unit T, to keep track of you."

"I've been with no one. Neither do I have anything I shouldn't have."

Ramiz pulled out a small electronic device and turned it on, then looked at her. "We shall see. Remove your clothes. I'll warn you, if you have anything, tell me before you undress, because if I find anything hidden in pockets, or strapped to your body, I'll cut your throat."

"I understand," she answered.

"Very well, pass me each item of clothing as you remove it."

Soon she was standing in front of him naked, while he checked her clothing. Being naked, did not faze Avril, she was used to it. Her last owner would often have her wear very little, serving drinks, when his friends came to the house, even allowing them to rub her bottom when she came close to them. After Ramiz had checked her clothing, running his electronic device over which could detect anything metal, even the smallest of items. He then began on her, first looking into her mouth, then running his hands through her hair, before having her do a complete turn. Satisfied, he told her to dress, Avril quickly doing as she was told.

"Right, it's time we left. Do I need to secure you?"

She shook her head. "No, I just want to go back to Beacher. I'll do anything you ask of me."

"Very well, we should go."

Outside Pascal's house, he closed the door and wiped it with a wet wipe. "Tell me, could you find where this man Erec hangs out?"

"I think so. It was pretty straightforward to get here, apart from turning off the main road and coming to this house."

"Let's try, shall we?"

Avril stopped several times, before recognising landmarks that had interested her on the original journey to Pascal's house, such as wall adverts, shops with lots of items she had never seen before and even the buildings. Soon they arrived outside the building Eric had taken her inside.

"This is where Eric brought me."

"What did you think of Erec?" he asked.

"Not much. He lied to me. Said he was taking me to the police station, but sold me for a few bags of heroin. If I had lied to any of my owners, they would punish me. I understand why he did. He has nothing and exchanging me, gave him the chance of clearing his debt with Pascal."

"It would have done, if Pascal had paid him what he promised, but he didn't, so I'm making sure he gets it. We want people on the streets to act as our eyes, so he needs to be confident we will pay. You wait here."

"I'm glad you don't want me to go with you, I did not want to see him again. They were in the far room when I came here."

He nodded and went inside, hesitating a moment while he got used to the dim light. Then he went through to the back. All three men were leaning against the wall dozing.

"Which one of you is Erec?" Ramiz asked.

"I am. Who wants to know?" Erec asked.

"You knew the rules. Find a child on the street, telling you she belongs to Beacher, you contact him, you don't offer to take her to the police, or sell her to line your own pocket."

"You sold Charlotte?" Fern demanded.

"Yes, why shouldn't I have? She is worth a fortune; then I noticed you didn't complain last night when you used some of the proceeds." He looked at Ramiz. "As for contacting Beacher, how could I do that? We have no mobiles. Better I put her with someone who knows how to get in touch."

Ramiz shrugged. "Whatever, but you see on this occasion the girl is under fifteen, and in France that's a long prison sentence if caught with her, so Beacher wants no loose ends that could get back to him, or risk you demanding more payment to keep your mouths shut. I trust you all understand?" Then he pulled a gun from his coat pocket, already with a silencer screwed to the barrel, and shot each man, finally finishing with a bullet to the head.

Coming outside, Avril was still where he had left her. "Did you find him?"

"I did, and he's been paid. Let's go."

Ramiz waved down a taxi, and they headed for a small airfield between Nice and Cannes.

"When we get to the airport, you're taking a short flight to an airport in Paris. You will stay with a lady Beacher knows well for about a month."

"So I'm not going back to the house Beacher had me working in?"

"Not for the moment. As far as anyone is concerned, you reached out for help and the woman took you in. You act your age, the husband will expect nothing from you, like you've done in the past, so don't offer."

"But I will go back to my life looking after a new owner?"

"Why, don't you want to?"

"Yes, I was happy with most of my owners. As for what I have seen of the outside world, this is not for me. It's frightening."

"Then Beacher will make sure you get an owner who will look after you well."

Chapter 21

Both Zoey and Jasmin remained in Nice for another two days, while Unit T's surveillance kept a watch on the church, but Charlotte never turned up. Karen had them both move on to the Torre del Mar complex, where she would join them in a day or so. Apart from the complex being secure, Zoey was to attend the private hospital owned by Karen alongside. Such attendance was mandatory for any girl. It also allowed a medical report to be added to the information held by Unit T.

Karen, with the information received from Zoey and government records, had first travelled to the UK, before she would move on to join them at the complex in Spain. Collecting her Range Rover from the secure car park in the basement of an apartment block she owned, that also had an apartment for her own use on the top floor, she set off for Oxford. An hour and a half later, she came to a halt outside a smart detached house on the outskirts of the city. In the drive was a BMW car, with a smaller car alongside. Karen walked up to the front door and rang the bell.

A man, she estimated to be in his early forties wearing slacks with a designer shirt, opened the door. "May I help you?"

"My name's Colonel Harris, Commander of Unit T," Karen began, at the same time showing him an ID. "Are you Reece Parsons, the husband of Daya Parsons?"

He frowned. "If you are looking for Reece, you won't find him here. Reece was my wife's first husband. I'm Mark Talbot."

"Your wife, is she here?"

"She is. What do you want of her?"

"That is confidential, unless she decides you can sit in on our conversation. As for your wife, she has a choice. I talk to her here, or at the local police station. I suggest here. Either way, we will talk."

He glanced at the black long wheelbase Range Rover blocking their entrance. Whatever Unit T wanted of Daya must be serious, with their commander coming? "You had better come in."

As they went through to the lounge, his wife looked up from a book she was reading.

"This is Colonel Harris, from Unit T, Daya."

She dropped the book, never taking her eyes off Karen. "It's about Zoey, isn't it?" she whispered. "I knew this day would come, and you'd be knocking on my door. Believe me, it's been a living nightmare."

"Who the hell is Zoey, Daya, and what's that person have to do with you?" Mark cut in.

"Before you say anything further, Mrs Talbot, my visit at this stage, is purely exploratory. Even so, you may prefer a solicitor to be present. It is also your decision if you want your husband in the room." Karen looked at Mark. "Mr Talbot, I require you to prove who you are by passport, or driver's license. Is it alright if I sit down?"

"Please take a seat. I'm also happy with Mark being here," Daya said. "Mark, fetch your passport please," then she looked at Karen. "I won't need a solicitor, Colonel, to tell you what happened. Before I begin, can you tell me if you are here because Zoey is seriously injured, or is she dead?"

"She is neither, Mrs Talbot, Zoey is in the care of LBNF. But I feel bound to make you aware; the charges against you are so serious, Unit T may apply for extradition for you to face criminal proceedings in the EU. I will not deceive you, under EU law, if found guilty, the punishment is a mandatory ten years with no remission. Although such a sentence could be increased, because of the age Zoey was taken."

"I can assure you, there will be no need for extradition

proceedings. I'll go voluntarily to face my punishment."

Mark had rushed out of the room and upstairs to find his passport. He wanted to be back and hear what this was all about. As he looked in the drawer, a little boy, aged three, came into the bedroom. "Who is downstairs, Daddy?" he asked.

"Mummy has a visitor, Daniel, please go back to bed."

Mark returned to the lounge, handing the passport to Karen. She looked at it, and then using the camera on her phone, took a photo of the front page, sending a text with it attached to Unit T.

"Perhaps, Mrs Talbot, you can tell me how Zoey, your daughter, ended up in a paedophile ring to be abused for four years? From the beginning, please," Karen, asked her voice cold without emotion.

"I met Reece Parson's, her father, when I was on a hen party in Spain. We had a week and were partying every night, sleeping it off on the beach. Reece tagged onto us, tall, muscular and fantastic looking, besides having all the flash, like the high-powered sports car, a villa to die for and he wanted me. In fact, he would not leave me alone. By the second night, he'd taken me to his bed, and I didn't object." She hesitated, as if thinking back. "I fell in love with him. He was everything a girl could want. When I returned home, he would call me every night. We talked for hours and soon I was returning, against my parents' will, yes, but I had to be with him. I could not tell them the one important reason I wanted to be with him: I was pregnant with Zoey. When he married me, they came round, accepting he was genuine and loved me. I never questioned where all the money was coming from to live the life we did. As time went on, sometimes he would be away for days, never telling me where he had been. Whatever he was doing, he was becoming more and more stressed. Things began disappearing from the house, valuable items, for no apparent reason. Even my jewellery went. One day he admitted to me he was broke, told me his business dealings had gone wrong, and he owed thousands to some particularly nasty men. He would never tell me what these business dealings were, but I think they were drug related, after I found a stash in the house. I was so mad, scared Zoey would find them and believe they were sweets, I washed them all down the toilet." Again, she hesitated, as if thinking back. "He went berserk when he found out what I'd done. Told me that was his get-out card to begin a new life, and I had destroyed it. If his business partners found out, they would kill him. We went on the run, left everything behind. Most was worthless such was our debt. I went to work and for three years, we were surviving, but unable to save. Reece began selling drugs to holidaymakers to keep our heads above water. Sometimes, we were so down we would use them ourselves. He became addicted. I was also relying on them to get through the day." She reached down to her handbag and pulled out a tiny picture, staring down at it. "I remember Zoey's eleventh birthday as if it were yesterday. The girl was so beautiful in her new party dress that had taken weeks to pay for. She had a fantastic birthday and gone to bed. Although thinking about it later, she seemed tired, but I put it down to the excitement of the day. We were both happy for her and began taking our usual quota of drugs. I remember at the back of my mind, people coming into the house, arguing with Reece, threats being made, but I was so far out the conversation going on between them would not fit together. I was being told to sign a sheet of paper. Reece was shaking me, telling me if I did not, they would kill him and Zoey. I panicked and signed. Then once they left, I fell into a drug induced sleep," she stopped. "Pour me a drink, would you, Mark? Would you like one, Colonel?"

"I'm fine, thank you. So when you came round the next day, what happened?"

Mark had given her a drink, and she took a sip before continuing.

"I found Reece face down on the edge of the table, out of it. I began tidying the room. There was drug paraphernalia all over the place, and I did not want Zoey to see it. Going upstairs to call her, wanting her to fetch fresh bread, so I could make us all a late breakfast, I found her room empty. I returned to the lounge shaking Reece, asking him where she was. He looked up at me, his words sending me cold. 'We are free of debt at last,' he said. I asked what he was talking about, it was then he told me about the man he worked for all those early years and kept us in luxury, how he had collected on the debt, the price, our daughter. You can imagine I went berserk, wanting to call the police, but he showed me the signed agreement. Said it was my signature on the paper agreeing to sell her for twenty thousand dollars. If I told the police, they would arrest me for selling our daughter and I would go down for at least ten years, maybe life because of her age. His last words terrified me. He also said she would be long gone by now and I would never find her, nor would the police. If I made a complaint and persisted in trying, they would kill her. He promised she would have a good life, better than we were offering, and she would never want for anything. We should be happy for her. I cried for weeks, the only solace for me, was my drug addiction, allowing me to forget. We split up. I eventually ended up in rehab, finally getting off drugs. What happened to Reece, I have no idea? Then I met Mark. We have a son, who I love."

"Tell me, what was the teddy all about?"

Daya looked at her. "You're referring to Zoey's stuffed toy she called Teddy?"

"Yes."

"Reece told me he'd put it in the plastic bag they took with her. It was such a tiny thing, but she loved Teddy. Has Zoey kept it all these years?"

"She has. It also served as the downfall of the man who had purchased her," Karen hesitated for a moment. "Thank you for your time. I will request that the UK authorities contact you to provide a written statement. I feel obliged to make you aware; assisting in the abduction of a minor makes your situation very precarious. I advise you to leave nothing out, or attempt to make excuses. Facts and facts alone will only help you now. Exact dates, names etc you can remember, even if they seem irreverent to you, may be important. Make sure you put them in the statement. The UK police will forward the statement to Unit T and our legal team."

"I understand, and I'm prepared to pay for remaining silent about her abduction. Tell me, would I be able to see Zoey?"

"That is not up to me. That is up to Zoey herself. I would not prevent it, if that were what she wants, but I advise you, do not push it from your side. In Zoey we have, whether she knows it, or not, a mentally damaged girl on our hands. A girl locked up from the real world for four years, she didn't even know what a mobile phone was, never had access to television or listened to a radio, besides being passed from man to man, constantly abused, holding onto her sanity with her only link to the past, a stuffed toy. At this stage, who knows what's going through her mind, and the last person she would want to meet could be you, although I may be wrong," Karen stood. "Thank you for your time. It is unlikely we will ever meet again, but I strongly suggest you arrange legal representation. EU law is complicated. The UK authorities will deal with Unit T. I'll see myself out."

After Karen left, Daya stared down at the photo.

"What have I done to my daughter, Mark?"

He shook his head. "What were you thinking? Believing it would all go away and no one would find out? The only way that would happen, Daya, would be if they had killed Zoey. Did you wish that on the child as well?"

"I don't know what I wished, but I've destroyed our life, our son. Even you could see what that woman thought of me. In fact, I do not think she believed anything I said. When your thinking becomes distorted with drugs, nothing is more important than your next fix. Not even your own kin."

"More to the point, Daya, what if Harris takes a deeper interest in how we afford this house, this lifestyle?"

"Why would she?"

"The crime happened in the EU, not that I know if Unit T can uphold it in the UK, now we have left the EU. If it can, it is well known among the people I deal with; Harris will go for your assets. Everything, this house, the warehouse, the cars are in your name, not mine. I could be out on the street with our son. You should have come clean years back and told me about Zoey."

"Karen Harris wouldn't do that, would she?"

"You'd better believe it, read anything printed about Karen Harris, and it soon becomes obvious she hasn't got where she has today by turning a blind eye. Her own charity's built on taking assets, maybe to a degree her own wealth, and she's worth millions."

"I'm going to prison, aren't I," she whispered.

"Not if I can help it, even if we have to move to a country where she can't touch us."

Daya did not reply. While she hoped, Mark could do something, when the time came to get out, would he leave his extended family in the UK for her.

Chapter 22

Joseph Hinder, manager of Torre del Mar complex, was standing in reception watching the entrance. He, like many of the managers who worked for LBNF, was always nervous when Karen visited a complex. Why that was so, he could not explain. After all, she would never show annoyance or frustration, although her comments could be quite cutting and very direct. Even Sherry Malloy, Karen's best friend, who had been with her for years, and the charity's general manager, was nervous when Karen was around. Karen would spot everything they had missed, but obvious when pointed out. This time he was ready for her, knowing she was coming, he had the staff go that extra mile in their work.

Sandy, who was Karen's first manager at the Marbella complex, put Karen's eye for detail down to her military background, the way she talked, with the expectancy that everything had to be, as she wanted, not how others interpreted her standards, which made Karen a very difficult person to work with. However, Karen would not raise so many issues if people would think for themselves. It often frustrated her that no one would make even obvious checks, as a matter of course, rather than her needing to point things out.

Jasmin came through from the pool area. "Karen's not arrived yet, Joseph?"

"No, security confirmed they'd collected her from the airport, so she's more than likely had them stop off somewhere."

"Well, she'd better get a move on. The restaurant closes for lunch soon, so I'll be going in without her," then she wandered away.

Joseph wanted to comment that for Karen, nothing closes, not even the restaurant, no matter what time she

165

arrived. However, no sooner had Jasmin left the reception area, when a car drew up at the entrance and Karen climbed out, coming inside.

"Good morning, Karen. Did you have a pleasant flight from the UK?"

"I did for a change. Mind you, I used a military corridor, which often makes for a more relaxing journey. It's getting so busy on the commercial routes," then she changed the subject. "Just to let you know, I'm not going to my apartment in the Marbella complex tonight. Can you make a room available?"

"We have no apartments, with Jasmin using the only free two bedroom apartment we had left, sharing it with Zoey, a new girl who arrived with her. Zoey is in the hospital overnight. Would it be okay for you to join Jasmin, or would you prefer we found Jasmin a bed in another apartment?"

"No, I'm happy to share. Can someone take my overnight bag to the room? Where is Jasmin?"

"She is around, in fact, delaying going to lunch until you arrived. Should I let her know you have arrived?"

"Yes, while I wash my hands? I have not been here for a while, so I will be looking around the complex. Already I have noticed our magazine is upside down on the rack. I suggest you talk to your staff. Don't give me the need to bring up such basic issues going forward," then she walked away.

Joseph rolled his eyes back in despair. How did he miss that, when he had been standing in the reception, and Karen had to notice it?

The restaurant in Torre del Mar was self-service apart from a small guest area that had waiter service. Opening from seven in the morning, until two in the afternoon, when it was closed for cleaning, residents could still purchase food from the poolside bar, until reopening once more for dinner from six until eleven. Catering for five hundred residents and staff from the Torre del Mar complex and another two hundred from the hospital next door, ensured that this was a very busy restaurant.

Karen joined Jasmin in the waiter service area of the dining room. A girl came through from the kitchen with a salmon salad along with a bottle of wine. Karen looked at the girl who brought it. "What is your name?"

"Rodica Cosmescu."

"You work in the restaurant?"

"I hope to," then she elaborated. "I begin my trial in a week, but they asked if I would come in today. If there is a problem with your meal, I can bring the supervisor to talk to you?"

"Yes, have her come to see me."

Rodica returned to the kitchens. "There's a woman with a blonde girl in the service area, asking for you," she told the supervisor.

The supervisor looked through the round visual panel between the kitchens and the restaurant. "God, that's all I need. That woman you talk about is Karen Harris, the bloody owner of this place. What have you done for her to ask for me?"

Rodica, to hear the actual owner was in the restaurant, made her nervous. "I've done nothing I know of. I've only taken their meals."

"Well, something's annoyed her. She expects perfection and can be very cutting in her remarks if she sees anything untoward."

Rodica suspected she might have lost her job, before she had even started. "Will she sack me?" she asked meekly. "I need this job."

"Who knows what goes through her mind? If she decides you are out, you are gone. Even Joseph could do nothing. I'd better see what she wants."

She went through into the dining area and waited by the table until Karen placed her knife and fork down and looked up at her. "Do you think long hair not tied back, dangling earrings and wearing jeans, is suitable attire for working in any of LBNF restaurants?" Karen asked.

"No, Lady Harris."

"I'm glad you agree with me, so why is Rodica dressed as she is?"

"Rodica was supposed to begin next Monday, Lady Harris, but the normal girl went off ill this morning and Rodica stepped in for me. I can assure you, I have ordered her clothing and it would have been here before she officially started work."

"For me, that is no excuse. You could have found Rodica something, rather than have her in the kitchens wearing outdoor clothes. Then even if you had difficulty in supplying clothing, why have you not insisted Rodica tied her hair back, remove her earrings and provided her with a hat? I expect LBNF kitchens to maintain the highest standards of hygiene at all times. Anyone not capable of maintaining even the very basic of hygiene regulations has no place in LBNF. Sort it out, please."

"I will, Lady Harris, and promise it will not happen again."

"Not promise, it won't. I will instruct Miss Malloy to make random checks for me going forward. Do not let me hear from her, that standards have slipped. Now leave us and have Rodica dressed accordingly, if she's to be here for the rest of the week."

"That was harsh, Karen. It took the supervisor aback, being accused of incompetence," Jasmin commented, after she left them.

"And so it should, as well as her being on very thin ice to continue in our employment. But please, never question how I run LBNF, Jasmin. I have been here minutes and noticed basic issues. The Torre del Mar complex is our flagship, it represents the high standards we offer for anyone being looked after by LBNF. This is also the only complex open for important representatives from governments across the world inspecting our facilities, in order to satisfy them, as to how we look after their nationals before they return home. Their reports are vital to ensure continued funding from such countries, and something that took me years of negotiations to secure. I can assure you it was an uphill task, to convince them, that their nationals, caught up in human trafficking, would receive the best possible care here. It was also the reason I purchased the hospital. Before then, with so many victims with medical issues, it was an area out of my control. Complacency, no matter how trivial, can quickly escalate, as happened in Unit T, resulting in a complete breakdown of security, so it is not acceptable. True, an upside down magazine, or a girl who has stepped in because of illness, working in a kitchen and wearing her outdoor clothes, may not be a prelude to a security issue, but in my mind, it is important flagging drops in standards to management. Such actions need to be stepped on hard, otherwise why bother having standards. We may as well let everyone do their own thing, turning up in virtual rags to cook the dinner. As well as putting out to the world, we are no better than a local charity with a few volunteers, struggling to survive, rather than a well funded professional organisation, more than capable of caring for often extremely traumatised victims of trafficking."

"You're correct, Karen, it was wrong of me to comment on what is a huge operation that must be the best in everything it does, and I apologise. We can't afford a repeat of what happened at Unit T."

"We can't, or rather I won't allow complacency to creep into LBNF, as happened in Unit T, no matter what level."

They carried on eating in silence. Jasmin could understand Karen's frustration, yet in some ways, it was of her own making. Sherry, with Karen wanting her out of Unit T, had been given the job of general manager, but in her view, the girl hadn't the management experience to represent Karen, because Sherry wanted everyone to be her friend. Her current role was a recipe for disaster. Added to this, Sherry, like all management personnel, had no authority to make changes without Karen's explicit go ahead, and to get such sanctions was virtually impossible, when even Sherry found it difficult to make any suggestions herself to Karen. Although, if anyone did, Jasmin doubted Karen would listen. It was her way or nothing. As for Sherry's position, it suited Karen to have Sherry looking after her interests. The girl was loyal to her and no one else.

"What happened when you went to see Zoey's parents in London?" Jasmin asked, after the supervisor had brought coffee and left them alone.

"The father is no longer with Zoey's mother. She got married again and our intelligence unit confirmed her new husband is who he claims to be. As for her story, most is shit, thought up over the years to cover-up her being party to the sale of her daughter. When I first talked to Zoey, she never mentioned either of her parents was taking drugs. Has she mentioned it to you, with no prompting?"

"No, is that what the mother's claiming?"

"She is, but in my view, yes, they were in financial difficulties, and yes, Zoey's father is more than likely to have made his money in the drug industry, as she claimed. I am convinced to get out of debt, both parents made a deal with Beacher to sell their daughter on her eleventh birthday. It stands to reason. They would have been aware just how much their daughter could be worth, seeing it happen with other families, working with Beacher. Then the mother was young enough to have another child, which she did, a boy."

Jasmin smiled. "I bet that annoyed her. There is not as much value in a boy as there is for a girl. So you believe she could have handed her daughter over, knowing the girl's fate?"

Karen gave an indifferent shrug. "I don't think she actually cared, the child was sold, end of story. Does it shock me what humans are capable of doing? It does not. Look at yourself, your parents was quite happy to dump you in a boarding school, not even allowing you to return home for half terms."

"You are correct in that way, the mentality is the same. They may as well have sold me, like Zoey, for what interest they had in me, as their daughter. Even when I left home, neither bothered, apart from a few Rand my father gave me, saying that's all I would ever get off them, so don't return asking for more." She hesitated a moment. "You know, I should have killed them for what they put me through."

Karen smiled. "Bit remiss of you then, after all, it's not that you're incapable of carrying it out."

"I suppose, but I've not done badly in my life, I have far more money in the bank than my parents will ever have, so I'll never need them. But going back to Zoey's parents, what are you going to do? I can't see you doing nothing."

"You can say that again. I have instructed Unit T's legal team to base the prosecution on my assumptions. It is up to Zoey's mother to prove otherwise. We have issued an international arrest warrant for her and her ex-husband, as well as frozen all her assets, not that her appointed UK lawyers were very cooperative on me doing that, reminding me a UK resident is not subject to EU law. I am also interested in what her new husband does for a living. They have an expensive house, fancy cars outside, with everything being in her name, so an investigation into his affairs is essential. If he's dealing, my other hat with the CIA would be very interested."

"You and your complex life, you're certainly untrusting, Karen. I'll give you that."

"I have to stand away, Jasmin, in anything I do. In the heat of the moment, it is too easy in becoming mixed up in the emotions of a broken family and loose direction. LBNF is committed to looking after Zoey until she is at least eighteen, as well as fight for justice and obtaining compensation, wherever I can get it from for her. Either way, that will cost us thousands. She may even decide to meet her mother and forgive her. That will be up to Zoey. Still, the girl has to be supported."

"She's hardly likely to want to see her mother, in her current frame of mind, unless it's to kill her. For Zoey, time has not diminished the hate of what her parents did. It would have been a living hell, and the more you talk to her, the more you realise how strong that girl must have been to cope. It did not break her, as we see so often, although convinced, when Beacher took her back at sixteen, she was going to her death. She had even accepted that, seeing it as a release. Both of us know that would not have been the case. A girl of sixteen already in the system and more than capable of looking after her owner has real value. You do not kill such girls. They are far too rare."

"True, Zoey is a very strong and confident girl, but as the reality of how much she has missed of her life, locked up as she was, becomes apparent, she will need help. Then Charlotte, the girl Zoey was with, interests me. With what little I have heard about her, this is another who has gone through years of abuse and come out stronger. What's with the modern girls, are they no longer the wimps, like the girls of the past?"

"I've got to agree with you there, Karen. These

young girls are proving to be very resilient. But where is Charlotte, has Beacher found her? A fourteen-year-old, with no money and in a city she does not know, cannot hide for long. One of your people on the streets should have come across her."

"Yes it concerns me, there have been no sightings. I suspect the reason being, she has already left the city. Unit T is going through CCTV at the railway stations and airports, including private ones, as well as street CCTV around the shelter. But it takes time and time is not what we have."

"Would there be any value going public? Do it through the police and keep us out."

Karen shrugged. "I considered that, but decided it was far too high a risk. French law regarding children under fifteen being used in paedophile rings, or prostitution, is even worse than our mandatory ten years across Europe, with a prison sentence of twenty years. That is a long time and for someone to find they have a girl the police are looking for, does not bear thinking about. They would kill her. We have to go softly, Jasmin. There is no other option. At least we're dealing with a girl who is already in the system, used to looking after her owner, so there is not as much panic, as with a newly abducted girl, with no parents screaming down our ear."

***

Following lunch, Karen wondered off to do her inspection. Jasmin went to see Zoey. More to cheer her up, hoping she would open up even more of her time with the paedophile ring. Karen had at this stage, kept away, allowing Zoey to regain confidence with Unit T through Jasmin.

While everyone in the complex knew all about Karen, very few had met her. So once they heard she was actually there, very quickly, Karen was engulfed with so many girls wanting to say hello, there was no option but to give up her inspection and talk to them. While this was going on, she received a text from Charles to contact him as a matter of urgency.

Excusing herself, Karen made her way to the main office area in the complex, using an empty office to call him. "What have you got, Charles?"

"We've been able to track Charlotte, to a degree. CCTV recorded her with a homeless man the police identified as Erec. This is where it gets messy. A suspected drug dealer called Pascal was found dead by his wife, when he failed to collect her from her mothers. Police have informed us that two cameras, owned by other householders that looked down the street to Pascal's house, captured Erec taking Charlotte to Pascal's on the same day she ran from the shelter. The following day, a camera captured a man leaving Pascal's house with Charlotte. The police did not recognise him, but after the police sent us the footage, we did from our database. His name is Ramiz Shaban, a man we have down as a low-level contract killer. When the police went to an abandoned building, that once housed a printing company, and a known location both for Erec and Pons to hang out, they, along with another man called Fern, were found dead. Each shot twice, once through the head."

"A contract killing for certain; it is also interesting that Ramiz Shaban was around, with Pascal dead as well. Such actions point to whoever has Charlotte is attempting to close all tracks leading to him or them," Karen suggested.

"Precisely, but later the same day, with your request to have all stations and airports watched, Charlotte was caught on camera with Shaban, putting her on an aircraft heading to Paris. He did not go with her. We've requested footage from Paris at the time the aircraft landed and we're going through it."

Karen was confused. "That's strange. She is on her

own, yet she did not approach the police, or talk to security at the airport."

"I agree, and I brought in our team of psychologists to suggest what may be going on in her head. The consensus is, after splitting with Zoey outside the shelter, with her perceived support gone, the girl was frightened, so she turned to the only person she knows for help, Beacher. They believe she is so confused, she has no idea which way to turn, but would feel safer back in the life she's lived for the past three or more years."

"Your team has done well, but the next stage is vital. We want to know who met Charlotte off that aircraft and vitally where she is now. I cannot see whoever has Charlotte going as far in trusting her to make her way to an address alone. We are looking at a girl, similar but even younger than Zoey, locked up for years with little knowledge of the world around her, making her unable to cope on her own."

"Those were my thoughts, Karen. I'll be back to you as soon as we have more information."

"On another issue, has there been any movement in Portugal around Beacher?"

"Not as yet, but a ship has arrived from Yemen with its next port of call, Maracaibo Venezuela, before doing the return journey to Portugal and then Algiers. If Beacher intends moving the other girls out of Europe, this ship returning to South America, and an area he knows well with many contacts, could be the one he will use. Maybe he's actually exchanging them for drugs."

"When does the ship sail?"

"According to the port, the ship is due to leave on Saturday."

"I'll need to consider what to do now. In the meantime, with such a brief window of opportunity, I want two units of Dark Angel troops in the area, along with enhanced surveillance on that ship. We must send the

175

troops very low-key. No one must know they are there."

"We can do that, Karen. Are you also looking at a lockdown of the camp, while this operation goes on?"

Karen thought for a moment. "No, we go on as if nothing is happening; if anything changes this end then I'll reconsider." Karen cut the call. Then she lifted the telephone receiver and called the CIA in Virginia. When they answered, she gave them a code number and asked to be put through to a Harley Meyer. While Karen operates with the CIA's local offices, her primary contact at their headquarters was Harley, a woman of Karen's age.

"Karen, we've not talked for a while. How are you? I understand you have taken back control of Unit T. Is that good or inconvenient for you?"

"The latter, I'm afraid, but it's only temporary while a new commander is engaged more in keeping with Unit T's philosophy. Otherwise, I'm fine, and your family?"

"They are all doing well, what I see of them, but we are in difficult times and our services are in great demand. Anyway, you are not one to call to talk pleasantries. What can I do for you?"

"Maracaibo in Venezuela, just how dangerous is that area of the country?"

"I'd not recommend a holiday there. Seriously, in the area there are many local gangs dealing in extortion against business and private homes. Zulia with suspected ties to the El Tren de Aragua are the most active in Megabanda. What is your reason for asking?"

"In Europe, a paedophile ring has collapsed. The girls aged between eleven and fifteen have, we suspect, been taken back by the person who supplied them to the circle. We know who that is, but as you are aware, to know is not enough. We need concrete information to act on; otherwise we are running around trying to catch our own tail."

"How did this collapse come about?" Harley asked.

"We have under our protection one of the girl's who had been in the ring for four years. Her information has proved valuable. This will lead to the arrest of most, if not all, members of the ring. The point is, they have pulled the girls out and we suspect they are back with the supplier. He's a large importer of heroin, with contacts in South America."

"Then we may know him. What's his name?"

"Beacher Marinez."

"Just a moment," Harley said, at the same time typing into her computer. "That's interesting. We know about him and he has ties with the Tren de Aragua. According to our files, he dropped out some years back; we suspected he was dead, but it seems not. Then by what you are suggesting, he could well be using contacts back here to build a nice little slot for himself. How long have you known about this man?"

"Unit T had its sights on him for some time," Karen told her, "but only in regard to trafficking, they weren't that interested in his drug operations. Although, to be fair, we had nothing solid on the trafficking side, just suspicions."

"It seems a ridiculous state of affairs to ignore drugs when that industry dwarfs the human trafficking business."

"I know, but if you look at why Unit T exists, it stemmed from me shouting that something needed to be done, backed up by lots of photos and articles about me in the media. So, in reality, I was lucky to get a specialist team on human trafficking. Although all the other European agencies were happy, Unit T took the less glamorous trafficking problems away from them. They would have drawn a line if we had included the drugs industry as well. Without that, they may as well had gone home and left it to us. Going back to Marinez, I am suspecting that the girls would be unusable in Europe, be it private purchases or brothels. So why not use his contacts in South America, to exchange the girls for heroin?"

"I'll go with some of your assumptions, Karen, but for one point. The girls of that age can be purchased in Venezuela for a few hundred dollars, except no one wants them. They are too much trouble, often underdeveloped and a child. Even the brothels would laugh, if they were offered them. Saying that, I could be very wrong and Marinez has some sort of arrangement where they can be sent that reflects their value."

"If my assumptions are correct, then the latter will be the case. Although at this stage I'm not sure if they are going on that ship."

"Listen, Karen, let's be positive and assume they are on it. Send me details of the ship. I have contacts in the country that can check the ship out, just in case you miss them. Then, at least there is a chance of us picking them up at this end,"

"I appreciate your offer of help, Harley. I'll do my best that it won't be necessary and we'll have found them before the ship leaves."

"No problems, I'm glad to help, and you take care, Karen. You're doing a good job over there for us and we don't want to lose you."

"I will, and then you make time for your family. You only realise their value when they're no longer there."

Chapter 23

A woman in her early forties approached Avril. "Are you Avril?" The woman asked Charlotte, who had been standing around in the arrivals hall at the airport.

"Yes, has Beacher sent you?"

The woman glanced around nervously. "Please don't mention his name," she began quietly. "But he has sent me. Shall we go?"

They left the airport, queuing for a short time at the taxi rank, before leaving in one. Travelling in silence, Avril spent the time looking out of the window, with so much new to her, she wanted to see everything. The journey of thirty-five minutes passed quickly, finally coming to a halt alongside a terrace block, with a mix of shops and double doors between, which gave access to floors above. Most windows had small balconies overlooking the street below. Avril was ushered through the double doors, and into a lift that took them to the top floor. Entering an apartment, the woman closed and locked the door, pocketing the key.

"My name is Jacqueline, Avril. Beacher has asked me to look after you for the next month. He has a great deal on and feels this is the best place for you."

"Yes, Ramiz told me I'd be here for a short time."

"That is good. Let me show you to your room."

They went through the main lounge and into a bedroom at the end of the corridor. A room barely furnished, with a double bed, a narrow wardrobe and a set of drawers.

"Inside the wardrobe are suitable clothes for you to wear around the house, underclothes in the drawers. Next door is the bathroom. Come with me."

Once in the bathroom, that consisted of a sink, a shower cubicle and toilet along with a narrow shelf that had on it a comb, brush and a razor, she turned to Avril. "When you're showered, sort yourself clothes from the wardrobe and drawers to wear, come through to the lounge. Bring the clothes you're wearing and we'll put them in the washer," then she left her.

Showered with her hair dry, Avril returned to her room, pulling open a drawer. Inside and still in packets, she found knickers and bra sets, along with suspenders, nylons as well as self-supporting ones. In another draw were T-shirts, shorts and jumpers. Opening the wardrobe, Avril found most of the clothing was short skirts, and short tops, along with jeans and two dresses. Shoes in the bottom were two to four inch heeled shoes, a pair of trainers and slippers.

Avril decided on shorts, a jumper with trainers. Now ready, and after collecting up the clothes she arrived in, she went through to the lounge.

"The clothes suit you, showing off your long legs," Jacqueline told her, when she came into the lounge.

"This is what I'd wear with my last owner. There seems such a variety of clothes in the wardrobe. Do they belong to another girl?"

"In a way, they are shared clothing for girls to entertain my gentlemen, apart from underwear. I have one ill, so you will take her place."

Excuse me, Ramiz told me I was coming here to experience family life, not entertain men."

"Yes, so I was told, but you see, Avril, no one has volunteered to recompense me. In fact, you are a nuisance, taking up a bedroom that could be used. That is unless you have money to pay for your keep?"

Avril shook her head. "I have nothing."

"Of course you don't, but you do have assets men pay a great deal of money for. I have regular clients, who like the younger girl. You will be expected to entertain them. Sometimes you will have an overnight."

"I'm fourteen. You cannot be serious in suggesting

I offer myself, many times a day, to different men. That would make me a prostitute, which I'm not."

"So what have you been doing for Beacher? Sitting on your arse all day, I'd never believe that in a hundred years."

"Since I was eleven, I've been placed with different men. I become part of the household, looking after my man. I cleaned the house, cooked our food and joined him in his bed."

"This joining him in bed, did that include him giving you a good shagging?"

"I suppose, if you want to call it that?"

"Not want, Avril, no matter how you wrap it up, if the man ends up with his cock up your fanny, he's shagging you. As it is, Beacher cannot take you for a month. When he does, you could be right, he will send you to one man. In the meantime, it will do you good to experience the other side of the industry, so you'll appreciate just what Beacher has done for you."

Avril sighed inwardly. She would never win; no one could care less about her feelings.

"Now that is sorted, it's time to eat. Come with me."

They went into the kitchen, sitting down at the table eating in silence, until Avril wanted an answer. "So how do I spend my days, sitting around until some man wants me?"

"I would like you to look at them as my gentlemen friends, Avril, please. As for what you do, in the mornings, first you sort your bedroom out, particularly if you have entertained a man all night, then into the bathroom, to ready yourself for your next. When ready, you come through to the lounge wearing a nice dress, sexy underwear, suspenders and high-heeled shoes. You seem to have good dress sense and have matched the shorts and top well. I like that in a girl. At seven tonight, your first man will be arriving.

You have had a long day travelling, so after food, maybe you should lie down until he arrives, then I will bring you through to meet him. I want to hear good reports. No sulky face, no objections if he wants to undress you himself, or even put you over his knee for a gentle spanking before you offer yourself to him. Do you understand?"

"If that's what you want, why not? It is better than sitting around bored. So how long have I got to entertain your gentleman for?"

"You have him all night. He will leave you by ten in the morning. Then you have the day off to prepare yourself in time for your next, arriving at seven. He will be gone by twelve the same night. You'll not have time to be bored, Avril."

"This is going to happen every day?"

Jacqueline placed her utensils down hard on the table. "Yes, but be warned, give me problems, upset my gentlemen, keep in mind, my son runs a brothel. Perhaps if you feel you are too good for this life, you could spend a week there, experiencing the seedier side of the profession. That will see you servicing at least fifteen a day, is that what you want?"

She shook her head.

"No, I didn't think you would, so get used to it and look after my gentlemen, because if I keep getting complaints, that is where you will go. Understand?"

"I understand."

"Now you're finished, get back to your room. I'll come for you later."

Chapter 24

Karen, still at the Torre del Mar complex, made her way to the manager's office. He had left for the day, and she had gone there for privacy, in order to talk with Charles at Unit T.

"Do we have anything on Charlotte, Charles?" she asked.

"Yes. Surveillance footage from Orly airport, showed she was met by a woman. Charlotte, in the way they talked, seemed to have been expecting her. They left the airport in a taxi. We were able to locate the driver, who told us he had dropped them off at a house in the Pigalle area. I suspect you know the area?"

"It's an area I know, not all for the best of reasons. Even so, if Charlotte has been taken to that area of Paris, they intend to use her. I also do not believe there is an intention for her to join the other girls taken out of the Spartes ring. Have you gone as far as identifying the exact house the woman took Charlotte?"

"We have. She was taken into a multi floor building with a number of apartments."

"Set up surveillance for a few days, and then we go in. Everyone who enters that building is to be identified."

"I've talked to our surveillance teams and although they could watch the building, to get inside would be very difficult."

"Did you obtain photos of the woman?"

"We did, but have been unable to identify her as yet."

"Well, keep on it. In the meantime, send me a copy of the photo as well as the location, and I'll take it from here."

Her words disturbed him. What did Karen mean, not that she would elaborate. Everyone, be it Unit T, LBNF or even individuals, all work on a need-to-know basis. If any part of a plan did not include you, you would be told nothing, only Karen had the full picture. Charles understood why. The industry they were fighting was awash with money and even for the most loyal, there is often a price that could buy someone's allegiance, but nothing could buy Karen's.

"That's fine, Karen, providing we don't lose the girl. I'll remind you, she is fourteen and in my view, Unit T should not delay in pulling her out."

Karen sighed inwardly. These people did not understand the world of trafficking. "I'm aware of the girl's age, but this girl is different. She has been in the system for a number of years. She is also comfortable with these people. Remember, she happily travelled alone to the airport. That's a public location, with an obvious police presence, and she approached no one. By her not doing so, we have the opportunity of identifying a number of active paedophile's, who can be the very worst of abusers. To take them off the streets for twenty years, cannot be underestimated as to its value. It may sound hard to you, Charles, but over the years, at times, there has been no option but to use the victims to get to the perpetrators. They are often our only way in. Even so, I would never use a girl not already entrenched in the system, she would have no value. Then a girl of Charlotte's age, for her owner, and I say the word owner, with tongue-in-cheek but appropriate, she is extremely valuable. In fact, she is at the most valuable age any girl could be. Then adding Charlotte's experience, she will be offered at over a hundred thousand dollars. So believe me, she will be looked after. Bear in mind to keep hold of such girls, as they tried with Zoey, they are prepared to kill. That, Charles, reflects their importance and how valuable Charlotte is."

"I had no idea girls went for such large payments. I must also bow to your extensive knowledge and experience, but please pull her as soon as. I have a daughter of her age and it makes my skin crawl to even think of what must be going through her mind."

"Don't let it, Charles. Charlotte being indoctrinated in her current way of life, she will have no concerns. Upset perhaps, with her orderly life being disrupted, when even after a small taste of freedom, you can see by her actions in the airport it had no effect on her wanting to escape from a life of what she perceives as safe. When we finally pull her out, Charlotte will be faced with months of professional help. Moving on, she is only one of a number in the hands of Marinez, who we risk losing completely. What progress do we have in Portugal, getting Dark Angel there and mobile?"

"Unit T troops are in place and waiting for a target from you and the order to go in."

"That's good. I am leaving first thing to join them. I'm currently receiving regular intelligence from my contacts on the street, as well as informers close to Marinez's drug distribution operation. While I have nothing yet about the children's whereabouts, he cannot make a move without me knowing. Anyway, we'll speak soon and I will update you."

After Karen went off the line, Charles leaned back in his chair, deep in thought. The short time Karen had been in total charge, he had felt out of his depth, beginning to understand that the normal rules of law and order, as well as decency and compassion. It seemed to him, the world Karen lived in was in fact a perpetual war, but a war with no rules? A war, he believed, if there were, no one would abide by them anyway, be it the criminal group, or their opponents like Karen. Both aware of a victim's value, each using them as pawns in the battle. He was beginning to feel uncomfortable, as she began drawing him in to the reality, where with Lang, such a war was so completely alien to a military mind, there was little option but to fail.

A commander of Unit T needs to be a risk taker. At times, a cold-blooded killer, or prepared to throw the victim to the wolves. If this was the case, did he want to be part of an operation where children may be abused, or killed, for tactical advantage? If he was, could he face his children, his wife, knowing he was becoming complacent in accepting Unit T, or rather Karen, using girls of his daughter's age?

***

Back at Torre del Mar, Karen joined Jasmin at the bar on a private beach owned by the complex. Being a weekday, while there were around fifty girls sitting around talking, it was relatively quiet. Most weekends, the beach bar hosts party nights for all the girls whose birthdays had been during the week, and it could get quite wild. These girls knew how to party.

The girl running the bar brought Karen and Jasmin vodka and tonics before leaving them alone.

"I want you to go to Paris, Jasmin. We've located Charlotte, but I suspect she will revert to being called Avril, now she is back under the control of Marinez."

"What area?"

"Pigalle. The problem being, she is in a multi apartment block."

Jasmin sipped her drink. "Do you think she's being introduced to possible buyers, or they are working her? After all, it's in an area where demand for a young girl would be high."

"True, but extremely dangerous to offer her around. The girl is fourteen, under French law that is twenty years if you are caught with her. I'd plum more for her being used by a discreet circle of paedophile's, or alternatively, as you suggested, being introduced to prospective purchasers. Having said that, I have the address, photos of the woman looking after her, and been in touch with one of my cells operating in the area. They have set up surveillance inside the building, allowing you to keep close to Charlotte, as well as find out what the woman's part is in all this. At this stage, she could be her minder waiting for Marinez to move her on. We just don't know."

"When do I go?"

"By train, first thing, I'm going the other way. There is no particular rush in you getting there. My people are still be working on getting inside the building to set up surveillance, as well as following anyone who calls at the apartment where they have her. So you'll have a complete picture going forward by the time you arrive."

"Then it seems you have quite a setup operating already?"

"I do, and unlike Unit T's surveillance teams, they are able to melt into the background. The only problem, I've geared it more for drugs, to suit the Americans, who, to be fair, have been my paymasters over the last months, but they are more than capable of backing someone like you."

"What are the rules of engagement?"

"None, you must go with your own gut feelings, as the situation changes. The only time you follow my orders, is when I decide we have enough intelligence to convict any persons visiting the apartment. Then we pull her out, your job, at that point, is to project the asset at all costs."

"I can do that."

"Of course you can, Jasmin, just don't leave too many bodies lying about."

They fell silent, taking time to drink their drinks.

Jasmin broke the silence. "What of Zoey? Is she remaining here?"

"What better place than to hide her among the girls? Tomorrow she's back in the complex and will remain on level three for debrief, until I decide the risk to her is no longer there."

Jasmin knew level three of the complex was the very high-risk area for girls whose pimps or cartels are still at large. Protected by a Dark Angel security Unit, there would be nothing lax in how they operate as happened at the camp. All were loyal to Karen. It was also a floor that even Joseph had no authority, and could not go on.

"You know, after a few days as commander, Unit T is back with a vengeance. I hope you made the most of your break, because you'll not be getting another any time soon," Jasmin commented.

Karen gave an indifferent shrug. "It's what we do, Jasmin, and we are very good at it."

"You mean you are. I am here, like everyone else, just for the ride. But I will tell you this: when I was working with the cartels, often listening to the derogatory way they would talk about you, they knew nothing. All the so-called big men brandishing guns, boasting to the leaders how, if given the chance, they would take you out, made me laugh. I would often urge the leadership to take up the idiots boasting as to how they would kill you and send them to face you. When push came to shove, none stepped forward, inwardly shit scared of going up against a professional killer. On a different subject and closer to home, is Farah going to follow in your footsteps?"

"I hope not, Jasmin, it has been a long lonely road I would not wish on anyone. Even so, I've a feeling she really enjoyed her time at school in the camp, as well as starting on her personal training to protect herself going forward. So whatever her future, I think she should have a stint in the military, if only to get it out of her system. In fact, she was over the moon to know I was back at Unit T, and is already asking if she was old enough to go on the firing range."

"It's your own fault. You make your life seem so easy to her. Whatever she does going forward, you must steer her away from covert operations. You and I know, no girl has survived more than two years. Okay, Sherry is an exception, but if it hadn't been for you going in, she'd never have escaped the many brothels she kept ending up inside, or she'd be dead by now."

"Perhaps, but I don't think so. Sherry is like me, she's a survivor, inwardly a soldier and a very good one when she puts her mind to it. She may have to bide her time, like us all, if I'd not found her, she would not have been held long."

Jasmin glanced at her watch. "You know we could talk all night, but it's time to call it a day for me, the last bus for the complex leaves in five minutes. Are you coming?"

"No, I'm walking back. It gives me time to think."

"You are armed?" she asked, obviously concerned.

"Of course, just get off, Jasmin, and make sure you're up to catch the early train."

Karen finished her drink and left the private beach, but not heading directly back to the complex, she decided to take the longer route along the public beach towards the town. Karen was happy to be alone. Since being a little girl, she had always been a loner, although to be fair at school, being a popular girl and particularly attractive, she had her share of admirers and for a short time was the head girl. Even so, with not finishing school because of her abduction, and her redirection towards army life, it should have been a catalyst for making friends. However, as well as using every penny she had to keep her charity running, often leaving her in debt each month, along with many covert operations, going out drinking with the lads when you can't pay your way, was never going to be the ingredients to a spectacular social life. Now, with so much wealth and power, it still served to work against Karen, with people actually being nervous around her.

Soon Karen arrived in the outskirts of Torre, with

the many bars and restaurants, some closing up for the night. A lad of around twenty, wearing shorts and T-shirt approached, handing her a small flyer. "Still time to cash in on our midweek offer of buy one and get another free," he urged.

Karen smiled. "Perhaps another day, I've work tomorrow."

He lowered his voice. "At least go in, and maybe buy a soft drink, I am down on my quota, it's been too quiet. Ten minutes won't zonk you out for work," then he grinned. "I'll even walk you home and tuck you up."

Karen laughed. "Such an offer sounds irresistible. In fact, the best offer I've had all week, not that it is going to happen. I'm far too old for you, but I'll go inside for a drink and up your quota."

He grinned. "Come on, you're not that much older. Besides, there's no law that the women needs to be younger than the man."

She came closer to him. Grasped his shoulders and turned him around. "Off you go. You have another two likely punters on the way. With your cheek, they probably will be following me in." Then she let him go and went inside.

Karen didn't really want a drink, but it was nice talking to him, and made a change to be treated normally.

A girl came from the far end of the bar, came over to serve Karen, but hesitated for a moment, then grinned. "Karen, what are you doing in here?"

"I've a buy-one-get-one-free flyer, given to me by a really cool lad."

"That's got to be Jonathan, he's cute isn't he and very hard to say no to?"

"He is, then the offer to take me home and tuck me up in bed tipped the balance. How can a girl say no to such an offer? Anyway, how do you know me?"

"Come on, I've seen your photo loads as well as read the magazine. I am in the Torre del Mar complex. This is my job. Not the best in the world, but at least I am working. My name's Radu Stibel and originally from Romania. What can I get you to drink?"

"I'll have a vodka and tonic, but a sealed bottle of tonic, please."

She quickly brought it back along with another glass and two bottles of tonic. "Are you out for long? I finish in twenty minutes. We could walk back together if you want?"

"Sounds good, but do me a favour. You have the second drink. I'm flying tomorrow and want to see the controls."

"Okay, but I'd not worry too much about being over the top. Our esteemed boss is not averse to watering down the spirits. Tells us it's stopping the punters getting too drunk, but also saves him a lot of money."

At that moment, the two women Karen had pointed the lad to outside came in. She smiled inwardly. He certainly had the gift of the gab.

Later, Karen was walking back to the complex with Radu. "Why haven't you returned home, Radu?" she asked.

"I can't. I come from a small village. They would soon pick me up again, and after a good thrashing, I'd be sent back to work on the streets in Cologne. I like it here; I'm safe, even saving a few euros. So, along with my compensation, which I really appreciate, I'll soon have my own little apartment."

"It's good to know you've a plan and we could help."

"I don't know how you did it, getting the charity together; well I do in a way, just dogged determination. I will miss the girls though. We have such a great time. Are you here Saturday? It's a big bash, being twelve girls birthdays this week to celebrate?"

"I wish, but work calls."

At that moment, they both heard a bicycle bell tingling.

"Oh no, it's Jonathan. He'll be mad. We usually walk back together. It's safer for me, not that the area is dangerous, but aged twenty with my past, you always feel a little nervous."

"Do you want me to get lost?"

"God no, we only work at the same bar. It's just that he lives this way, that's all."

He cycled past them and spun the bike around, dismounting. "You never waited, Radu."

"Sorry, Jonathan, I met someone I know and decide to walk back with her."

By now, he was at Karen's side and pushing the bike. "We meet again. It's fate, you know."

"Funny fate to meet someone you've just made a commission out of," Karen answered.

"Love is like that. I knew we were made for each other the first time we spoke. We should quit our jobs and run away to a commune and make love under the stars."

Radu nudged Karen. "He's always like this, falls in love with every attractive girl he talks to. Don't you, Jonathan?"

"No, that's all finished. This is the real thing. He suddenly pushed his bike away and went down on one knee. "Please, beautiful lady, let us walk in the moonlight and talk about our future together."

Karen had stopped and was looking down at him close to bursting into laughter, but thought better of it. She had no intention in mocking him.

"The offer sounds idyllic, Jonathan, even more so with the possibility of this blossoming romance of ours, ending up with us making love under the stars. But can I take a rain check on your suggestion? I'm a bit busy this week?" offering her hand, to pull him up.

He grasped it, stood and looked sad as Karen walked on to catch up with Radu. "Story of my life, I should kill myself," he called out with obvious despondence.

Karen stopped alongside Radu and looked back. "Come on, it's a bit bad if you're not prepared to wait a week for me, when I was thinking more of standing at the altar with flowers, rather than in front of a coffin."

He grabbed his bike, catching up with them both. "I like your humour, my type of girl. Am I going to get a name, or are you going to be a girl of mystery?"

"Should I tell him, Radu, or leave him frustrated all night?"

"Christian name won't harm. You don't want to frighten the life out of him," she answered with a grin.

"I'm Karen, not really a romantic name, I'm afraid. Then this is where we part company and where I am staying. It was good meeting you, Jonathan. While I'm gone, will you do me a great favour?"

"Anything, Karen, I'm putty forever in your hands."

"Take care of Radu for me."

"I will, Radu and I look after each other. Isn't that right, Radu?"

"We do, good night, Jonathan."

He gave her a hug, followed by Karen, before cycling away.

"He likes you, Radu, but doesn't know how to tell you?" Karen told her.

"How did you see that?"

"Believe me, it was obvious. He never took his eyes off you, all the time he spoke to me, as if he wanted to say the words to you. You could do much worse. Just give him a little encouragement, when I'm back, let me know how you got on."

"I will and thank you for not mocking him. He's really sensitive, you know?"

"Yes, I sensed that."

They both entered the complex.

Chapter 25

Jasmin arrived in Paris, taking the local train to Pigalle. The address Karen had given her turned out to be a patisserie with a cafe area. Going inside, she found a table and ordered coffee along with a nice looking cake. Jasmin was always partial to a fancy cake covered in cream.

Ten minutes after she arrived, a woman, Jasmin estimated to be in her forties, came into the cafe. She looked around and walked up to her. "Jasmin Dlamini?" she asked in French.

"Yes, and you are?"

"Emma Köhler, we have a mutual friend in Karen Harris," she replied, at the same time showing Jasmin her mobile phone. On the phone was a message from Karen, along with a photo of Jasmin. "May I join you?"

"Of course, would you like coffee? I have already ordered. Can we also talk in English? I'm not good in French and we'd be very slow."

"Thank you. Coffee would be most acceptable," Emma, answered in English. "Do you have a Unit T ID? I know this is not exactly a Unit T operation, but Karen said you would be carrying one."

Jasmin passed it across. Emma looked at the ID and at Jasmin, then checked her mobile, ensuring the number Karen sent her by text was the same as on the ID. "Thank you" she said, handing it back.

"You're very security conscious. I like that in people I work with," Jasmin commented.

"In the world we live, take someone's word and you could be dead the next day. Information in the underworld is a bartering income. Often the seller has no interest in who buys, it is all about who pays the most. Then the fools who believe they can sell to both parties, do not last long."

Conversation stopped when a woman approached

the table, taking their order. After she left, they carried on.

"You've been with Karen for a while?" Jasmin asked.

"A few years, I was down on my luck, my parents dead, my husband killed in a gang fight between rival groups trying to increase their distribution area for hard drugs. Overall, I was a mess. Twenty-eight, completely broke, taken by a pimp to work the hotels. He worked me for five years, servicing shit, often ten a day and no time off. Karen pulled me out, gave me time in one of her complexes and a little compensation after the pimp was jailed. I work as a cleaner in a number of houses now," then she gave a hint of a smile. "Let's just say they are special houses, the occupants of interest to Karen. And you?"

"I take contracts, nothing more, apart from protecting Karen."

"That is good. She needs such people. Karen exists in a dangerous world."

"Karen's not alone. We all do, but it is useful to have the power Karen wields behind us. What is happening with the young girl? Have you any close access?"

"I have, or rather, the cell has. An elderly woman who lives alone in an apartment on the floor below has reached a financial agreement with Karen. She has left us the key to the apartment and taken a short holiday to visit a sister in Belgium."

"So Karen spoke to her?"

"She did. In fact, the woman was more than relieved to find that something was going to be done about her neighbour, and even more so, when she heard Karen would be calling her personally. She told Karen the apartment was constantly being visited by different men. Some even knocked on her door looking for the apartment, not realising they were on the wrong level. Anyway, she left this morning. We have installed pinhole radio cameras in the passages and one looking at the entrance door of the apartment, the girl is inside. Karen was estimating a two-week operation. But she would call the woman, who owns the apartment we are using, if it looks like we could overrun."

"This all sounds extremely efficient and typical of Karen. Do you really need me?" Jasmin asked.

"We do, you should realise we're not trained in the use of arms, nor do we carry weapons, We operate under the radar, keep Karen updated as to what is happening in our area and at times run a surveillance operation like this. Weapons have been used around this girl so Karen wants protection, just in case things turn nasty, both for us or the girl."

Jasmin gave a hint of a smile. "That I can do, how many apartments are on the block?"

"Eleven. We have identified a time when most are at work, enabling you to slip in unobserved. That is three twenty this afternoon. Until then and following your refreshment I will take you to wait at my home."

***

Jasmin joined two other people in the apartment. One male called Alexander, and a female called Bettina. Both were of German origin, with Alexander operating the camera feeds and Bettina communicating with yet another centre. Although neither of them seemed prepared to enlighten Jasmin as to where, or who, Bettina was talking to. Jasmin felt a little uncomfortable, and had the impression she really should not be with these people, with everyone obviously part of a cell that technically didn't exist. In her view, they were part of a secret world controlled and owned by Karen. Everyone who was part of this world had total allegiance to Karen. Anyone else was on a need-to-know basis, as far as information was concerned, and no more. She could understand why, after hearing Emma's

197

story, Karen had pulled Emma out of the gutter, given her a new life and purpose. That was worth a fortune in trust and loyalty. She wondered if Bettina was the same and maybe Alexander?

"To keep you updated, Jasmin, "Bettina began. "We logged a man coming to the apartment last night at around seven, leaving this morning just after ten. We have his address and currently we are looking for a name, along with where he works. At twelve today, another man arrived. He remained until half-past three. Because this apartment has been used as a brothel, before the young girl arrived, we cannot assume they are for her. Karen is checking the names on her database. If they are known or suspected paedophiles, then they are there for the girl."

"Do you have the name of the woman who owns or rents the apartment?"

"We do. It is a Jacqueline Nguyen, aged forty-two, but her name is not on the rental agreement. It is rented to an Axel da Silva. We have nothing on him as yet, but the information has been passed to Karen, she will pursue it if necessary."

Jasmin sighed inwardly, again a brick wall in Karen's world. Even these people will never know what she does about it. "With two men going into the apartment, don't you think it is reasonable to assume they are using the child?" Jasmin suggested.

Bettina shook her head slightly. "We never assume, it has no value, Karen requires us to be precise in anything we say, or do. The evidence we collect, has to stand up in a courtroom, otherwise we are wasting our time. You need to understand, visitors have been coming to the apartment long before the girl arrived. We don't know why, or what for."

'And that's telling me,' Jasmin said to herself.

Conversation was brought to a halt when Alexander

cut in. "We've another visitor, a male."

They all looked at the screens. Jasmin was not happy. This, in her view, was getting out of control. There was a fourteen-year-old in the apartment, not an adult. She left the room, going into a bedroom, calling Karen on her mobile.

"Problem, Jasmin?" Karen asked.

"I don't like it. The girl already has had three visitors. This cannot go on, Karen. She's a child."

By Jasmin's mood, Karen realised she was now out of her depth. "For a start, we don't know that. You are also showing traits you actually have a heart under that hard exterior, which I always knew you had, but would not admit it. You may have had the belief you know the sex industry, but you don't. I can assure you, working on the fringe, taking out the odd trafficker for a cartel, does not prepare you. You are now at the sharp end, the reality where children as young as ten, even younger, are exploited, killed, or raped. It is a dirty and often brutal industry, Jasmin, and I don't like it, the same as you. When I first joined Unit T, I would often be sent on covert operations. On one such operation, I met a few girls of Charlotte's age, held by a cartel. I laughed and talked with them, and while their lives must have been a living hell, they were happy. My naivety in the industry, as well as stupidity in believing I was helping, but not understanding what these men were capable of, sent them to their deaths. I have to live with that, as well as watching the final girl, I seem to remember aged ten or eleven, murdered before being placed in a body bag, probably for dumping out at sea. I have always believed I could have saved them, Jasmin, if I had not hesitated before going in. The only good thing to come out of their deaths, if you can say it was good, was that it led me to their persecutors. What I do know, no girls will be used again by those people; I killed the lot of them. Going back to your concern, we can only do what we can. We lose many on the way and yes, we may lose Charlotte, but believe me, Charlotte can cope. This has been her life for at least three years. To pull her out now, because of a conscience, leaves more girls vulnerable to this type of men, who believe they are safe. Everyone who goes through that door, if it turns out they raped the girl, will soon be off the street, be it a contract, or the legal route. When the time comes, if it is needed, you do your job. The others, with you, know what they are doing. We will bring her out very soon. That's a promise."

"Why are you always right? I'm supposed to be immune, a contract killer with no thoughts for the sanctity of life?"

"So you say, but in the harsh world of human trafficking, you're a pussycat. I bet you can still count how many have died by your hand. Me, I lost count years ago, except it is in the high hundreds and they still keep coming. Take my recent time in Singapore. I shot and killed four. Some could have had families, but in our world, it means nothing. Live by the gun and you often die by the gun. Even so, no matter how hard we try, we cannot ignore the reality that every victim is part of a family, wanted or not. With our intervention, that victim's nightmare will come to an end, one way or another. Whether she walks out, or is carried out in a body bag, is often beyond our control. All we can do for the victims is our best. Always remember that."

"Is not that I'm a defeatist, Karen? It's when I know I could walk in there and bring her out?"

"Of course you can, the same as me, or the local police, but if we did, what would we find? A woman claiming she was asked to look after a homeless child. We have no idea if Charlotte would back her claim, shout rape from the rooftop, or even if Charlotte was prepared to leave with us. Each possible scenario could leave us helpless in moving forward. Keep in mind, Jasmin, Charlotte made her own bed by not asking for help from the authorities at the airport, when she could. So now, she becomes the pawn in a dangerous game. If she is lucky, she will come out unscathed, but that is not your problem. It's mine, and mine alone, to make that life or death decision."

"You'll sort it somehow, Karen. How are you doing your end?"

"I'll tell you tomorrow, it's a bit fluid at this moment in time. Anyway, I've got to go."

"Okay, take care."

Jasmin sat on the edge of the bed, after cutting the call. She liked to portray to the world that she was in control of her life, tough and uncompromising. However, since becoming involved with Karen, she was witnessing the consequences of criminal groups who had been her paymasters for some years. She was annoyed with herself, for ignoring what was really going on, but after talking to Zoey and now Charlotte's predicament, it had really hammered home to her just what Karen had faced over the years and why she was like she is. Not that Jasmin believed Karen was indifferent in her thinking, more realistic to know she will lose at times, as well as win. Yet to be in Karen's position, where at times the route she takes, can decide if a child lives or dies, that she could never do.

Chapter 26

Karen dressed in jeans, T-shirt and a bomber jacket arrived at Lisbon Portela airport in her private jet. A car was there to take her to the local barracks where two units of Dark Angel were waiting. Both units, assembled in the camp's main hall, came to attention as she entered.

Standing on a small stage, she nodded to the lieutenant who brought everyone at ease.

"First, let me apologise for not being in uniform. I am moving on from here to join covert operatives, where a uniform would not be appropriate. Why are you here? A girl aged fifteen escaped from a paedophile ring known as Spartes. The ring and the supplier of children to the ring panicked, and the supplier began pulling the girls out. I believe we are looking at twelve girls aged from eleven to fifteen. This is all we know, apart from who their supplier is. There is no doubt, for the supplier, these children are extremely valuable, but they also have a great deal of knowledge. That means to obtain their maximum value, they will be offered to buyers outside Europe. Our underground army, made up of informers, covert operatives and surveillance teams, are working very hard, to not only locate the children, but if we miss them, find where the supplier intends sending them. What we do know, they are certainly in Portugal, or heading here. It is possible, but again we have no hard evidence, they are to be shipped to South America. There is a ship docked here, bound for Maracaibo in Venezuela, due to depart on Saturday. Where it is heading, would be ideal for this ship to be used to transport the girls. Your job will be to search it, or if we locate the girl's location earlier, bring them out. On your side, it will be a waiting game. I do not need to remind you, the children's lives, first depend on our covert operatives giving us solid intelligence, followed by your professionalism in extraction. Has anyone any questions?"

"I joined Unit T under the command of Major Lang, along with others in these two units. We have never been in this position before, commander. What are the rules of engagement? Can we use our weapons to defend as well as engage?"

"Soldiers new to the Dark Angel units will form the search teams, ones who have been on operations before will act as protection, although everyone will carry weapons and can protect themselves if challenged. Exchange of fire between us, and criminal gangs, is very rare, but when criminals are desperate, there is always that possibility. Follow your lieutenant's orders. None of us is here to be a hero. I want everyone to keep to what they have been trained to do, remain safe and return home."

No more questions were asked, and Karen left the room.

One of the new soldiers turned to his mate. "It all sounds a bit iffy to me. Then she looks a scruffy individual, certainly not commander material."

His friend nodded his agreement. "I'm with you there; I can't see what's so special about her. Listen to others on the camp and most are happy she is back, and supposed to be the best. In my view, they should never have let her return. Lang was a good soldier, knew his stuff and she had the gall to fire him."

Another soldier sat to one side leaned across, his voice low. "Such negative and degrading talk about our commander will see you out Dark Angel and maybe the camp. Colonel Harris holds the top bravery awards a soldier can be awarded across eight countries, including the USA's Congressional Medal of Honour. No soldier in the world can compete with that. Our colonel also trains with us and she is not supposed to be the best, she is. Given the choice, I would trust her to protect my back anytime.

She has no fear, as well as being on the front line for fifteen plus years. Very few soldiers spend so long in an active combat role. Even with this operation, you can guarantee she will lead us, if her security detail will let her, and believe me they have their work cut out preventing it."

***

Karen left the camp by taxi to the Amadora area of Lisbon. While prostitution is legal in Portugal, it was illegal for a third party to be involved. Even so, most engaged in prostitution, be it a male or female, would normally have a minder to look after their interests, technically paid by the prostitute, which made it debatable, if that person fell into the third party definition. Of course, the major European criminal cartels dealing in drugs and prostitution were not concerned with what was legal, or not, and were already in Portugal, along with local criminal groups like Beacher Marinez.

After the taxi dropped her off, she walked down a side street and entered a bar. Karen immediately recognised the woman she wanted to meet, going over to her and sitting down opposite. The woman was in her late fifties, still dressed in typical clothes worn by prostitutes to show off their assets, although she looked tatty and rough, the clothes dated and dirty. Her hair bleached, her face showing the hard life she had lived, failing in her attempt to hide it by make-up.

"It's good to see you again, Helga," Karen said, as she sat down.

"And you, Karen. You look well love; the break has done you good."

"Everyone keeps telling me that, but quick enough to have me return to leading Unit T."

"Your attempt to leave was premature, Karen. You knew your work was not finished."

"I suppose, and then I was getting a bit bored. Do

you want a coffee, or something a bit stronger?

"A large gin would be most welcome."

Karen went to the bar, ordering a black coffee for herself, returning in a few minutes with their drinks.

Once Karen was sitting down, Helga lowered her voice. "You asked me to look into Beacher and where he's based? Most of the girls know him, but he is very elusive, with none knowing where he actually lives. But not all is lost. I called you last night because I hear the man who works with him called Javier, is at The Two Cats club for one of the club owners fortieth tonight. It is not a closed club as such, but they do have private rooms, often booked by parties looking for a little privacy. The club is owned by two men. One is called Davi, the other Santos."

"Is the birthday party to be in one of the private rooms?"

"I don't know, but since talking to you, my friend Leonor told me she had an invitation from Santos. She has been told, if possible, to let a few girls know they can get in free, if his name is mentioned. He wants to make up numbers. Davi believes it is only him and a few friends, but Santos is making it a big party. I realised this could be an in for you, so I told Leonor I might know someone who would go. I am sorry, Karen, I took a bit of a liberty, telling her you are a high-class escort taking a few days holiday. I also used your normal cover name, Amber."

"That's fine. In fact, if I decide to go, there will be two of us, both purporting to be escorts working across Europe."

"Even better, and being escorts, you will be expensive."

"We are. As for this Leonor, is she going there as a prostitute and available, or as a friend?"

Helga looked a little embarrassed. "To tell you the truth, people like Davi, only have prostitutes hanging around. He is not one for relationships, more shag and forget, with no complications. Javier is the same. He is not after hangers-on either. Even so, they are not the type to pay the woman, but most accept that because they are introduced to clients who pay, and I mean pay, it can be very lucrative for a working girl offering a few free samples so to speak. Now you know the situation, any doubts, Karen, keep well away. If they see through you, they can be nasty people. These are also very experienced men in reading women. You would be there as a professional escort, not a girl off the street. Your demeanour, your answer to a question, as well as showing off your assets in the way of sexy clothing, has to be as expected. Use your surveillance people, I know you have, or send others in. At least you'll find out which one, among Davi's guests, is Beacher's business partner Javier, and he could lead you to Beacher."

"I understand, and I'll consider what you say. If it means I need to go in, I know the ropes. After all, over the years I've been forced to work in brothels as well as work the hotels. You learn how to handle your clients, in order to avoid punishment that is always hanging over you. My only hesitation in going in myself is ending up with someone of no value, but having to play up to him in order to remain in character? What I'm asking, Helga, with a choice of many girls, some as young as eighteen, am I too old to even have a chance to attract Davi, or Javier?"

"Not at all, Karen, you'd easily get away with early thirties, and Davi is not the sort of man who likes young girls. They are too full of themselves and giggle a lot. He prefers them older. You and your friend will be new to the area. Everyone will want to try their luck, particularly Davi and Javier, and they get to choose who they take before anyone else. One thing I'll warn you about, Davi's so full of himself, believing he's god's gift to women, he seems to think it is his right to take a girl up into the private office, or even out the back of the club, into the yard and give her a good shagging, up against the wall. A few girls have told me that. If he does, show him you're more than capable of giving him a good time, then he'll have you taken back to the house, to continue with you later."

Karen hated this sort of talk, but this was the real world of prostitution, where you are there to be shagged, not look pretty.

"God, that's all I need. My back up against a yard wall is not the sort of location to show your capability, beyond a lot of gasping, as well as telling him how good he is in making you come."

Helga grinned. "I've done it for years that way, Karen. The odd gasp and urging has always earned me a few extra quid." She stood, looking down at Karen. "Think about it while I go to the toilet. These days I have to go more often. It's a bloody nuisance." She left Karen alone.

Karen was thinking about what Helga had said. If the truth was known, she was no closer to finding Beacher, or the girls, even with the assistance of her informers as well as Unit T's intelligence unit, and time was running out. Whether she liked it, or not, this was the only possible lead to locate Beacher, that had presented itself, it had to be followed up.

Helga returned. "Have you made a decision?"

"I have. Where do we meet Leonor?"

"Outside the Two Cats club, at eight tonight, I'll give her a call to say you're coming and bringing a friend. Take care, Karen. Such people are not worth your life."

"I will," she replied at the same time, pushing two hundred euro into Helga's hand.

"Thanks Karen, that's my rent paid for the week."

"You're welcome. When I pay for the drinks, I'll leave another gin behind the bar."

She stood and nodded to Helga. After stopping for a

moment at the bar, she left."

Helga watched her go, and then called Leonor.

"You know these girls?" Leonor asked, after Helga told her they would be outside the Two Cats at eight.

"Only one, called Amber. I knew her mother. She died about three years back and Amber joined a Paris agency who books girls for the very rich. These are top class girls, Leonor, and only here for the next few days, calling on friends before moving on. Amber went out of her way to call on me, which was thoughtful."

"Thanks for mentioning it; it gets me out of a problem with Santos, who's been a bit difficult lately in allowing me in."

"Why's that?"

"He's after a bigger cut out of the prostitutes earnings, but demand is down and the punters have been playing us off against each other, getting lower rates. Sign of the times, I suppose, when there is not much money around."

***

After Karen left Helga, she took a taxi to a hotel. This hotel was not where she would normally stay, being a three star in a back street. The room she headed for was on the top floor by the fire escape. Knocking on the door, it was opened, and she went inside.

Inside the room were three males and a female. The males were former Dark Angel soldiers working directly for Karen and part of the team who looked after high-risk girls in the Torre del Mar complex, but sometimes called upon, as Karen's protection and backup, in covert operations.

The last person, Elvia Weib, aged twenty-nine, was originally from the German Democratic Republic. Attractive and commanding very high fees as a high-class escort and often engaged by Karen for special jobs.

They all gave Karen a hug, John pushing a can of

beer in her hand. "Thanks, John, just what I need," she told him, taking a drink. "Right, the plan; Elvia and I, are to meet a prostitute known as Leonor, outside the Two Cats club. Inside is a party going on for one of the club owners, but it will possibly be attended by Marinez's business partner, Javier. We cannot be armed, although both of us will have our special mobiles and watches on us, so we can be tracked. It is up to you and the lads to protect us."

"Is this a general nightclub, so anyone can go inside?" John asked.

"To a degree, apparently there are suites that can be booked for private parties. I'm not sure if they are to be used for the birthday party."

"Isn't it a little risky you going, Karen? After all, it is more than likely Marinez will turn up as well. He could know what you look like?" Frank commented.

"Of course there may be a possibility, but with a little titivating away from my usual boring look, providing we are not sitting at the same table, which is highly unlikely, then I'll get away with it," she shrugged indifferently. "Besides, with Elvia at my side, he'll not have eyes for me."

No one commented. This was Karen undermining herself as usual.

"Right, where's my case?" Karen asked.

John pulled it from the far side of one of the twin beds. Karen took it and went through to the bathroom.

Frank looked at the two lads and shrugged. "We keep very close to her. You need to warn us, Elvia, if you suspect trouble."

"I know her from old, Frank. She will be fine; I'll make sure of that."

Fifteen minutes later, Karen came out of the bathroom. Karen had changed into a short tight, slightly flared dress, self-supporting nylons and four inch heeled shoes, showing off her long slim legs. She also had on a wig. Black, long and straight with a sweeping side parting covering one side of her face, the other side behind her ear, as well as a darker tone of make-up, red lips, and more importantly, her deep blue eyes were now brown with contacts. This was not the usual Karen in any respect.

"I've got to admit, I thought I knew you, Karen, but you don't look like you at this precise moment," Frank commented, with added agreements from everyone else.

"It's what women can do. The point being would I pass as a high-class escort, Elvia?"

"For an escort, working at the level I do, servicing men in their forties and older, you'd not be short of clients. The younger men, maybe not, you look like you're at the very top of your profession and out of their reach, fee wise that is."

"I'd certainly be that, but we are after the older man, who has money and can get any amount of younger girls. Let's hope such men see something different in us," Karen commented, before glancing at her watch. "Time we moved. Check our trackers, Frank."

He did a quick test, along with their watch winder signal system. The system was very basic. Every half hour, both girls would press the winder button once, which would send a single bleep to a receiver Frank carried. The single bleep would tell him all is well. Two bleeps on the move. Three bleeps need help, but can assist. Four bleeps, indicates help is needed urgently, but cannot assist. No signal at all in an hour, then they go in no matter what.

As a cover for Elvia and maybe herself, they would be staying at a hotel with service apartments attached. Such a location was important in a number of ways. The quality of the service apartment had to reflect their supposed income. They needed a location to bring back Davi, or Javier, if either of them preferred somewhere more private rather than Davi's house. The apartment must also enable them to come and go without entering through the hotel foyer. This apartment suited all requirements and Karen had already set it up inside, with a suitcase full of clothing, items in the bathroom, including condoms and lubrication with a few valuables in the apartment safe. While the apartment may never be used, it would complete the deception if needed.

Chapter 27

Beacher came through to the lounge, where Javier was strolling through emails on his phone.

He looked up. "Have you talked to Jacqueline since Avril arrived?"

"I fucking have, and do you know what the stupid bitch has been doing?"

"Go on."

"She's using the girl."

Javier frowned. "I thought you told her to keep the kid low-key?"

"I did, anyway I'm not taking any shit from her. I've told Ramiz to go and hook Avril out, leaving no proof she was ever there."

"Drastic, don't you think?"

"No I bloody don't. I have an offer on the table for a hundred and fifty thousand from a client in Dubai. He was impressed Avril never did a runner at the airport, realising this was a girl who had accepted her life and could be trusted. Now the only way to convince Avril I had not sent her to Jacqueline to be used, is to let her witness Jacqueline's punishment. It has to happen, Javier, otherwise we wave goodbye to the money."

"You're right, those who don't follow instructions must be taught a lesson. By the way, it is Davi's do at the club tonight. Are you going?"

"Not the club, but if he's going back to his house later and bringing women, not in their nappies, I'll go there?"

"You know, Davi, if he goes back home, he'll not have any woman much younger that thirty. Younger ones give him a complex, but more the truth; he can't keep up with them."

Beacher laughed. "It's a poor do, when even the little blue pills can't keep you at it. Give me a call if there's anything worth coming for."

***

Leonor, standing around outside the club, glanced at her watch yet again. The girls Helga told her about were late. Had they decided against coming? She hoped not, after telling Santos she had arranged for extra girls. Just at that moment, a taxi drew up close to the club entrance and Karen, along with Elvia, climbed out.

Leonor ran up to them. "Please tell me one of you is Amber?" she gasped.

Karen smiled. "I'm Amber, this is Elvia, and you must be Leonor?"

"I am. I'd nearly given up on you."

"Sorry, it's our fault, we don't really know this area and didn't realise how long it would take to get here," Karen lied. She had deliberately delayed coming early, wanting Frank and Jim to be inside the club when they arrived. They had been waiting with John, for the signal that the lads were in the club.

"No problem, at least you are here now. Let's go inside, and then I'll tell you what's supposed to be happening."

The club surprised Karen. Very plush and even at this time busy. They followed Leonor through doors at the far end of the club, into a wide passage, with a double door going off each side and at the far end, a door marked kitchen. Above each double door was written the name of the suite. They went into one. This was empty, and Leonor closed the door.

"Not sure if Helga told you, its Davi's fortieth, he's part owner of the club. There will be a small celebration when he arrives, in the private suite on the other side of the passage, before the party carries on in the main club. Initially there will be about forty in the suite, along with a number of girls, which includes us. We are there really

213

to mingle, with most of the guests being male. Some of us will have a chance of being invited back to his house. It is spectacular and understand it's worth close to two million, so that says it all. All the important people will be there, so the possibility of lucrative introductions is very high. Helga tells me you are escorts. This could be good for you both, don't you think?"

"Unlikely, Leonor, we don't do one nighters. Most of our work is on private yachts, or long weekend business functions. I cannot see the people who frequent here, or even local dignitaries, forking out thirty thousand plus to book us. But we're happy to party for a change, without having to please a client, so you'll get no complaints from us, nor will we step on the local girls toes taking their business," Karen told her.

"Wow, that's big money. I wish I could get into that, but looking at you two, I'd have no chance."

Elvia smiled. "It's not all partying, Leonor. It can be hard work pleasing some of the clients. They can be very demanding, believing, by forking out that sort of money, they own you."

"Yes, I suppose, everything in this business has a downside. Nothing is easy money. Take me, I do the hotels, you go on a supposedly single client booking, only to find him with two friends, all wanting to shag you."

"So all that's expected of us tonight, Leonor, is to mingle, with a bit of flirting, keeping everyone happy?" Elvia asked.

"That's the idea. Some could have the belief, with you being prostitutes, you're punting for work, but I would think you've had your fair share of those and can handle them?"

Karen glanced at Elvia. "Not a problem in that, is there, Elvia?"

She grinned. "It'll be fun seeing them try."

"Are we likely to be introduced to the people that matter, Leonor, like the owners and maybe their important friends, rather than the hangers on?" Karen asked.

"Of course, Santos was quite taken when I told him I'd arranged for two high-class escorts to come. He is bound to want to show you both off to Davi. Then Javier Schneider, who Davi plays cards with, is the most important guest. Not sure, what he does, but it is bound to be illegal whatever he's into. He is also loaded, along with his business partner, Beacher Marinez. Beacher's more a card player and one to avoid. Not that he comes to the club very much, but if the party carries on at Davi's, he could turn up. I understand he never really goes there for the women; he prefers to get a card game going with other guests and screw them for everything he can get. That can go on all night."

"So if we go to the house and this Beacher's there, should we be avoiding him?" Elvia asked with interest.

"I would. He is a sadist, prefers the older women, but seems to have the idea he can treat them like shit, often laying into them with his leather belt. Some say he is really into very young girls, but that is just the talk, not that I'd be surprised. He likes to hear a girl squeal and most girls of school age do a lot of that. I will point him out if we go, so you know to keep well away. The last thing you want is spending a month, to allow the bruising to disappear."

"You can say that again. We're booked for the next two weeks on a yacht in the Caribbean, the owners a regular and pays well." In fact, Elvia was not lying. She was booked on such a trip with Karen. Meaning it could even be verified through her agent, if it was needed to get out of a situation in proving they really were escorts. Karen, under Amber Foster, was also registered with the same agency, listing a string of bookings. However, what Elvia did not know, Karen had a share in the agency, using it as a means to verify her identity in covert operations like this. Then, following this operation, Karen, as Amber, will become unavailable and a replacement sent.

"When you say most of school age, that's sick?" Karen commented.

"Maybe, but believe me, it's getting harder with so many even younger than sixteen looking to pay for their top of the range mobiles and fashion clothing. Only last week, Santos sent me on a hotel booking. I was to meet another girl there. The client had me performing in front of a few of his friends with her. Only later, while cleaning ourselves up in the bathroom, before we were due to join the clients in bed, did she admit she was fifteen. Believe me, you would never have known, apart from her obviously still learning the trade. I was terrified for the rest of the night, in case the police raided the room. I would have gone down for even touching her. When I complained later to Santos, he just laughed, saying, if that was what the client wanted, that is what he get's."

The door opened and Santos came in. "So this is where you are, Leonor? I'm assuming these girls are the ones you told me about?"

"They are, Elvia and Amber. I was just giving them the lowdown before going through."

He nodded, and then turned his attention to Karen and Elvia. "I'm told you're escorts, tonight is a party. I don't want to see you punting for clients. We have our own girls."

"This is our break. We're not interested in adding more clients to our list. We have enough, thank you," Karen came back at him. "But if you have your own girls, we'll stay for a single drink and move on."

"I'm meaning girls around here belong to us. Their job is to look after my clients. We don't allow ones not working for us attempting to take them over. With many

216

working away tonight, you're only here to make up the numbers. You also remain in the club until I say you can leave. If Davi says you join him and his friends at his house later in the night, you go. Any objections on your side, I will have you both thrashed. Have we an understanding?"

"Some bloody party night, when we're being forced to stay," Karen came back at him.

"Then you shouldn't have entered the profession. Prostitute, call girl, escort, whatever you choose to call yourself boils down to one thing. Your life is no longer your own, your body belongs to whoever pays for it, meaning you will always be told what to do; you do not tell us what you want. So get yourselves into the other suite and mingle. Davi's due in ten minutes," then he left the room.

Leonor shuffled uneasily. "Sorry about that. He can be obnoxious, as well as play the big man at times. But it's all talk. Just ignore him and have a good time."

"We will. Let's go and see who's arrived, shall we?" Karen answered.

The room was already filling. A bar ran along the back, with two people behind making cocktails and pouring drinks. On another wall, a buffet was laid out, although still covered. The average age in the room, Karen estimated to be around forty, with the majority of women obviously over thirty. She was relieved. At least she wouldn't stand out, as she suspected she might, if the girls had been in their twenties. In fact, Elvia would be one of the youngest in the room.

Collecting vodka and tonics from the bar, after Leonor drifted away talking to others in the room, Karen and Elvia also moved from the bar, at the same time looking carefully at men already standing around, and glancing at others entering.

"I've not seen you two around here. Where have you

been hiding?" A man of around five feet four commented, as he approached them,

Karen looked at him for a moment. Apart from being nearly six inches smaller than both of them, his casual clothes were obviously expensive, his gold-rimmed glasses, designer. "We were invited by Leonor. Do you know her?"

"I do, very well in fact, she gets work off me. What are your names?"

"I'm Amber; this is Elvia, and yours?"

"Tolga Doherty, everyone around here calls me Tog. You're both on the game the same as Leonor?"

"We're escorts; we don't do the hotels like Leonor."

"I see, you work the posh end of the market. Then you certainly look more upmarket than the scrags around here. What's your fee?"

"Our minimum hire is one week. We charge twenty thousand dollars plus expenses."

He raised an eyebrow. "For both of you, that sounds low for escorts, I presumed at the top of their game."

Karen grinned. "We believe we are, but sorry to disappoint. That fee gets just one of us. So what are you into?"

"I have an agency, here in Portugal, for women like you. With a client list prepared to pay far more than your fees, plus a nice little bonus. I may try one of you out later. If I like how you perform, I'll give you plenty of work."

"Thanks for the suggestion, but I think we'll give it a pass, we're already fully booked for the rest of the year and don't want more," Karen came back at him.

He shrugged. "That's a foolish attitude. How long have you left? A few years and then you are only good for cleaners. Earn while you can, never sell yourself cheap. I'll mention you to Davi, maybe have you both join us later at his home," then he walked away.

"Sounds ominous, Elvia, what do you think, he's lining us up to entertain him later?"

"He couldn't be much plainer. Do we bail after Javier has been identified? I wouldn't be able to stop laughing, with him trying to shag me."

"I'm with you on the laughing bit, but I need to think, let's mingle more. If there's a chance of Marinez being at the house, while I don't fancy going, knowing what could be in store, we're here to identify him. Once we have, it will be up to the lads to follow him back to his home. I'd not expect you to go to Davi's house, you should bail, claim you don't feel well and get out. The lads and I will see it through."

"It wouldn't look good. Anyway we've had no firm invite as yet, then there's still time to see how it pans out, this guy Tolga could be all talk."

A few men had spoken to Karen and Elvia, and while neither girl encourage them, they did not push them away, not wanting any confrontations. Davi came into the room. There was spontaneous cheering and everyone began singing happy birthday.

Karen looked at the man. Around six feet, well built, wearing slacks and T-shirt showing off his biceps and arms covered in tattoos. The singing soon died down with most shaking Davi's hand.

The buffet had also been made available, and Karen, along with Elvia, took the opportunity to move away from men hanging around them and fill their paper plates, drifting off to eat.

Another man entered the room, going over to Davi embracing him, before accepting a drink. Both were talking quietly together, as they walked over to a table with seating set around. They sat down and for them food was brought.

"That maybe Javier," Elvia commented in a low

voice.

Karen nodded her agreement. Again, this man, like Davi, was tall well built and by his bulging arms under a long-sleeved shirt, he worked out.

Leonor joined Karen and Elvia. "The man with Davi, is Javier, do you want me to introduce you both?" Confirming what they had both suspected.

"Yes, we should at least wish Davi a happy birthday," Karen answered.

They followed Leonor, coming to a halt in front of Davi.

"Who are these girls, Leonor," Davi asked, who had been watching their approach.

"This is Amber," she answered, grasping Karen's hand and pulling her forward. "And her friend is Elvia, both are escorts, working all over the world."

"Hi, we came over to wish you a happy birthday," Karen said.

"I've had enough of that," he retorted curtly. "Anne, Bamby, get lost, let my guests sit down." The two girls, glared at Karen and Elvia, but said nothing, quickly standing and walking away. Karen and Elvia took the vacated seats.

A waiter, seeing the new girls sit down, remained close, in case Davi ordered drinks. Davi looked at him, "Don't stand around, fetch clean glasses and fill them with my champagne," then he turned to Karen. "Tog said you're high earners. What's your agency?"

"We're with Priour Chausse."

"I've heard of him, not that I knew he had clients out of France."

Karen shrugged. "We wouldn't know who he deals with; we go where he sends us."

"You should talk to Javier's business partner; he has some very wealthy clients, most from South America. He would guarantee you five thousand a day, less commission. What do you say, Javier?" Davi asked.

"They'd have to be fucking good to command that sort of money. Are you both that experienced?"

Karen answered for them both. "We don't get complaints; if we did Priour wouldn't use us. As for the opportunity of earning more, we would be fools not to look into it. So in my mind, there can't be any harm in talking to your business partner."

"Then you will join us when we leave, to complete the night at Davi's home. After I mention you both to him, he could be interested in meeting you," Javier told her.

Champagne was brought, and the talk became more general. Soon everyone was drifting into the main club area. Karen and Elvia came out of the room, followed by Davi. Javier went the other way, through the door marked kitchen, and into Davi's office. Closing the door, he called Beacher.

"Bored already then?" Beacher asked.

"Piss off, why should I be bored, there're loads of girls here all gagging for it."

"Then go and fuck one. Why are you calling?"

"Two girls brought by Leonor could be of interest. Apparently, Santos panicked with most of our girls working tonight, asking Leonor if she knew of any girls interested in a party. Leonor had asked Helga, among others, and she recommended them. Would you believe they claim they are escorts, working for Chausse in Paris? They are both good-looking girls and clients would certainly pay money to use them, but high-end escorts, in my view, unlikely."

"Are we talking about the Helga, who works the streets, and is like sixty?"

"Not quite sixty, but yes that's her."

"How the fuck would she know any escorts, particularly ones who work for Priour?"

221

"Those were my thoughts. Sent by Harris do you think?"

"I'm already ahead on you with that. But why would she waste her time sending girls to a party for Davi? He's the only one around here, as clean as a whistle, apart from a bit of hustling of wealthy punters. Harris wouldn't be interested in that."

"Unless Harris had spoken to Liberty and Davi isn't the target but me. Talk around the street could well have alerted her that I would be there. After all, Davi and I go a long way back; I'd not miss his fortieth."

"That is a possibility I could accept, after all we suspect she is onto us, not that she'd have any evidence to go further. So it could well be a spot of fishing, to see what comes out the pool so to speak," Beacher said, after some thought.

"I don't like being watched. What do you think we should do?"

"Could we use them?"

"If they shag as good as they look, then yes, we could."

"So how about we stick two fingers up at Harris and snatch them from under her nose?" Beacher suggested.

"Sounds good to me, we can always use a couple more."

"We could, but keep in mind, if they do work for Harris, she will have a means of keeping track of them. I will get Duarte to run down to the club, with his scanner. He can claim it's a security check, because they are going to Davi's house."

"Good thinking. If they really were escorts, dealing with the very wealthy, they would be used to being checked. But you mentioned Davis house, do we really want them there?"

"Of course not, I'll have him take them to the

entertainment house. Assuming they are plants, nothing has to go with the girls to the house, such as watches, mobiles, compacts; in fact, I'm thinking that we shouldn't even let them take their own clothes. Harris is a sneaky bastard and knows all the tricks."

"I'm with you there, then Duarte will enjoy having them strip off, he likes bringing such women down to no better than a common prostitute. But leaving naked, is going a bit too far. Providing he checks them carefully, as well as leaving their valuables behind, that would do."

"Fair enough, now that is agreed, is Davi putting a game together later?"

"He was talking about it, are you coming?"

"I will, have him line up a few wealthy mugs and the usual girls as their companions."

Chapter 28

Karen and Elvia, left the private suite, going through to the main club area after being handed a plastic strap to wear around their wrists, indicating they were guests of Santos. They found, by showing it at the bar, they could get free drinks. In the main club area they were plenty of men of their age wanting to dance with them.

A security man approached, after they came off the dance floor with two men. "You're both wanted in the office. Follow me," he demanded.

They glanced at each other, not sure as to why, but followed him through the door marked 'kitchen', and into the office. A man, they had not seen before, was already inside. The security man, who brought them from the main area, remained standing by the door.

"My name's Duarte. I look after security. I've been told you are going onto Davi's house. Girls we don't know, I like to be sure that they aren't carrying cameras, listening equipment, even personal weapons. We also check with their agency they are who they claim."

"If you want, but we carry nothing like you're describing," Karen told him.

"Claim what you like. It changes nothing. I have a job to do. Empty the contents of your handbags onto the desktop, remove your watches, and unlock your phones."

They both did as he asked. While Elvia's phone linked to Karen, under the name Amber, Karen's phone had numbers to Unit T and her own operation. To get over this problem, depending what unlock code you entered, the phone would display typical apps and messages a girl would have on, not the other numbers. Then, while both phones were capable of being tracked, they could still do this even if the battery was removed. Not that the phones indicated this, nor were they top of the range, but a regular smartphone that could be picked up anywhere.

After going through the contents and checking the bags, Duarte looked at the phones. Seemingly satisfied, he placed them back on the desk.

"Remove the dresses."

"What's that all about? You have checked our handbags. It's obvious we're not carrying anything," Elvia asked.

"Seems like they want us to do a striptease, kinky are you?" Karen added, looking directly at Duarte.

"Yeah, like we never see women naked in our job, so don't feel flattered, we're not that desperate to see prostitutes, the other side of thirty, strip off. Even so, I want you both down to your knickers, proving to us you are carrying nothing, or we will do it for you. Either way, you'll not leave this office until we're satisfied," he came back at her aggressively.

Karen like Elvia, had no concerns in taking her clothes off, she had lost count how many times over the years she'd done that, allowing a man to carry out a so-called inspection of her body. They both began undressing, soon standing in front of him in knickers.

Duarte checked the dresses carefully, and then had them both do a complete turnaround, before running his hands through their hair.

While checking Karen's hair, he felt the wig and pulled it off. "What's this? Don't like your own hair, maybe trying to look younger than you are? Can't blame you, with no longer the body of a twenty-year-old, the wig must boost your ego," he mocked.

Karen said nothing; after all, while she may look after herself, no one could stop the obvious signs of ageing.

"You'll not need it tonight." Duarte carried on, bringing Karen out of her thoughts. "Get dressed. We will keep everything on the desk, including the wig. Ask for them when you leave Davi's house in the morning."

Karen was now worried. If Javier saw her without a wig, would he recognise her? Then what if Beacher was going to the house, even if Javier didn't realise who she was, Beacher might. But what could she do, apart from brave it out and hope they don't?

Another man came into the office, and once dressed, led them out, through the rear yard into the back of a van. With Duarte sat in the back with them, the van set off.

***

A short time later in the club, Davi was ready to leave, when Javier joined him.

"Small problem with the two escorts, Davi. We were unable to get a conformation they worked for the agency, no one was picking up. You know, Beacher, he likes to be sure a woman is who she claims, particularly turning up out the blue."

In fact, Javier had lied to Davi. They did get conformation, but he and Beacher had other plans for them.

"That's no problem; it's going to be more a card night, anyway. So what has happened to them? Have you told them to go?"

"Not quite. With them having no immediate work, he took pity, so he decided to take them over and use them. By the beginning of next week, both will be working in one of his houses. If they're no trouble and prove they are capable, he'll set them up in an apartment and have them working the higher class clients."

Davi grinned. "He's getting soft, not so long ago, if a girl lied, he'd have beaten the fucker so bad, she'd not be working for weeks."

"Maybe, while that's always an option going forward, more of a reminder as to who owns them, business always comes first, and we are a little short of experienced women in our operation."

Davi, already disinterested in their fate, glanced at his watch. "It's time we were gone. With luck, the mugs coming to play will lose a lot."

"No luck, Davi, they will."

***

Frank glanced at his watch. The regular half-hourly signal from both girls had not come. Then, while he had seen them around the club earlier, they had been gone for some time, yet there had been no watch signal, of two pulses, to say they were on the move.

"This doesn't look good, Jim, we should return to our car and check if Karen's phone is being tracked by Unit T."

After leaving the club, John joined them.

"Have you seen either girl leave, John?" Frank asked.

"Not by the front. There have been two delivery vans, which turned down the road at the side of the club. Both have left."

"You have the numbers and times?"

John handed him his notepad. "Yes, I also have photos on my mobile."

Soon they were inside their car. Frank talked to Unit T's intelligence unit, then after cutting the call, turned to the others.

"They're checking and will call back. They've had no direct contact with Karen either."

"This is not good, Frank. If either girl couldn't get to her watch, Karen might have been recognised?" John commented.

"If she has, she's dead. Karen knew the risks and was prepared for the possible consequences." Frank answered quietly.

They fell silent until an app on Frank's phone came alive. It showed a map of the local area and a small flashing blip moving along a road away from the club.

"Looks like Unit T have a fix. Let's go and find them," Frank told the others. They set off at speed, but before they caught up, the blip still flashing as it updated, came to a halt. The journey took them to a side road. Parked outside a house was a small car. Frank's local scanner was indicating both phones were actually in the car. However, there was no one inside. With no one on the street, Jim forced the boot open. Inside, they found the carrier bag Duarte had put the girl's valuables in. Taking it back to their car, Frank checked through it. "It doesn't look good. Their handbags and contents, including watches and mobiles, are in this bag, as well as Karen's wig. We have to assume they know who she is." Frank glanced at the house. "Let's go and talk to whoever lives there."

With the two lads standing on either side of the door, Frank rang the bell. At first, no one came, until he rang it once more. Then the door opened slightly, prevented from being opened wide by a chain.

"What do you want? It's late," a woman asked.

"Do you own the car outside?"

"My husband does. Why?"

"I was passing and thought I had better let someone know it's been broken into. The boots open, as well as the doors."

"Thank you, he's out back, I'll have him check it as soon as he comes in," then the door shut.

Frank glanced at John. "Go round to the back. We'll move away from the door, to see if he comes outside."

In fact, the house belonged to the other man who was with Duarte, when the girls were in the office. Duarte had him put everything on the desk in a bag, including the phones. They intended to sell what was sellable, sharing the spoils. After all, where the girls were going, they would have no need of valuables.

The man was not outside; he was actually in the

bathroom. When he came out, his wife told him about the car. He was livid, storming out of the house, leaving the front door wide open. Once at the car, he found the boot open, the carrier bag gone. Being a bouncer who had come to the end of his shift after the girls left, he was a big man, not afraid of anyone, but looking around there was no one to be seen. Slamming his doors shut, along with the boot, he returned to the house.

Back inside the house and going into the kitchen, he stopped dead. His wife was standing, with Frank's gun at her head. Jim was leaning on another wall of the kitchen, holding his gun. Both guns had silencers fitted.

"Please, Nilton, don't do anything stupid. This man told me he will kill us both and our children," she begged.

"Touch my children and I'll take you apart," Nilton shouted at Frank, ignoring his wife's words.

"And how are you going to achieve that, when you're lying in a pool of blood alongside your wife?" Frank asked him quietly, "You can't, so take a seat and answer our questions. Then you may all live."

Nilton realised the stupidity of his statement. These were obviously gunmen and would have no issue in killing a child. He sat down. "What do you want?"

"The items in the bag, we found in the car boot, belong to our friends. Why are they there?"

"I was given them to take to the charity shop. You can have them if you want, it saves me doing it."

"Not good enough, look towards the door."

Nilton went cold. At the entrance to the kitchen, his little boy was standing in his nightclothes, to his side, John.

"This is no time to be the big hero protecting others. It is a time to think of your kids. I want the truth, because each word we consider a lie, we start shooting, beginning with the children. Four lies and you are all dead. Then we move on to the owners of the club; so any idea that you have bargaining power, you don't. Someone will break, before the night is over."

"Tell this man everything, Nilton, you owe Davi nothing, and he's certainly not worth the lives of our children," his wife urged.

Nilton sighed, she was correct; his children were worth the world to him. "A man we know as Duarte works for a Beacher Marinez, and came to the club. Beacher did not trust the two girls who had suddenly turned up. We were to make sure they had no weapons, or communication devices, and Duarte was to take them away. I was given their valuables to sell. That's all I know."

"Where was he taking them?"

"I've no idea. I work for Davi at the club. Beacher's business partner Javier was in the club tonight and going to Davi's house later, to play cards; you should ask Davi or Javier where the women are."

"What's the address?"

"I can tell you where Davi lives. If fact, I'll draw a map, providing you go and never come back."

"If the address is good, you won't see us again. Believe you would be doing anyone in that house a favour by sending a warning that we are coming, think twice, if you value your family. We will know and we will return. Now the address and we're gone."

After they left, Nilton looked at his wife after she had taken the boy back to bed and returned to the lounge. "Do you think I've done the right thing, in telling them I knew where Davi lived?" he asked.

"Why would you ask such a stupid question, when our children's lives are at stake?"

He shrugged. "It's just that we owe a lot to Davi, giving me a job when no one else would, and those people were obviously military. There's only one group who uses such people; that is Karen Harris."

"He may have given you a job, but you work long hours for very little and as I said earlier, you owe nothing, certainly not our lives. If that lot were sent by Karen Harris, stay out of it, this is not our fight. So get any remorse out your head, Davi makes his own bed, and as far as we are concerned, no one came to the house tonight."

Chapter 29

Karen and Elvia were sitting quietly in the back of the van, Karen considering her next move. Duarte leaned down and pulled two narrow gold looking bracelets out of a bag on the van floor.

"Hold, your hand out," he told Karen. She did as he asked, and he clipped one of the bracelets around her wrist. Then he did the same to Elvia. "These are your ID's showing you've been checked."

"They are pretty crap bracelets, is this the best Davi could do?" Karen commented.

"They have a use," was all he said.

"How far is Davi's house? We seem to have been travelling for ages," Karen asked.

"I wondered when you would notice. But you see there has been a change of plan, you are not going to the house, you have changed agency. You now work for Beacher Marinez."

"This man Marinez, does he usually have girls snatched off the street, forcing them to work for him?"

"You've not been snatched; it is a change of agency. You're to work in one of his entertainment houses."

"You mean a bloody brothel. We left those sorts of places years back," Elvia cut in.

"Hardly a brothel, at these houses, he runs stag weekends, small business conventions and the like. You will both be offering lap dances, personal services, and all-night companionship for his important guests."

"How much is he paying for this work?" Karen asked.

Duarte grinned. "You get fed, free accommodation and a day off a week. No actual money, your earnings are absorbed by your keep."

"What sort of accommodation and food amounts to

twenty thousand a week? You'd better be telling him he pays the going rate, or we walk," Karen told him.

"I'll mention it. In the meantime, you work and show him you are worth your demands. Of course, you may be thinking it is possible to overcome me, or like you say, walk out of our houses. It is not going to happen. That is where our bracelets come in. It may look a bit cheap, or crap as you commented, in a way it is. That is if you look at it as a fancy bracelet, but it's a very important part of your control." He pulled a small fob from his pocket, pressing one of the buttons.

Suddenly, Elvia was hit with an electric shock that very nearly threw her off the seat. It stopped, leaving her shaking.

"Good isn't it, how about you, Amber, do you want to test it out?" pressing another number on the fob, this time it was Karen's turn to experience the intense shock, leaving her like Elvia, shaking.

Duarte, disinterested in their obvious discomfort, carried on talking. "We'll arrive in about five hours, stopping for a short break for me to take over the driving. Be warned, all the security at the house has one of these fobs. Any objection, on your part, in what you are told to do; you have only experienced the weakest signal, it can go up three times that strength, and then you will know about it. They also have a punishment cellar, there a woman is taught a lesson she will never forget. But the odd one who does, from that day on, control is by drugs. It is up to you, work hard and you will get to enjoy your days, be difficult, and then your future becomes more of doing everything we want of you, just for your next fix. So while we travel, think carefully about what I've said."

Karen knew this was a real problem. While it would seem Beacher would not see her tonight, going forward, he may well turn up at this so-called entertainment house. It was time to see if Duarte could be bribed.

"How much does this Beacher guy pay people like you?" Karen asked, after remaining silent for ten minutes.

"What's it to you?"

"I was only thinking; it's bound to be a pittance, to what he's taking, particularly if he doesn't even want to pay us. So if we are to be stuck in a place earning nothing, it is not good business, how about you and I making a deal?"

"What sort of deal?"

"Let us go and in return you get fifty thousand."

He sniggered. "You've got fifty thousand. Where is that coming from?"

"From being paid thousands a week, what do you think I do with it, piss it up against a wall like men would? After all, when we're on assignment, it's all in, we spend nothing."

He sat for a moment in thought, before looking across at Elvia. "I'll not take less than fifty for myself, what of my mate? Can you pay him the same?"

"I could do twenty thousand. He'd not know you got fifty," Elvia suggested.

"Do we both get a shag?"

Karen sighed. "Are you taking the piss? We are offering seventy thousand tax-free in your hands, yet earlier in the office, you were comparing my body to a young girl, in a derogatory way. Now you want to shag us. If you want us, you pay for it like anyone else. After all, you'll not be short of money."

"Fuck off, I've never paid for a woman and don't intend to start. You're both prostitutes, so include personal services as part of the deal, or forget it."

Karen glanced at Elvia, who just shrugged; this is how she made a living, but not Karen. Then it was more than likely they'd both have been used by someone tonight, so she couldn't see her risking a possible get out by refusing.

"Very well, you get your shag," Karen finally answered.

Duarte banged on the panel between the cab and the back. The van pulled to a halt, and the driver came around to the back, opening the door. Duarte climbed out and they walked away, after locking the back of the van, so the girls could not escape.

"Beacher would castrate us if he found out," Gabriel, the driver, commented, after Duarte told him about the deal.

"We aren't going to let them go, idiot. Yes, we will take the money, yes; we will give them both a good shagging. After all, they have the looks and a body to go with it. So after they transfer the money, they are back in the van."

"How do we get them back in the van?"

"We need to check the payment is in our banks. They must wait in the van, while we go to a cash point. But once back in the van, I will use the shock from the bracelet to disable, and then we will use the handcuffs. You're not telling me, two women would have any chance in overcoming us?"

"They wouldn't, but do you think they would fall for it?"

"Two stupid prostitutes, why not, they'd be more interested in walking away, not looking at potential problems in doing that. Apart from which, they could hardly expect us not to check our accounts, before letting them go."

"That all sounds good, but I can't see why I get less money. I want fifty as well."

"That's why I told you what they'd offered. I am not risking one of them blabbing how much more I'm getting, and we end up arguing. We get equal amounts. They'll have no choice and just have to dig deeper."

The two men, after agreeing, went back to the van.

"How are you going to pay?" Duarte asked.

Have you got my mobile?" Karen asked.

"No, they are back at the club."

"Then we should return to the club for the mobiles, or to our hotel. We left our debit cards in the room safe. We can transfer the money by phone, or we can go to the bank tomorrow and collect cash."

"Going back to the club is not possible. We'll go to your hotel, but Gabriel here gets fifty thousand, the same as me, or you forget it," Duarte told them.

"I also want my shag," Gabriel cut in.

Karen looked towards Elvia. "How much can you do?" she asked, with a quick blinking of her eyes to indicate she had a plan.

"Thirty-five tops, unless you can wait ten days for money from my savings account to be released."

"Okay," Karen told Gabriel. "I'll make up the rest for Elvia. As for your shag, choose between yourselves who you want. If both of you want the same woman, that's fine, but you still only get one shag each, This is no marathon, or all night session, you shag until you come and that is it, but no longer than half an hour. Take longer or decide to want to take us both, you pay our day or overnight fee of two thousand euro, the same as any client booking us."

"Yea, like we will be forking out that sort of money. But piss us about in that half hour and you'll feel my leather belt across your backs," Duarte told them. "Tomorrow, you'd better fuck off, out of Portugal. When we tell Beacher you escaped, he'll be looking for you."

"We're going anyway, or we were, so by weekend we'll be gone. The hotel's back in Lisbon."

"Won't it look strange us all walking into a hotel?"

Gabriel asked.

"We're not in the hotel, but staying in one of their service apartments," Karen told him. "The entrance to the apartments has a number coded lock entry, as well as the apartment. No one will see us enter, or leave."

"Then let's go," Gabriel urged Duarte, more than happy with what he had heard.

They turned back the way they came, with Duarte in the back of the van.

Arriving outside, where Karen and Elvia were staying, with the van parked up, Gabriel pulled open the back door. "Time to pay," he said with a grin.

***

Once inside the apartment, Karen went over to the room safe and was just about to key in the code when Duarte called over to her.

"Don't open it, I'll do that, just in case you have a weapon inside," he told her.

"We're bloody escorts, not gangsters, but if that's what you want, I'll give you the code."

"I do, what's the number?" he came back at her.

Opening the safe, all he found was around a hundred euro, a debit card and a passport under the name of Amber Foster, along with an envelope with Elvia's name on. Inside the envelope, a small amount of cash and her debit card.

"It's time to pay." He told her with a grin across his face, at the same time passing over the debit cards.

"Before that, the bracelets, remove them. Our agreement must work both ways, so once paid and you've had your shag, you leave," Karen demanded, all too aware, after they had been paid, the bracelets would be high-risk if they still had them on. Although in reality, even left on, it would make no difference as to the inevitable outcome, apart from adding a possible painful experience. Karen had a plan to conclude this standoff, in her favour, even if Duarte decided to renege on their deal.

"I'm not taking them off yet," Duarte told her.

"Why not, and if not now when?"

"After you've paid and before we give you both a good shagging."

"Trust is not one-sided; it has to be from both sides. We are giving you all our savings, and the use of our body. Leaving the bracelets on, means we are offering everything, yet you are not prepared to go as far as even removing the bracelets. Why is that? Afraid we'll suddenly become dangerous adversaries, cut your throats, or maybe throw you out of the apartment?" Karen mocked.

"Yeah, like that would happen from you two," Gabriel came back at her. "Do it, Duarte, we're wasting time," Gabriel urged, giving Duarte a wink, although neither girl saw him do it.

"Hold you arms out," Duarte told them.

After they had been removed, Karen asked for their debit cards.

Duarte pulled out a wallet from his pocket and removed a card, and passed it to her.

"And yours," she said to Gabriel, "unless you want me to transfer my payment and Elvia's to Duarte's bank account?"

"What do you think, Duarte?" Gabriel asked.

"I'm not into mixing up payments. You get yours and I get mine."

Gabriel handed Karen his card.

"Don't forget we're listening to what you say," Duarte reminded her.

Karen looked at him. "Touchy aren't you. First you had the belief I'd a weapon in the safe, now you think by transferring money with an automatic bank system, I'm going to tell it to call the police."

"Just pay the fucking money," realising what a fool he was making of himself, after all, they were escorts nothing more.

"Give me your mobile. I can hardly call from the apartment phone," Karen demanded.

Karen keyed in the telephone number on the back of her card; with Duarte checking it was the same. Everyone watched as she keyed in an access code and password, followed by Duarte's account number. After that was accepted, she made a payment to Gabriel's account. Then she cut the call. "I've paid your shortage to Gabriel's account, Elvia. You just need to pay him the balance," Karen said, passing her the phone and Gabriel's card.

Minutes later, the transactions were complete.

"How long will it take for the money to get there?" Gabriel wanted to know.

Karen shrugged. "I've no idea. I have never done it before, probably ten minutes. You'll have to check."

While Karen was doing her transfers, Elvia had made coffee in a jug. "Anyone want coffee, with a tot of spirit from the minibar? There's no milk," she asked.

They all had coffee, each pouring in whisky, or brandy, using miniatures taken from the bar.

Duarte downed his drink quickly. "It's time for the next part of our agreement. Who do you want, Gabriel?"

"I'll let you choose."

"Then I'll take this cocky one, I want to see if she's everything she claims," he said, grasping Karen's arm, propelling her towards one of the bedroom doors. He glanced back. "Have fun with Elvia. If you can't cope, send her through," he mocked.

"Like that will happen. You'll probably be the one who fails, and end up sending me Amber to finish what you couldn't."

"I've told you, if each of you want both of us, you

pay," Karen cut in.

"Fuck off and get in the bedroom," Duarte demanded, hitting Karen across the side of the head with his hand.

She never reacted, But once inside the bedroom, Karen carried on through to the en-suite bathroom with Duarte following.

She glanced back at him. "Would you like to check inside my washbag, in case I've some sort of weapon?" she asked cuttingly, offering the washbag.

"I'm getting fed up with your constant mocking. Anymore of it, I'll give you a hiding you won't forget," he told her, at the same time snatching the bag off her, pouring the contents into the sink. Inside were all the things an escort would use, such as condoms and lubrication. Plus the usual items, toothpaste, toothbrush, soap and a facecloth. From the start of this operation, everything had to be perfect. There was no room for error, even down to what had been left in the bathroom.

"Satisfied? Can I get myself ready now?"

"Yes, and be quick about it," then he left her alone.

Karen was disappointed. Her backup team will now know she was in the apartment. Why had they not called back, following the call she made? Unable to answer that question, but suspecting there must be a genuine delay on their side, it left little option, but to continue the deception. Karen hoped her plan would have avoided Duarte taking her to his bed, although to be fair, earlier in the night, she had been faced with working in a brothel, with all that entailed, until she found a way out. So in a way, while she did not want sex, particularly with Duarte, this was the better alternative. Quickly undressing, she stood for a moment in front of the mirror, combing her hair. It had been nearly ten months since going with a man in this situation. Then, like now, offering sexual services as part of a covert operation. Karen was used to being slapped about, often receiving punishments, making her submissive, when she hesitated in doing anything a man demanded of her. In fact, if she really thought about it, ninety per cent of her sex life had been with strangers and mainly men in their late fifties and sixties. Always easy for a young girl, but at times, she would end up with a man younger, more viral and demanding, which while still forced to go with him, she would react positively and work hard to please the man. With the telephone still not ringing, delaying any longer, in joining Duarte in the bedroom, may raise a suspicion that all was not quite right. Sighing inwardly and after using a little lubrication out of a tube around and inside her vagina, and on the nipples, Karen grabbed a condom and left the bathroom.

Duarte had already removed his T-shirt and slacks, leaving just the pants. "About time you were back, I'm already getting a hard on."

"I'm here now. Shall I put your condom on? Then you can tell me how you want me?" she asked with little interest, the packaged condom in her hand.

He took it from her. "I'll do it myself." He dropped his underpants and began working the condom on, all the time talking. "Since I first saw you, I could sense the way you looked down on people like us. This arrogance did not last long; soon begging me to get you out of the shit, as well as offering yourself as part payment. I bet that sticks in your craw?" he taunted.

Karen, indifferent to his verbal attempt to pull her down, shrugged. "That's crap, I never offered myself as part of the deal. You demanded I did. Then it's only a shag, and believe me I've lost count of how many times I've been shagged by strangers over the years, but once I wipe their body liquids from between my legs and pull my knickers up, they're forgotten. As it is, you've had your money, so get on with it," Karen came back to him.

"I'll certainly be doing that," he said, grabbing hold of her, turning her to face the bed and pushing her to the edge. "Bend over, hands on the mattress and spread your legs," he demanded.

Karen did as she was told. While she hated it this way, at least she would not be bouncing up and down on top of him, forced to look at the satisfaction, which would be written across his face, in taking her.

"Further, I want your bottom well up," he shouted, pushing down lower with his hand on her back. As she did, he immediately began slapping her bottom with his free hand. The slaps were hard and stinging.

"Take this as a taster, because if you don't get rid of the obvious contempt, you have of me, I will finish this session with my belt. After that you'll not be able to sit down for a week," he said aggressively, at the same time moving directly behind her, gripping her hips, while he worked himself inside.

Karen closed her eyes, when he began to shag hard. Unexpected and impromptu punishments, as she had just experienced, always took her back to her early years, when such aggression, and the need for it to stop, would make her submissive, wanting to please the man. The same with Duarte, who was not gentle in the way he was treating her. Even so, from experience, most men going at it this way, were unable to pace themselves, the abuse never lasting long before prematurely satisfying himself, and she would be discarded, bringing their agreement to an end. But Karen soon found Duarte had no such intention by suddenly stopping, pushing her away from the bed. "With the punishment and you relaxing, you're turning out not to be a bad shag, so maybe you really are worth your big fees. Get yourself astride and work your fucking arse off," he demanded, as he lay on the bed.

Karen still concerned, as to why the mobile hadn't

rung, did as he asked, and soon they were at it again, He'd pushed her arms up above her head, arching her body back, thrusting her breast forward, before reaching behind gripping her buttocks preventing her from slowing, or pulling out. While she believed the abuse would be finished so much earlier, it was obvious that was not going to be so easy with Duarte. Then with her decision to avoid more painful punishment, by working hard to please him, her body was beginning to react to his demands. Karen was building up her own orgasm and at this rate; she could not, or did not want to prevent it happening. But yet again, he stopped. Karen could not believe he wanted more from her, as he pushed her off, having her lay on her back while he positioned himself between her legs, gripping her breasts and again working inside.

It was obvious he knew how to work a woman, all Karen could do was lie back, enjoy the experience by allowing her own orgasm to take her over. In reality, no matter what she thought of the man, he had gone so far, she did not want him to stop.

It was at this time, his mobile began to ring. Karen could not believe the phone would begin ringing at this precise moment. While she was expecting it, it could not have been at a more inconvenient moment and she really did not want him to answer. Except, not to do so, could be intensely embarrassing for her.

Even so, Karen had no choice in wanting him to ignore the phone; Duarte had stopped, pulled out from her, going over to a dressing table on the other side of the room. He suspected the call maybe from Beacher checking up on them, a call he could not ignore. However, after looking at the number and finding, it was not Beacher, or a number he recognised, Duarte turned back towards the bed.

Karen was still in the same position on the bed as he had left her. Now they had stopped, it was essential he answered the call. "You're not going to answer? Maybe it's something to do with the bank transfer, if you don't recognise the caller?" she suggested.

"Fucking better not be," he said, grabbing the mobile. "Who is it?" he shouted down the phone, after answering.

"Miss Amber Foster?" a man asked calmly.

"Do I sound like a fucking woman?" he shouted.

The man apologised, told him he was calling from the bank and could he speak to her.

Duarte mumbled some incoherent comment, before looking across towards Karen. She had, by now, climbed off the bed and was standing watching him.

"It's the fucking bank. You'd better not have fucked up my payment, otherwise, it is definitely the belt for wasting my time, before being taken to where you were supposed to be going in the first place."

"Charming, so now you not only want my money, apart from fucking me, I'm to be beaten yet again. What is next? Pass me to your mate for good measure?"

By now, he was inches from her, slapping her hard across the face. It stung, but she had no intention of him knowing he had hurt her.

"If I decide he can have you, with or without this call that will happen. In the meantime, less of the wisecracks and sort it out. Remember, I'm listening to every word."

He dropped the mobile phone onto the bed.

Karen, ignoring his comment, picked it up, confirming who she was to the caller. The man asked the usual security questions. "Can you confirm how many transactions you have made?"

"I have made two transactions."

"And do you want an immediate transfer, or delayed?"

Karen hesitated. Did she want to continue with Duarte? Even though he had been aggressive to her, which was not new, yet she was beginning to enjoy her time with him. Her only problem in asking for a delay, she would no longer be in control of the situation going forward.

"Immediate please," Karen heard herself saying.

This is all in order, Miss Foster. I confirm transfer has been verified and will be made immediately."

Cutting the call, Karen handed the phone back. "They were confirming my earlier instructions and paying."

"Fucking idiots, of course you're paying, so why ask again?"

"If you remember, the original calls were all electronic, so maybe because they were such large amounts, they're checking I'm not being scammed or forced to pay. Ironic, don't you think when I am?"

"Then it's a good job you kept your fucking mouth shut. Fetch another condom and stop wasting time."

"I'm going to have a pee first, then I'll bring two, in case someone else calls and another falls off," she mocked.

Without even waiting for him to agree, she went through to the bathroom, shutting the door and swinging the catch over. Going over to the sink, she used a sponge from her toilet bag to press cold water on her face, where he had hit her. Duarte's violent retaliation was her fault, but at the time, it felt good saying it. After a few seconds, she used the sponge to wash between her legs and quickly dressed, closing the toilet lid to sit down and wait.

Seconds later, there was the sound of the bedroom door opening and shouting.

"On the floor, face down or I shoot," came the demand.

Karen stood. At least it was over, besides acutely aware that if she had not managed to get him to answer the phone, her people would have come in to the bedroom to find him shagging her. While this is what the industry is all about, it still would have been embarrassing, to be caught in that position. Karen came out of the bathroom to see Duarte face down, his hands secured behind by a large tie wrap.

"Cutting it a bit fine there, Auguste, you could have found me in a very compromising position," Karen said to him, at the same time attempting to make out by her words, they had prevented her from being raped.

"Sorry, we were closer to the club and about twenty minutes from here."

Karen now realised why she had been forced to go as far as she had. Twenty minutes was a long time waiting for assistance? "That's fine; at least you're here now. Give me ten minutes, to find more suitable clothes," picking up her suitcase to take into the bathroom. "Also, have this piece of shit put some clothes on, as well as the other, and secure them in the lounge."

Soon she was back, wearing jeans and a top, both Duarte, with Gabriel, were in the lounge. Both secured and sitting on kitchen chairs. The three men who came to Karen and Elvia's rescue were, Auguste, Marin and Joseph. All belonged to the French unit of Karen's private army, tasked as her covert support, that even Frank's team did not know of. This was one of Karen's need to know operations and Frank's team did not need to know she had made additional arrangements, beyond his. Now they were standing around, all holding guns with silencers attached.

"I bet it was a surprise to be caught with your pants down, Duarte? But you see escorts can afford to pay for protection. Anyway, you still have a chance to hold on to your money, if you're prepared to give me information?"

"You'll get nothing from me."

"If that's your choice, I'll just make sure Beacher is aware, that you both took money to let us escape. Knowing his reputation, you may last the week, so it's a spending spree then die."

Gabriel looked at her. "Why would you do that? We intended to let you go in exchange for payment."

"You could at least give both of us some credit, and admit you never had that intention?" Karen came back at him.

Gabriel smiled, but said nothing.

"Right, times moving on, what's it to be live or die? Personally, I am not bothered. Although to be fair, the world's better without your sort."

"Who are you really, and why do you want information?" Duarte asked.

"Sorry to disappoint, in suspecting we are something more than escorts, we're not. Although we are at the top of our game, meaning for the next few years, we can command a great deal of money. It's what you said earlier that concerned me."

"What?"

"This Beacher guy will be pissed off by our escape and will be looking for us, even after he kills you two. You can see I have protection, normally from clients who seem to believe they can cheat us. They soon learn, girls commanding the money we do, can afford to retaliate against someone who believes they can take over our lives and work us free. So we strike first. Beacher will pay for believing he could take Elvia, and me, after we had done Leonor a favour to make up numbers, as well as possibly ending up later servicing Davi's friends. So he will be sent a warning to keep away from us, or face the consequences. I also want the address of where we were heading originally; it gives us an additional hold over this man Beacher, if he believes we could send people to cause trouble with his clients."

Gabriel grinned. "I've got to see this, Duarte, a few so-called gunmen taking on Beacher. He'll tear them apart."

"You're right, he will. Tell you what, Amber; we will give you his address, as well as where you were heading, although I'm betting, next time we go there, we'll find you and Elvia installed, working your arse's off. That's on condition you let us walk, as well as keep the money you've transferred."

Karen smiled to herself. The arrogant fools, but why should she care. Information was needed, and once she left the apartment Amber would disappear, until her expertise was called on in another operation. "I've told you what we want, give us the information and you can go. But be warned, you have our money, do not for one moment have the idea you can tell me a load of rubbish. I have your card numbers; we will find your address and collect our money in cash or kind. Marin and you Joseph take Gabriel into the bedroom, Auguste and I will take Duarte into the other. Once in the room, both of you write down the addresses. If they match, you can leave. I can't be fairer than that."

A short time later, the two men left, accompanied by the lads.

Elvia joined Karen in her bedroom.

"I assume the call you made tonight, as well as mine, wasn't directly to our banks?"

"Correct, although both cards do work in an ATM, the number is an emergency number that is monitored by our covet operation. A certain password and number I keyed in would inform them to make a transaction for me, or if I put in a different code, it would indicate I was in trouble and needed assistance urgently. It also confirmed, in the code, they were not looking at triangulating the mobile I was calling from, but the hotel apartment I had rented for the operation. Once they were outside, they called again pretending to be the bank checking on the transfer, but in essence, confirming two transfers, meant there were two assailants. If the transfer was to be immediate, they should come inside immediately, or delay until I called them in. Of course, they already had the apartment code for the door. Just one of the ways I can summon help."

"You're getting really smart these days; you must tell me how else you can get help. I assume you didn't fancy Duarte taking you, deciding to terminate the operation rather than delaying?"

Karen shrugged. "Unfortunately, with their delay getting to us, he'd already started. But I am like you; one man is much the same as the next. Then I am not averse to having sex forced on me or fussy who. Such luxury was knocked out of me years ago. The only issue to consider, was there an advantage in the operation moving forward, in allowing my time with Duarte to continue. I decided there was not. He would not disclose anything useful without being forced. In fact, I don't believe they would have let us walk away, rather take our money, shag us, and still send us to the brothel, or whatever he liked to call it."

"I'd agree with you there. Mind you, they do have your money."

"What money, the transfer never got passed our operations room, after all I never gave the correct passwords," she answered with a grin. "Besides, by the time they find out nothing's arrived, it will be too late, we'll be gone. I have already sent a text to a Dark Angel unit of Unit T to go to the house we were heading. The other unit will surround Beacher's house, waiting for my order to go in. Which reminds me," pulling a mobile out of her pocket left by Auguste. "I need to contact Frank, he'll be panicking. With Frank, that's dangerous, he kills people."

"I think all your private army does that, Karen."

She smiled. "Maybe, but that's what it's all about. They take one, you take one of them and so it goes on." Dialling a number, Frank answered. "Frank, Karen. Where are you?"

"Where am I, we're currently looking for you and heading to Davi's house to take it apart? Apparently Javier is there and possibly Beacher Marinez, so we intended beating the shit out of them for your whereabouts."

"You've done fantastic to get as far as you have, but a change of plan, don't go inside. We already know where he lives. I've sent a Dark Angel unit to Beacher's house, waiting for him to return."

"I'm okay with that, Karen, provided you're alright? We were concerned as to your safety when we found your wig, with the mobile and watch."

"Yes, I admit, I didn't consider that could happen. Although, the man who took me, could not have known what Karen Harris looked like, or probably never considered I could have been her. I will tell you all about it when we meet. I'm also using a temporary mobile, until I get my own back, you should have picked up the number."

"I have. We have yours and Elvia's mobiles, including your watches. Anyway, take care, Karen, talk soon."

"We will," then she cut the call.

"Sorted, Karen? Was Frank onto us?" Elvia asked, after Karen pocketed the phone.

"Sort of, they had located where Davi lived and knew Beacher would be there. He would have got out of them where we were being taken; they are ex-Unit T and know how to make someone talk. Mind you, I hope Jasmin is having better luck than me."

"She'll be fine. You have them on the run and they know it. So get it all wrapped up in a few days and come with me to the Caribbean. Think about it, free drinks, food, plenty of sun and swimming, and we get paid along with wild nights," Elvia urged.

Karen laughed. "You know it sounds good, I really wish it were possible."

"Just excuses, even I know that you'd not be missed for a few days, so it is possible. You just have to make it happen."

"We'll see. It's time to move on and get answers."

"You mean you're not going to bed, don't you ever sleep? I'm knackered," Elvia asked, aghast at the thought.

"I'm a commander, with troops in the field awaiting orders. The luxury of sleep does not come into the equation. We'll drop you off in a place of safety, so you can get your head down."

***

Duarte along with Gabriel, after leaving the apartment in their van, pulled up a distance away. Duarte took his phone out.

"Who are you calling?"

"Beacher."

"Why?"

"Think about it. We have a brilliant excuse to tell him about the girl's protection. Say the van was forced to stop and with them having guns, we had no chance. So we win all ways, money in the bank and we are off the hook. We can even tell him their protection will be coming for him. That will give him a laugh."

"I like it, call him, make his night."

"Why do you want Beacher?" Javier asked, when Duarte called.

"To tell him we had trouble with the escorts."

"What trouble?"

"They had fucking protection. Forced us to stop, and three men got out with guns. With me in the back, when Gabriel saw the guns he could do nothing. Then when they left, the older one, Amber, told us to tell Beacher she was coming for him. He would pay for attempting to abduct them. I laughed; they have no idea who they are taking on."

"We never laugh, where gunmen are concerned. Return to Beacher's house and join up with his guards. It is possible they are not who they claim to be. The three gunmen you saw may not be all of them."

"Just a minute, we never agreed to take on gunmen."

"While we pay you, you do what you're told. So make sure you go direct to the house otherwise expect a visit, which won't be pleasant," then he cut the call.

Duarte told Gabriel what Javier said.

"I'd not worry. I bet the girls were all talk, and now running like scared rabbits."

Chapter 30

While Karen had been out of contact, Jasmin had her own problems. Beacher's instructions to Ramiz to bring Avril out, resulted in him turning up.

Jasmin was first alerted by Bettina, looking after the surveillance while Alexander slept. At first, they decided this was yet another man visiting. That was until half an hour later he left the apartment, along with Charlotte.

"What do we do, Jasmin, stop him?" Bettina asked.

"My instructions are to keep Charlotte safe. That means I follow. When you finally get hold of Karen, let her know. Is the car still outside? Emma hasn't taken it has she?"

"It will be. It's there just for this sort of situation, not transport."

By this time, Ramiz was at the door leading onto the street. Jasmin was also on her way down, hesitating a moment until Ramiz, with Charlotte, actually left the building.

***

Thirty minutes before this happened; Ramiz had gone directly to the apartment with Jacqueline opening the door to his knocking.

"Beacher's sent me, we need to talk?" he told her, before she could ask who he was.

"You'd better come in. Do you want a drink?"

"Coffee is good, no sugar," he replied, following her into the kitchen.

As Jacqueline made the coffee, she wanted to know why he was there. "So what's the problem with Beacher?"

"He's receiving information that Avril is being used. He specifically told you to look after her, not use her."

"Maybe he did, but he didn't offer me any money to do that. I have a nice little business going here. A young girl hanging around, while I look after my clients would not work. So why can't I use her? She's no virgin, and is only doing what she's been doing over the last years."

"Then you should have asked for payment. He has had offers close to a hundred and fifty thousand for her. Your stupidity could have got her injured, by one of your clients, which would write off such money. Do you think he's going to sit back and allow that risk to continue?"

"Then pay me. I am not talking about a few euro for her food. I want compensating, if I can't bring clients here."

"You don't need any compensation. I am taking her with me. How much has she earned?"

"Oh no, Beacher's not getting her fees. That is mine. Anyway, she is in her bedroom. I'll tell her to pack anything she has."

After she left, Ramiz pulled out a gun and began screwing on a silencer. The woman in his view was a fool. Beacher would have made sure she was paid well, for looking after the girl. But like many in this industry, when they have a girl who can earn cash, they use her without any thought.

Avril came into the room, followed by Jacqueline.

"I'm told, I'm to leave with you, is that right?" Avril asked.

"It is. Beacher gave instructions you should not be used, and he heard that was not happening. Have you got everything?"

"Yes, I don't have much. Everything's in the carrier bag."

"Very well, wait for me outside the apartment, while I settle up with Jacqueline."

Avril left the room, standing outside the apartment in the corridor. Last time she was sent out of a room, someone died. This seemed to be fast becoming the norm around her, but what could she do.

While Beacher had told Ramiz that Avril should see Jacqueline's punishment, for not following his orders. Avril was fourteen, he had no idea how she would react seeing someone shot, maybe go into hysterics, or not allow him to take her out of the apartment quietly. Such risks were not advisable where he was taking her.

After Avril left, Jacqueline was keen to make out she had come to no harm. "You can see the girl's fine, so when you see Beacher, you can assure him I've looked after her."

Ramiz stood. "That's unnecessary, Avril will tell him herself. For you, it is the end of the line. Workers who ignore instructions have no value." Then he pulled out the gun and shot her. Finally, he fired a second bullet to the head.

Joining Avril, waiting where he had told her to wait, they left the building, climbing into a car already parked up.

"Where am I going?" she asked.

"I'm taking you to Portugal to meet your potential new owner. He lives in Dubai; this man is to be your permanent owner. No longer will you keep changing every few months. He's coming to Portugal to meet you."

"Do I have a choice? Say I don't like the man?"

"All Beacher's girls who come of age have a choice. But do not just discount him; he is very wealthy and you are a lucky girl to have been put forward. Accept him and you will have a very different life, nice clothes, no working in the kitchen, or cleaning the house. Beautiful homes, holidays on private yachts. This has been what Beacher has had you working towards, since leaving home, all the time gaining experience in keeping your man happy. Keep an open mind, no man is perfect; even so, some have far more attractions for a girl than others, such as I've listed."

"I suppose, and then I'm never going home, so I

have to live somewhere."

"Course you do, so why not in relative luxury?"

They fell silent. Avril leaned back, closing her eyes. Her time with Jacqueline had been a wake-up call, to what her future could be, servicing many men rather than one. If Beacher had found her the one man, she must take the opportunity and not complain. After all, while Zoey had told her about Unit T and the charity LBNF offering her freedom, a chance to do anything she wanted, but to what end? Living in cheap accommodation and having to work five days a week to survive. Why would she want that, when there were men prepared to take her in, give her everything? She was old enough, as well as capable of looking after a man, making him feel special. Yes, this is what she wanted, no matter what.

"You've gone quiet. What are you thinking about?" Ramiz asked.

"Not so much thinking," she lied. "More relieved that I'm away from that woman. I am a one-man girl, not one after another. So the man living in Dubai will suit me."

"He will, and like I said, what she put you through, should not have happened. Beacher has kept his word and will look after you."

"Do we have to go on an aircraft to Portugal?"

"We do. It is over a thousand miles away, so even in an aircraft it takes two and a half hours. I will be coming with you. You'll not go alone."

By now, they had arrived at the airport. While Avril waited inside the entrance, Ramiz took back the hire car, before joining her, going directly to the check in desk.

***

Jasmin was more than annoyed with Karen not responding to her calls. Then Unit T, it seemed, had no idea where she was either. Even so, she had no intention in losing sight of Charlotte. While she followed the car, Jasmin was considering taking the man with Charlotte out, although she was also interested in where they were heading. So her natural instinct, in reverting to a contract killer, had to be curtailed for the time being.

Pressing buttons on her mobile, Jasmin called Bettina.

"Are you still in sight of the girl, Jasmin?" Bettina asked.

"I am. Is Emma back yet?"

"She is. Do you want to talk to her?"

"Not so much talk, but we need to check the apartment. Have her knock on the door, with some excuse. The last time this girl was removed from a house, the occupant had been killed. Beacher likes to close all loops back to him."

"We'll do that and come back to you."

By the time Bettina called back, Jasmin was parking up at the airport. "What have you found?" Jasmin asked.

"Professional hit, we are packing up and leaving. There is no point remaining. Where are you?"

"At the airport, I am going to try to get on the same flight. If it isn't possible, they will not be allowed to leave Paris. We cannot risk losing sight of her, without Karen having in place people to meet the aircraft. If I can get on the same flight, I will go with them and text the car park level I've left the car, so you can collect it later."

"We understand."

Jasmin watched as Ramiz and Avril went to the desk. After they walked away, she joined the small queue that had formed behind them.

Pulling out her ID, she showed it to the girl behind the desk. "Unit T, a few passengers back, a man with a young girl booked in. What is their destination?"

"Do you have a name?"

"The girl may be travelling under the name of Avril

Dumas."

The girl keyed in the name. "You're correct, an Avril Dumas along with a male Ramiz Shaban are booked on a flight to Lisbon. They depart in an hour," she answered after looking at the screen.

"Can you get me on the flight?"

"One moment," the girl went onto another screen. "I have a place in business class. Do you want it booked?"

"Yes," she answered, pulling out her credit card.

The girl smiled. "I don't require payment, I can charge the ticket directly to Unit T. May I have your ID in order to scan it?"

Jasmin passed it across.

"Who shall I put down as sanctioning the purchase?" she asked.

"Colonel Karen Harris."

She looked up at her. "You know Karen?"

"Very well, we often go out together."

"I'd love to meet her. She's so inspirational to all girls."

"She is, but I think you'd be surprised if you did meet her. She's very down to earth, no airs and graces, just a normal young woman."

"I can imagine, particularly when you see her interviewed on telly, she's so relaxed. Are you watching the young girl?"

"I can't confirm that officially, but between you and me, we do have an interest in her and where she's heading."

"I understand. Are you carrying a weapon?"

"Yes."

"Do you have a Unit T licence?"

"I do,"

"Then, before you go through security scanners, please inform them. The weapon will be taken off you during the flight, secured, and returned to you in Lisbon," she told Jasmin, passing back her ID as well as a boarding pass. "Have a good flight and look after the young girl."

"I will. Thank you."

As the girl told her, security checked her Unit T licence and stamped a warning on the boarding pass. While she kept hold of the gun in the terminal, because of the dangers of firing a gun in a pressurised cabin, she would need to hand it in before boarding. Walking through, Jasmin had no issues in being seen. She had not met Charlotte, nor did she know the man with her. This made it easy to remain close to them, spending the time reading a magazine she had picked up while ordering a coffee. Food would be provided on the aircraft, so it was pointless buying food, although she really was very hungry.

Jasmin, after failing to contact Karen, decided to try Frank's number. He answered. "Where is she, Frank?"

"Karen has just come off a covert operation. She does not have her own phone back yet. Can I help?"

"Charlotte's on the move. She was collected by a contract killer, who killed Charlotte's minder, and they are now on the way to Lisbon. I am following. Do you think this is the break we were hoping for, and Charlotte is going to join up with the other girls?"

"It's possible, Jasmin. Stick to her like glue. I can have you met at the airport, if you think it has value."

"It does, I can't rely on taxis to follow them. Can you get word to Karen, she may decide to hold off on whatever she's up to, until we find out where Charlotte is heading."

"Who knows with Karen? But I will get a message to her; she may even call you direct. When are you due in Lisbon?"

"Around thirteen hundred hours."

"I'll have people there to meet you."

"Very well, I'll call you later."

Chapter 31

Karen joined her Unit T troops close to Beacher's home. She had a surveillance unit in a position that would allow them to watch the comings and goings to the house. The property consisted of a large house set in acres of land with a high wall at the perimeter, along with a few outbuildings.

Frank called Karen on the temporary mobile, to inform her of his conversation with Jasmin.

"In view of that development, we will keep our operation on hold, Frank. Charlotte could be the key we are waiting for. Although, I cannot understand why the girl had to be pulled, she was safe where she was. Unless Beacher never intended her to be used, then it would make sense, deciding to bring her closer to keep an eye on her."

"Those were my thoughts, Karen. Has Beacher returned from Davi's house?"

"He did, along with Javier. Also, the two who abducted me, turned up, so we have to assume Beacher knows someone is coming for him."

"Was it wise to let them go?"

"There wasn't much option. As far as they were concerned, Beacher is up against three minders working for two escorts. I cannot see him believing two escorts would employ minders off their own bat. So he will not lose any sleep, just maybe try to find out who owned them. He'll certainly not be expecting fully armed combat troops to descend on him."

"Yes, I can see your logic. Even so, Karen, when they go in, you stand back. You have very competent lieutenants working in the Dark Angel teams, who are more than capable of taking him down."

"God, you sound like Jasmin. Has she been schooling you?"

"I don't need schooling to know you of old. You

have already taken unacceptable risks going in with Elvia, although to be fair, your ability to bring out the greed of such people to your advantage got you both out. I should not need to remind you, you are thirty-seven, Karen, and once again, Unit T's commander. If you want out, you have to trust people to walk in your footsteps, with you leading from behind."

"You're right, but it's hard to step back. I have been trained as a combat soldier. Such training never goes away."

"I don't disagree, which is why I joined your private operation. Except with the two men who abducted you both at Beacher's house, it's imperative they don't associate your recent actions with Unit T."

"Don't worry, Frank, I'm not intending going in. They will not see me. Anyway, I am off for breakfast and getting my head down for a short time. Our next step in this operation is to see if Charlotte's arrival can help."

Karen, of course, certainly did not want Duarte to recognise her. He would not be able to keep his mouth shut that he had shagged the famous Karen Harris that was certain, particularly when he found no money had gone into his account.

***

Javier came into the lounge, where Beacher was counting currency.

Beacher looked up. "We took them for twenty thousand, last night, bloody idiots allowing girls to hang on their necks in a card game."

"They were, particularly when the girls belong to us. It really does beggar belief what must be going through their tiny brains, when a young girl only has to show a bit of leg to send them into fantasy raptures. But back to business, Ramiz called to say they were on their way, landing around lunchtime. What do you want doing with

Avril?"

"That is good, and the timing's just right. Her new owner is also on the way and due later today. We will put her in a five-star hotel, nothing downmarket. Text Ramiz to have him meet you at the airport. You take her over from there. Go to the main shopping area and select something smart for her to wear, as well as nice underwear. Avril has to look her best when she is presented. To do that, we also need a hairdresser."

"Then we should use the Lapa Palace. They have a spa, so she can spend time in that. I'll arrange a hairdresser to go to her room."

"I agree. It is ideal. When you introduce Avril to the buyer, give him time to check her over and if he wants her, which he will, do the deal and take the money, then the girl's his and she's out our hair."

"I leave her with him?"

"Of course, he's got a private aircraft. It is his problem how to get her out the country. We're not a delivery service for the likes of those people."

***

Avril and Ramiz arrived in Lisbon to be met by Javier. Avril knew Javier from when she was first taken, so she had no problem in getting into his car, while Javier spoke to Ramiz.

"You have done well, Ramiz. I will be taking Avril from here. Beacher wants you back at the house. We took two escorts last night, but it turned out they had minders. Three in fact, all with guns, the girls claiming the minders worked for them. Beacher does not believe that, and he is currently finding out who owns the girls. Once he knows, you are to take the owner out. Beacher wants the girl's back, to work in his entertainment house."

"Sounds my sort of job, rather than being a childminder. I talked to Avril on the flight. She's quite intelligent for her age, although very naive about the real world, but that's understandable."

"Well, she'll soon be gone. Her new owner is on his way. Is your car still here?"

"Yes, in long-term parking. I'll go and collect it, then get on my way." He hesitated, pulling out a passport from his pocket. "This is Avril's, you'll need it."

"Good thinking, I nearly forgot that."

Javier joined Avril in the car and they set off.

"Where are we going?" she asked.

"You, young lady, are coming with me to a shop to find you more appropriate clothes to be wearing in a five-star hotel. Then it is the hairdressers, followed by a spell in the hotels spa for a massage and treatments to relax you. Tonight you are having dinner with me and another man who has flown in from Dubai to meet you."

"Is this the man Ramiz told me about?"

"Correct, but it all hinges on you giving a good impression. You have had a taste of what happens to girls who fall by the wayside, after Beacher's mistake in believing Jacqueline would look after you. I assume you don't want to go down that road?"

"No, it was horrible. I'll do my best and show him I can be attentive and loving."

"Of course you will. It's in your interest and I don't believe for one moment you are a fool."

They fell silent and soon they pulled into the car park of a large clothes store. Shutting the engine off, he turned and looked at her.

"I will select a few items for you to try on. If anyone asks, not that I am expecting anyone to, say you are my niece. The same as when we go to the hotel. You will be on your own in the underwear department. I want no running to me, asking if I like your choice, girls would never do that, unless the man has some sort of sexual relationship with her. Even so, I do not want to see you come back to the counter with tiny see-through panties, or bras pushing out your tits, as your paedophile friends liked. You are a fourteen-year-old, not a hooker, so you will choose nice underwear, to show off your figure, yes, but appropriate for your age and no nylons or suspender sets. Have you understood?"

"I understand. My favourite colour is blue. May I have a dress in blue, please?"

"There is no reason why you can't select the colour. I am more interested in the style. You need to look your age but grown up rather than the other way, as a child." He glanced at his watch. We only have an hour to get to the hotel. I've a hairdresser coming to the room, so it's time to move."

***

By the time the aircraft landed in Lisbon, Jasmin had a direct link to Karen. Karen had also arranged a vehicle and someone to assist in surveillance.

Currently, they were following Charlotte after she joined Javier. Not that Jasmin knew who he was, although she had sent Karen the car registration, which was being checked. The person with Jasmin, and part of a Unit T surveillance team was called Michael. Aged twenty-nine, Michael had worked in surveillance for ten years. He was also very good-looking, and Jasmin suspected Karen had deliberately made this choice to find her a man. Not that Karen would admit it, or that she would fall for it, but Jasmin thought it sweet all the same.

"That's strange. They are turning into a clothing store car park. Don't say he's going to buy her new clothes?" Michael commented.

"Or they are checking no one is following. Drive past and park up. I'll wander back on foot," Jasmin told him.

Jasmin entered the store. It was large and quite busy, enabling her to melt in with existing customers. Watching Charlotte it soon became obvious, the man with her was deciding on what style of clothing he wanted her to try on, but allowing her to make the final choice of colour. Finally, after a visit to the fitting rooms, where she had come out a few times to show him how she looked, a decision had been made. This was followed by Charlotte looking around the underwear department, while the man stood close to the tills, ready to purchase everything selected. Again, Jasmin notice Charlotte was comfortable around this man, as if she knew him. However, with the use of a mirror used by customers, Jasmin was able to take his photo, through the mirror, to send to Karen. She may be able to identify him.

Seeing Charlotte returning to the man with undergarments, Jasmin left the shop and joined Michael. "They purchased clothing and should be out in a few minutes."

At that moment, her mobile began to ring. It was Karen.

Jasmin gave her an update.

"The photo you sent was of a man called Javier Schneider, Beacher's right-hand man. That would be why she knew him. They probably met when she first was sent to Beacher. The purchase of items of clothing, shoes and underwear sounds odd, unless she is not heading to join the other girls, but being presented to a potential buyer. If that's the case, she's a waste of time, taking us no closer to finding the other girls."

"What do you want us to do, pull her, or let the girl move on to a new owner? She seems happy enough, particularly after watching her sorting clothes, that girl has no concerns."

"Maybe she doesn't, Jasmin, but the law is the law concerning minors, I have no option, but to uphold it. Even so, letting her run, so to speak, there is a good chance she will lead us to her new owner. Then we strike. Realistically, that could be days, or weeks away, making it more of a surveillance operation, rather than protection. If you want out, I'll bring in others."

"Not so much out, but my skills are not directed towards long-term surveillance," Jasmin hesitated. "For the time being, let's see where she's heading, then if it looks like it's going to be protracted, we'll decide then."

"Very well, keep me informed."

Jasmin leaned back in thought. While she understood, protracted surveillance was not her type of operation. In a way, she felt responsible for Charlotte. This was brought about by talking to Zoey and understanding the way Charlotte would be thinking. The girl wanted stability, let down by her parents; her only comparison would be the time she spent with the paedophile ring Spartes. If Beacher was offering her more of the same, Jasmin believed, in Charlotte's mind, this could be the stability she'd already experienced and now wanted. Already shown in the shop, in the airport, in fact everywhere where a girl in panic would seek help, Charlotte never did. Yet, even if it were best for the girl to remain in an environment where she was comfortable, Karen could not allow it to happen. Like it or not, she had to step in, that was the law. Yet there was also another aspect in this. Was Karen's delay in stepping in too soon, because she wanted a financial return beyond taking a paedophile off the street? After all, if she hits the man taking her, she would not only send him down for ten years but also strip him of his assets. Something she had done a great many times, which not only covers Unit T expenses, but also LBNF receives the balance, besides giving the girl some compensation to start a new life. In Jasmin's view, this often complicated what at times could be a simple arrest and conviction.

"They are turning into Lapa Palace hotel. That is a five star plus hotel and rooms can cost hundreds a night," Michael commented, bringing Jasmin out of her thoughts.

"Then she's being sold, either today or tomorrow, that's for certain. Beacher would not have her brought here for nothing, or for a protracted time at those room rates. Drop me off and park up. I need to know the room they are in," Jasmin told him.

Chapter 32

"Ramiz a word," Beacher asked, popping his head into the kitchen, seeing him sitting there with a coffee and a slice of cake.

Ramiz finished off his coffee and went through to the lounge.

"Javier is tied up tonight, so I have a small job for you," Beacher began. "We've a number of girls, who have been delivered today to our warehouse. They are to be taken out of the country by ship. The ship is due to leave on the first tide, you along with Duarte and Gabriel, are to oversee them being loaded into a container tonight. Once the container has left, the two women who have been looking after the girls and bringing them to the warehouse are to be eliminated, along with Duarte and Gabriel. No one must know the girls were ever in our warehouse, or where they are heading."

"The women I understand, but Duarte and Gabriel, why them? They'd never talk?"

"True, but their demise is for a different reason. They can no longer be trusted, allowing themselves to be overcome by two escorts and their so-called minders. They claim it was three minders with guns looking after the two girls. They must think I'm stupid to fall for that sort of crap. More like they were given a few euros by the escorts to look the other way as well as thinking up this story, so as not to admit what they had done. Tell me, have you ever heard of three gunmen looking after a couple of escorts before?"

"One minder, possibly armed, yes, but three of them, that's ridiculous."

"My thoughts as well, so, like I said, it's better getting shut rather than beating the truth out of them."

"This container, is it coming on a lorry?"

"Yes, then it will go through to the docks and be loaded on the ship. Why?"

"What of the crew on the ship, as well as the lorry driver, won't they know about the girls?"

"Of course, but I've already made arrangements for their silence. You sort this end out and the girls."

"How long will they be in the container?"

"What's it to you? You just make sure they leave. Then tidy up."

"So I'll not even know what ship, or where they're going?"

"If you want to know, then yes, but with all possible leads being cut, such knowledge is not to be advised. After all, we couldn't have you carrying that information around, could we?" he answered with a hint of a smile.

"I'll see to it," Ramiz said, and then he left the room. He did not like threats, particularly when he was taking all the risks. Beacher needed to watch his mouth; otherwise, he would forget that they were supposed to be working together. Going through to the back, he found Gabriel watching a game of football. "Where's Duarte?" he asked.

"Out back, having a fag, why, do you want him?"

"Yes, you're both coming with me. We've a job."

***

Once on their way, Duarte asked where they were going.

"We've a few girls to load inside a container at the warehouse. They're apparently on their way to another country."

"Why's he doing that, when we need girls in most of the houses?" Duarte came back at him.

"We do as we're told. Beacher is paying the wages, so he'll know of the local shortages. Anyway, I hear you two lost two women, so you can hardly complain about Beacher."

Duarte glanced behind at Gabriel, before answering.

"Maybe we did, but it's all right for you, you carry a gun. When you're faced with three gunmen and you're unarmed, you do as you're told."

"How did that happen? I understood the girls were at the club and due to go on to Davi's house. Why would they have any idea that they were not going there? I assume they carried nothing, like a mobile or weapon?"

"Of course we searched their bags. Beacher also wanted them stripped, to check they had nothing hidden, besides leaving their mobiles at the club. He did not believe they were escorts for some reason. He was wrong. Neither of them was bothered stripping, but once in the van, one of them called Amber, was bright enough to realise they were not heading to Davi's. After I told them where they were heading, this Amber offered us fifty thou to let them go," he grinned. "Gabriel and I talked, and upped it to fifty grand each with a good shagging thrown in. After all, we would never let them go. They'd have still gone to the house, less their savings and with a good send off."

"Fair enough if they fell for it, which I presumed they did?"

"Yes, paid us online using their debit cards. The one called Amber was an arrogant bitch. It felt good knowing she did not want me to shag her, but after a good slapping across her bottom, she knew what she was doing, and turned out to be pretty good. It's a pity I never finished her off, before the three gunmen burst in."

"How did the gunmen know where the women were?"

"We went back to their hotel apartment to get their cards. How the gunmen knew we were there, god knows, but they did. Then, something else came to me later. She had to know they were coming. When she came out of the bathroom, she was dressed. That woman knew we were finished."

"Interesting, so they just upped and left with the gunmen?"

"No, we left. That was after we had given them Beacher's address and the entertainment house they'd been originally heading."

Ramiz listened to what happened in the apartment. The more he heard, the more serious doubts were forming in his mind. "You're telling me, all they wanted was Beacher's address and the entertainment house?"

"Yes."

"Why? What was their reason?"

"The one called Amber, told us someone had to pay for attempting to abduct them, so Beacher was going to pay. Both of us laughed. How would three gunmen take on Beacher? Mind you, we did call to warn Javier what they'd said."

"What's confusing me is how did they call for help? Whose phone did they use, then are you sure it was the bank they dialled?" Ramiz asked.

"They used my phone and were certainly talking to an automated banking service," Duarte told him. "I called my bank the same as Gabriel the next day. The bastards never paid any money into our accounts."

"Tell me," Ramiz said. "This number, they dialled. Where did it come from?"

"It was on their debit card. We are not that daft to allow them to dial any old number. I also watched it being dialed," Duarte answered.

By now, they were turning into the industrial area where the warehouse was located. Stopping outside the warehouse, Ramiz told them to go inside, and check the girls out. He would join them shortly.

Ramiz sat alone in his car, deep in thought. Everything he had heard, in his view, sounded odd. While he accepted, an escort would have a number on her phone to call for help. He had never known any to go as far in setting up a number, pretending it is a bank, as well as have the number printed on a card. Such arrangements pointed to a professional organisation, with various ways for the woman to call for help, without alerting anyone around her she had done that. Accepting that to be the case, were they escorts, and what organisation was behind them? In his mind, only one operation would have such elaborate arrangements, to look after their covert operators. That was Unit T. With such a possibility, he needed to talk to Beacher. Pulling out his mobile, he called him.

"Are you at the warehouse?"

"I am, but you need to listen to what Duarte has just told me?"

"What?" Beacher asked.

He reiterated to Beacher what the two men had said. "I don't like it, gunmen, and ready printed bank cards with a number to call for assistance, points to Unit T. Only they have the capability to put two women in the field with backup, in fact I think the three gunmen the lads met maybe the tip of a larger force. You know Harris is back with Unit T? I am not sure if she has actually taken over as commander, but she will be controlling it, and this is typical of her type of operation. This was similar to when Unit T took the Marinate gang down, and Harris was their commander. She sent prostitutes in then."

"You're reading in too much. Just get on with the job. I have contacts who would immediately know if Unit T moved any troops, and they would call me. As for Harris being back running Unit T, unlikely, there are many powerful people in Europe, who intend it not to happen. Anyway, I have work to do. Call me when the girls have gone and you've tided up the mess," then he cut the call.

Ramiz could not believe the audacity of the man. Either he was a fool, or he already knew of the threat and had a way out, leaving everyone else to face the overwhelming might of Unit T. No criminal group, once Unit T had a target, could bring enough experienced gunmen to take them on. Then if that was not enough, Unit T was also able to call on all EU countries military to support them, making the potentially ridiculous situation of Unit T being able to put thousands of soldiers in the field. He looked at the warehouse. There was no way he intended being caught with a number of children with the possibility of Unit T being close. Mandatory ten years, maybe more, for loading a few kids onto a lorry, was not his plan for the future. He started the car and drove away.

Inside the warehouse, Duarte and Gabriel found ten girls sitting around on the floor, with two women handing out small bottles of water, taken from two plastic shrink-wrapped cartons, along with a chocolate biscuit each.

"Who the hell are these? None look older than fifteen," Gabriel gasped. "It's no wonder Beacher wasn't going to use them around here."

"I don't like it. It is one thing taking girls in their twenties, but very different taking young children. This lot is jailbait with the key thrown away," Duarte commented.

"Were has Ramiz got too?" Gabriel asked, looking around and seeing he had not followed. "He should talk to Beacher and find out what is happening," he commented, at the same time, walking over to the pedestrian entrance of the warehouse and looking out. The car had gone, but a lorry carrying a container was approaching the warehouse, beginning to turn around in order to reverse in.

Gabriel went back into the warehouse, going up to Duarte. "He's fucked off, leaving us here. Now the fucking container has arrived. What do we do?"

Duarte was thinking, when the sound of a vehicle horn went off.

"Come on, Duarte, make a decision. The driver

wants the shutters opened."

"I'm off. If Beacher, or Ramiz, hasn't the guts to sort the children out themselves, I am not taking the fall for them. You can stay if you want."

"No way, let's go."

Both ran outside, but stopped dead. They counted at least ten soldiers, in combat clothing, their steel helmets sporting the Unit T logo. Each soldier held an M4 carbine, all directed towards the warehouse.

"On the ground, face down, hands above your heads," the lieutenant in charge, demanded.

Both men never hesitated, with a soldier quickly approaching, pulling their arms down and handcuffing them. Other soldiers pushed past, entering the warehouse. In minutes, the two women were brought out in handcuffs.

Now more vehicles were beginning to arrive, including police and ambulances, followed by the press. Quickly, the police were setting up barriers, keeping onlookers, and press well away from the warehouse.

The prisoners were taken away in police vehicles. A short time later, Karen arrived, joining the lieutenant.

"A report, Lieutenant," Karen ordered.

"My unit was assigned, with a surveillance team, to follow Ramiz who led us to this warehouse. Two men, who were in his car, remained at the warehouse and he drove away. Ramiz was stopped by the police, and is currently being held for questioning. Inside the warehouse, we found ten children being looked after by two women. Both women and the two men have been arrested and taken away by the police. We have a coach on the way, but meanwhile each girl is being checked over by paramedics. All have been found to be in good health, but they are very confused. A Unit T aircraft is due to arrive in two hours at the airport to transport the children back to Unit T's camp."

"You have done well. Carry on Lieutenant, I have to

leave you, and move on to another problem caused by this gang."

He saluted her and Karen left.

Chapter 33

Charlotte came out of the bedroom of the hotel suite to see Javier, with another man. Both were sat down, but stood when she came in. Dressed in a slightly flared blue dress, with three inch heeled shoes, her hair still long but styled, Charlotte looked and felt good. For her, this was an important meeting; the man was her future, a future she wanted.

"Ah, Avril, let me introduce you to Mr Karimi, he's specifically flown in from Dubai, to meet and talk to you," Javier said.

"It's nice to meet you, Sir," she said directly to him.

"And you, Avril. Please call me Reza. How old are you?"

"Fourteen."

"You know I'm looking for a young girl, to come and live with me? Before you answer, such a girl would be expected to learn my language, follow my religion, as well as joining me in the bedroom. Is that your understanding?"

"That has been my life since eleven. I have been taught a number of languages by previous owners and looked after them both by cleaning, cooking and entertaining them in whatever way they demanded. So yes, I understand what is expected of me, in exchange for living in your house."

"That is good, but before I agree to take you home, following light refreshments, Javier has allowed me to take you into the bedroom, so you can show me just what you have learned to keep your man happy. Are you in agreement to do that?"

She smiled. "I've no objection in you doing anything you want with me, in order to convince you of my loyalty."

Javier glanced at his watch. "Time is a little tight for me, Reza, food is still twenty minutes away. I propose to move forward, you should first look Avril over." He turned to Avril. "Avril, remove your dress, show Reza how nicely developed you are, then take him into the bedroom."

Javier had warned Avril this would happen, and she must not object in any way. To do so, she would be returned to a life similar to her experience with Jacqueline. Before Rexa arrived, he had Avril walking up and down the room, wearing only her bra and knickers, with heeled shoes, at the same time being guided in how to show herself off to her best.

Without delay or hint of objection, Avril walked up to Javier, so he could unzip her dress, allowing it to drop to the floor.

Now in the underwear purchased in the store, sexy yes but discrete and still in the heeled shoes showing off her long slim legs, she did as she'd done earlier, doing a few turns. Finally, after picking up the dress she went over to Reza, offering her hand. "Would you like to take me to the bedroom?" followed by a smile.

"I would," he answered grasping her hand and taking her through, shutting the door.

Javier sat on the settee, drink in hand, turning on his smartphone. Unknown to Reza and Avril, he had left two small cameras in the bedroom. He sat watching them undress and both climb onto the bed before Reza began to shag her hard. However, watching them was no kinky action by Javier. Their time together was being recorded. Reza was a very wealthy man, the girl fourteen. Such a recording, would over time, extract far more money than what he was paying for Avril. In Beacher's and Javier's view, while the man may be shagging the girl behind closed doors, a video of him actually doing it, is undisputable proof where talk is not.

***

The food arrived shortly before Reza came out of the

bedroom, leaving Charlotte to tidy herself up.

"Well, was I right, could the girl shag?" Javier asked, while finishing off a sandwich.

"You were; that girl is extraordinary, she knows just what a man enjoys."

"Of course she does, it took three years of training to get her like that, and offered to you in her prime. So we have a deal?"

"We do, full payment is in this small attaché case," he answered, picking it up and passing it to Javier, as well as a key, which he pulled from his pocket.

Javier stood, took the case, resting it on the settee opened it up. Quickly he checked the money, before closing the case. "It's been good doing business. When you tire of her, we will have a replacement with similar training waiting. Now I will leave you two together. The room is booked until the morning. Take her back to bed, or leave for home, she's yours now."

"We'll also be leaving soon. My aircraft is waiting for me. Is her passport in order?"

"Yes, and under the name of Avril Dumas. It has been made by the best and she has already been through airport security once today without any issues, so you'll have no trouble taking her to Dubai," he said, at the same time pulling the passport from his pocket, handing it to Ramiz.

At that moment, Avril came through from the bedroom, dressed once more.

"Good news, Avril," Javier began, "Reza is more than happy with your performance, you now belong to him. Look after him well and have a good life."

"I will, thank you for allowing me to show myself off."

"You're welcome."

With nothing more to say, Javier left the room.

"We will eat, Avril, then leave."

"Where are we going?" she asked, at the same time sitting down and taking a sandwich.

"I have a house in Dubai, another in Iran. You will remain in Dubai, there you will complete your education. I want a girl, when she is older, to be at my side on business trips. You girl will see the world of the rich."

"Can't we remain here tonight; I've lots more to show you?"

"While that is a very attractive proposition, unfortunately it is not possible; my aircraft is already booked for departure. It is a long flight, and I do have an area for sleeping fitted out, we will continue getting to know each other during the flight."

Finishing their food, they left the hotel after booking a taxi.

Arriving at the airport, while they had no need to book in, they were still required to go through immigration and security at a private area reserved for non-commercial flights.

The immigration woman looked at Charlotte's passport, then up at her. "What is this man's relationship with you?" she asked casually.

"He's my uncle; we are joining my parents already on holiday in Dubai. I couldn't leave earlier, I had exams," she answered. If asked, Reza had told her what to say.

"Just one moment," the woman left her small booth going through to an office.

Reza had already gone through and was waiting nervously when Avril did not follow immediately. He approached an official.

"Can you check on my niece, my aircraft is on a tight schedule?" he asked, in an attempt to get her pushed through.

"I will find what the delay is, Sir," the officer said,

and walked away.

Soon he was back. "If you could follow me, Sir, immigration has a few questions before your niece can join you."

Once in a small interview room, an official came in, shutting the door.

"What is the problem?" Reza wanted to know.

"The name Avril Dumas has been flagged as a person of interest to Unit T. We are currently checking if your niece is the girl they flagged, or another girl of the same name."

Reza inwardly was panicking, if Unit T had flagged the girl and there was even the slightest suspicion, he may be here for hours with a lot of explaining to do. It was time to bail and leave her with the airport authorities.

"I'm a busy man; my aircraft is already schedule for departure. I was doing her parents a favour in taking her to them in Dubai. Just how long will it take to confirm this is not the girl Unit T are looking for?"

"Unfortunately, Sir, normally when we are dealing with Unit T, and being based in France it can take an hour or more. However, I understand Unit T has a representative in the area and our department is attempting to obtain local clarification. I will go and see what is happening for you."

"Do that. Otherwise, she will have to remain with you. Her parents will need to sort a ticket on one of the commercial flights. I cannot afford to wait."

"That is possibly the answer, Sir."

"Excuse me, what are you saying?"

"If you can provide us with contact number along with the name of the hotel her parents are staying, we will talk to them, to obtain conformation Avril is their daughter, and they are aware she's travelling with you."

"Unfortunately that is not possible. They are staying with me, yes, but for the next two days are on a safari in the desert. Communication is virtually impossible, which is why I collected her."

The man's tone changed. "So you intended to leave Avril with us, in the hope we can contact her elusive parents, who seem to have no interest in their daughter?"

"I didn't infer that, they are on holiday and I'm looking after her until they come off safari. It's you who are making it impossible for me to do that."

"Let me talk to my supervisor and see what can be done."

Five minutes later, the man returned. "I have good news; Unit T's representative has arrived. They will no doubt positively confirm Avril is not the girl Unit T are looking for. As soon as they give the green-light you will be on your way."

"That is good news. I look forward to meeting this person."

The supervisor left the room; shortly Jasmin came in, shutting the door behind her.

"Mr Karimi, my name is Jasmin Dlamini from Unit T," she began, at the same time showing her ID. "I'm here regarding a girl who came with you to this airport calling herself Avril Dumas."

"Calling herself?" he cut in. "This girl is Avril Dumas, and carrying a passport in that name. She is clearly not the girl you're looking for."

"If you had given me a chance to finish, whatever her passport is saying, the girl accompanying you is not Avril Dumas, she is in fact Charlotte Lucas. Charlotte was handed over by her parents to a Beacher Marinez at the age of eleven and has been used for some years by a paedophile ring. Marinez partner, a Javier Schneider, who you met in the Lapa Palace hotel, had taken Charlotte with him to meet you. Money was exchanged and you are currently attempting to remove a minor out the country using a false passport."

"That is ridiculous, but you are correct, I did meet a man I know as Javier, he asked if I would take Avril to Dubai, where her parents are waiting. He suggested I claimed she was my niece, as sometimes officials are cautious of a young girl travelling alone with a man, in particular when leaving the country aboard a private aircraft."

"I should tell you, Mr Schneider was arrested leaving the hotel carrying a small attaché case you were photographed taking into the hotel. It was found to contain a hundred and fifty thousand euro. Was this money for the purchase of the girl?"

"It certainly wasn't, I was settling a debt, following a business arrangement. I told you I was doing him a favour taking Avril with me."

"Did you have sexual intercourse with Charlotte?"

"I did not, if that's what she's claiming, she's lying."

"Charlotte, or who you call Avril, is saying nothing. That is usual, the girl is scared, however there is no getting away from the fact she is fourteen and a minor, and cannot insist we allow her to leave the country until we are satisfied she is not being trafficked. Additionally the passport she presented was not good enough to fool immigration, and found to be a forgery. That is a criminal offence. She has been arrested on the charge of attempting to leave the country using a forged document. Charlotte is facing a prison sentence, unless she can convince the court of her innocence, or the people with her today admit she had no knowledge of the deception and Charlotte truly believed the name of Avril Dumas was her registered name."

He gave an indifferent shrug. "I didn't know Avril wasn't her name, if she has deceived the authorities as to her true identity, then she should be convicted. Also, if this was an attempt by Mr Schneider to get Avril, or whoever you claim she is, out the country using me, I thank you for your diligence. As for your question about me having sexual intercourse, and Avril confirming nothing happened, along with me explaining what the payment was for, I cannot see why I am being delayed in leaving. You can sort out Avril's problems and relationship with Mr Schneider without me," he said, coming back at Jasmin, with a hint of satisfaction on his face.

"You are correct, without Charlotte's admission she was raped, with or without her consent, you would be free to leave. Providing we are satisfied, you were not part of a conspiracy to take Charlotte out the country. To that end, Mr Karimi, the delay in me talking to you, was to allow forensics to give the hotel suite a check. What was found, led me to ask the questions I have, in particular if you had sexual intercourse with Charlotte. Why did I ask? Charlotte had been with a paedophile ring since the age of eleven. During that time, she was abused constantly. A habit of hers was never to throw a used condom down the toilet. Apparently, it would often block the drains, so she was always told to use the bin. That is where a used condom was found, in the hotel bedrooms en suite. Being a five-star hotel, it is unlikely that bins are not emptied before a room is made available to a client. This evidence has been sent for DNA testing. To ensure you are telling the truth, we will require you both to take a DNA test," Jasmin hesitated. "Additionally the forensic search also revealed two tiny surveillance cameras hidden in the bedroom of the suite. It has been confirmed by our technical department both were attached, by wireless, to Mr Schneider's mobile telephone, recording what was going on in the bedroom. Need I say more, or would you like to change your claim that you and Charlotte did not have sexual intercourse?"

Reza shivered inwardly, Unit T had him, even if he could argue against taking a DNA test, a recording of him in the bedroom would convict him. "I didn't know she was fourteen. Avril readily consented; in fact urged me to take her."

"Based on that admission, Mr Karimi, you will not be allowed to leave the EU as you have arranged. I suggest you engage a lawyer to represent you. The police will soon be here to take you into custody, where you will be formally charged by Unit T, for the attempted abduction of Charlotte Lucas as well as having sexual intercourse with a minor. That Mr Karimi in the EU is ten to twenty years with all assets taken." Jasmin stood, turning to leave the room.

"You lot set me up," he called after her.

Jasmin turned. "I don't set people up, Mr Karimi, your own arrogance, believing you can come to the EU and purchase a child for you own sexual gratification, set you on a collision course with Unit T's commander, Colonel Karen Harris. On my part I'm licensed to kill and believe me, people who destroy the lives of an innocent child, totally relying on adults to keep them safe, I would have no compunction in squeezing the trigger."

"I know of Unit T and their commander's so-called holier-than-thou attitude, she's just as bad as the ones she takes on. In my country, age is not a barrier. Avril is already sexually active and wanted to come with me. The girl wanted the finer things in life and she would have got them. She would never have starved or needed to work, her life would have been perfect and you have taken that away from her."

Jasmin gave a hint of a smile. "I don't think so, you see while you rot in prison. Karen Harris will use your assets to complete her education."

"Ha, my assets are outside her jurisdiction, the girl will get nothing."

"You believe Karen Harris won't be aware of that?

Apart from the fifty million in the aircraft sat on the tarmac, Unit T will make a request that you relinquish a considerable amount of your assets to them as compensation. Refuse and Karen will apply to the European court that you remain in prison until you do. That, my friend, could be as long as being carried out the prison in a coffin. Think on that, before you make such bold statements. As for Charlotte, when she is old enough, she will leave LBNF a wealthy woman. She will be able to make her own decisions on how to live and not have a life of servitude forced on her. So yes, by taking Charlotte to your bed, your plans for her will be fulfilled, but not, I hasten to add, to include you," then she left the room.

Two police men came in the room, arrested Karimi, and led him away.

Chapter 34

Beacher being no fool, realising with Blake Fellows death and the escape of Liberty his operation had gone seriously wrong. Unit T was knocking on the door, and he knew they would not go away until he was caught and taken to prison. However, careful planning over the years had allowed him to skim large amounts of money from his businesses, all of it safely stashed in various locations across the world, out of reach of the EU authorities.

The call from Ramiz, while he had openly discounted his concerns, had been the signal to get out. The actions of the escorts were not normal, confirming to him Unit T was closing in. Not waiting to collect anything from the house, apart from a bundle of ready cash, after all his real wealth was not there, Beacher went through to the kitchen area. A number of his security people were sitting around eating.

"Come on lads, get yourselves outside, I'm hearing another group is on its way to sort us out, are you going to let them?"

Everyone said they would not, quickly moving out into the grounds, with weapons, to face this so-called threat.

Beacher had not joined them; he went through to the garage pulling a large cover from something in the corner. Underneath the cover a flex wing microlight aircraft. He dragged it out into the centre of the garage, checked it over, ensuring the fuel tank was full. Then putting on warm clothing, helmet and goggles he pressed the garage remote control. This did not open the front but the rear door of the garage. This was a design put into the house, with not only a roller shutter door at the front of the garage, but one of equal size at the back giving access into the extensive garden. From the back of the garage ran a long tarmac path, more than wide enough to take the width of the wheels of his microlight. When the door opened fully, he began pushing the microlight outside. Once outside, and after starting the engine, Beacher climbed aboard. Using the path as a runway, he opened up the engine, and in seconds, he was up. Glancing down Beacher smiled inwardly. Maybe this was an odd way of leaving, yet it had many advantages. A vehicle could be followed, or stopped. Even though he had the space to allow a helicopter to land, there was always a chance it could be hijacked, or the pilot panic and give in. His microlight was manoeuvrable, under his control and a top speed of over a hundred miles an hour, it would be very difficult to track

***

Around an hour and a half after setting off, Beacher came down, landing close to a small private airport. Leaving the microlight and discarding the warm clothing, he walked through the gates into the airport, going over to an aircraft parked with other private aircraft close to a small building. Pulling a key out, he opened the door of one and climbed aboard, quickly checking over the aircraft readying it for departure. Happy everything was in order, he left the aircraft, going to the small building. A man sitting behind a desk put down a paper he was reading.

Beacher walked over to him. "The name's Touati, here is my flight plan to Adrar in Algeria. I want to leave as soon as possible."

The man took the flight plan and picked up his phone, talking for some time before replacing it. "That is in order, Mr Touati. The fee is three hundred euro and use of the runway twenty-five."

Beacher pulled out a wad of notes, counting out the fee of three hundred, along with the extra twenty-five. The man checked it, making out a receipt. Beacher left the building. Soon he was in the air hugging the Portuguese coastline, before passing over Morocco, heading into

Algerian air space. Beacher knew he was free, out of reach of the EU authorities and in particular Unit T.

***

Back outside Beacher's house in Lisbon, Unit T troops have been given the order to go in. Karen was on her way to join them. Not that she would lead, but follow them in. However, she was also disturbed by an intelligence report of a microlight, apparently taking off to the rear of the property. Although there was no conformation, if it actually took off from inside the grounds, or from the area beyond.

In some ways, Karen was not that bothered. If Beacher had gone, there was no rush to locate him. This business was like a drug, once they had a taste, they could never leave for long and soon returned with the belief Unit T had forgotten all about them. Unit T never does, they would be in its database forever.

The lieutenant in charge of the assault on Beacher's house watched Karen's car came up the drive. She climbed out and he saluted her.

"You report, Lieutenant."

"We met slight opposition, but it quickly became apparent to them, they faced combat soldiers, so they gave up. We've no casualties; the opposition, a few simple injuries but nothing life-threatening."

"Beacher Marinez, was he in the building?"

"No, Colonel, he'd already left."

"And the other occupants, where are they?"

"The police have just taken the last of them to the station."

"Very well, shall we go inside?"

Karen walked around the house. It was nothing special and obvious this was not where Beacher had been spending his money. Even so, it would raise a few thousand towards Unit T's costs and compensation for the girls, along with all the paedophile assets as each was pulled in and identified by the girls.

Minutes later Jasmin joined her.

"Sorted out Karimi then, Jasmin?" she asked.

"Yes, he's been charged and is now with the police. He's got a very smart aircraft you'd like."

Karen gave a hint of a smile. "Has he now? I will have to have a look at it. In fact we'll impound it and I'll fly it back to Unit T myself."

"I thought you would. I hear you've muffed your part of the operation and let Beacher slip through your fingers. Bit lax on your side don't you think?"

"Yes well, I've never had someone do a runner using a microlight. You've got to admit that's a first."

Jasmin grinned. "I don't believe it, he really did, and you're not having me on?"

"No, our people are talking to air traffic, in an effort to find out if they have any idea where it came down. Personally, he will be long gone; you cannot track such aircraft unless you have prior-warning one was going to be in the area. Such an escape must have been planned by Beacher, as part of a plan to get out the EU fast."

"Then find where he's gone and put a contract out, I'll take it and finish the job," Jasmin suggested.

"In this case, I agree, you have the contract. Because of him, we have twelve traumatised children and somehow we have to put their lives back together. Which reminds me, how is Charlotte?"

"She's mad and I mean mad at you interfering in her life, actually screaming obscenities when she was told she wasn't leaving with Karimi. I will tell you this, Karimi had painted a life for her that every girl dreams about, and she could not care less how old he was, she wanted that life desperately. Mind you, when I spelt out the reality of her facing a long prison sentence, by attempting to leave the country with forged documents, and only your intervention could keep her out, she calmed down and apologised."

"I can understand that, after what she's already had to endure; but you and I know it wouldn't have lasted and she'd be pushed aside for a new girl, probably ending up in a brothel, or her throat cut. Not that she would believe such a thing would happen. Even so, like it or not Charlotte will have to face the reality she is still a child, and the path she follows now will be very different. Mind you, once back with the other girls, many she must have met, Karimi will soon be forgotten."

Jasmin frowned slightly. "Maybe you are right. Both Charlotte and Zoey have amazed me, with their resilience and very definite view of life. It makes you wonder if any of the others are like them."

"It does, and I've a feeling both girls would make very good candidates for our ongoing operations. With age on their side, looks and experience, a girl off the street would take some training to get to that level."

"I can't disagree with you there. In fact, I would like you to keep an eye on Zoey's progress. I'm considering her to work alongside me."

Karen smiled, "You really believe by the time Zoey is at an age to join you, I'll still be here? No way, I'll be long gone."

"Oh, come on, what else would you do? You've had your little tantrum, and walked away, now it is time to buckle down and sort out some of those men entrenched in the EU, attempting to get you out. That will be fun turning the tide on them."

"I suppose, and then I was sort of bored with nothing to do. There is another point in this, without me you're out of work."

"That is a very good point, it's really handy flashing my Unit T ID and the airport authorities letting me keep my gun, as well as freebie air flights."

"God, you say I'm tight, and you're trying to save a little from your millions."

"So what are your plans? When is Farah back from school?" Jasmin asked, changing the subject.

"She's not back for two weeks. I have a day or so at the camp sorting the paperwork out, then I was thinking of taking time off, perhaps going to the Caribbean for a change. What about you?"

"Back to London, I was actually asked out on a date and accepted before you had me help you out, so he took a rain check. Your plan of a short break sounds good, but going away on your own, odd. What about asking Sherry to go with you?"

"No, she's got a lot to sort out with LBNF. It would suit her for me to be out her hair, the girl gets very nervous when I am around. Anyway, I like being on my own at times. I can do what I want for a change, without any telephone calls. I might even get a makeover; maybe change my hairstyle and colour, so as not to be recognised, and live a normal life. Are you hungry?"

"I'm always hungry, where are we eating?"

"You've still got a room in the Lapa Palace hotel?"

"Yes, just in case we needed a surveillance base, why?"

"Let's eat in the restaurant and stay overnight while my people sort out Karimi's aircraft for tomorrows flight back to Unit T."

"Wow, you want to eat at a restaurant that doesn't do a two for one deal. This has got to be a first."

"Maybe, but I'm told they do a good steak, besides you booked the room so the dinners on you," she answered.

"God, I'd hoped just once you'd be a little more adventurous in your choice of food."

Karen gave a hint of a smile, but made no comment.

She was back in control of Unit T. This time it was going to be very different, with the backing of the CIA, as well as a very motivated private army behind her.

Spartes Connection

I hope you have enjoyed this book? With Karen Harris back in control, will she remain in command, or hand over the reins to someone else? After all, the world is still not safe and she has a target in the EU.

If you are new to the Karen Harris books maybe you would like to know more about Karen? How and why she formed the charity LBNF? Where the money she has came from? Maybe you are interested in how Karen first met Sherry, or how Karen became involved with the contract killer Jasmin?

While the first two titles are a must-read in understanding Karen, all the other titles are stand-alone, yet follow Karen on the journey to where she is now. Listed below are the key titles in the series where her friends and sometimes her enemies become part of her life.

The start of Karen's journey....... The People Traders

Why Unit T was formed ....The People Trafficker

How Karen financed LBNF .... Unit T - Special Forces

Karen meets Sherry Malloy .... Goin Goin Sold

Karen becomes Lady Harris....... The Royal Grandchild

The loss of Karen's parents .... Nigerian Connection

Karen looks for her sister Sophie ..... Russian Connection

Karen and the contract killer Jasmin ... Circulo

Karen meets Midnight .... Covert Operator

Karen's worth £500,000,000 ..... Jasmin - Contract Killer

Books by the Same Author

International Crime featuring Karen Harris

    The People Trader

    The People Trafficker

    Kreisen Cartel

    Unit T Special Forces

    Goin Goin Sold

    The Royal Grandchild

    Nigerian Connection

    Russian Connection

    Italian Connection

    Romanian Connection

    English Connection

    Irish Connection

    Spanish Connection

    German Connection

    Circulo

    Jasmin Contract Killer

    Covert Operator

    Contracted to Kill

    Chinwe

    Hoxa Cartel

    Salakau Connection

    Spartes Connection

Crime

    Girl in a Web

    Corrupt Money

Romance

      Catwalk Supermodel

      Gemma's White Cliff

      Fantasy

      Plagarma

      Timeless Chamber

      Tall Ship Magic

Fairies

      Sparkle and the Insect Collector

      Sparkle and the Hole in the Ground

      Sparkle and the Whirlwind

Audio

      Nigerian Connection.......... 15 Hours

      Russian Connection............ 9 Hours

      Romanian Connection ...... 11 hours 20min

      Italian Connection............... 11.5 Hours

      Corrupt Money.................... 7.58 Hours

Read the first few chapters of all the above books free at:

http:// www.keithhoare.com

www.ingramcontent.com/pod-product-compliance
Lightning Source LLC
Chambersburg PA
CBHW030424180626
46812CB00005B/2163